Luther's Own

Book 3 From the Brother's In All Series

By

Gina Rose

Edited by Brian Cross & Sybrina Durant

Luther's Own

Copyrighted 2014

Paperback
ISBN-13: 978-1508570196, ISBN-10: 1508570191
Ebook ISBN-13: 978-0-9906537-8-3,
ISBN-10: 0990653781
Paperback ISBN-13: 978-0-9960940-9-2,
ISBN-10: 0996094091

BISAC Codes:

FIC027000   FICTION / Romance / General

FIC027070   FICTION / Romance / Historical / Regency

Dedication

This book is for my good friend Patricia Broadway because without her enthusiasm it might never have been completed. She quite literally made me do it.

Thank you for driving me forward, Pat.

Gina Rose

Prologue

1803
Dunheath, Scotland

"Quit following me around, brat," Luther Rollins, the young Marquess of Huntley told his little fiance as he tried to navigate the precarious path to escape her detestable presence.

The young girl giggled with pleasure at the knowledge that she had annoyed him. How she loved to torment her future husband, it was so easy to do, after all. So what if it was the only way to gain his attention? It was a game worth playing as she adored him so completely. Of course, pigs would fly before the mischievous eight-year old-girl allowed him to know her true feelings.

"See if ye can make me," she taunted as she jumped up, pulling his hair as she did before dashing a broad circle around him, making rude gestures with her tongue.

It was clear she was enjoying the game of catch me if you can, a game for which he had no inclination to play. The young man believed that his father must have been utterly mad to have subjected him to such nonsense. Ah, my horse is just over there, he observed with renewed determination in his awkward steps of evasion.

"You are an insufferable creature," he growled as he tried to make his way past her, stumbling and dodging ineffectively as he went. God's bones! Why must she be so persistent?

If only he could get to his horse to make good his escape then he could leave this cursed place to be rid of her once and for all. Perhaps I should catch her and tie her to a tree! The thought pleased him for it would serve her right.

"Lass, leave yer betrothed alone now and come back inside," a booming male voice called from the doorway of the old keep.

"Do as your father bids and go inside," Luther commanded as he yet again tried to make his way past her.

"I dinnae know why my father thinks ye would be a good husband. Just look at ye!" she taunted.

Of course, she would not give up the chase so easily. If nothing, she was a determined little thing. Does she never tire of running in circles? He marveled at her tenacity while caught between the desire to stick his long leg in her path to fell her or wring her impudent little neck.

"I shall marry you when my bones turn to dust ... quit pulling my hair," Luther growled again, this time completely exasperated by his inability to get away from her.

"It looks like a pile of angry snakes," the girl teased then yanked it again for good measure before darting off to the keep.

Relieved that he would be spared further humiliation at the hands of the bothersome delinquent, he braced himself for what would no doubt be an unpleasant confrontation with her father.

"Get inside lass for I would speak to young Luther," her father commanded.

Roslyn MacClarent, daughter and sole surviving heir of Fergus MacClarent, Laird of Clan MacClarent, Earl of Dunheath took one last opportunity to harass her future husband by bending over and wagging her buttocks at him before going inside her home. The girl needs a good thrashing, Luther mused as he watched the little hoyden go away. He breathed a sigh of relief when she was out of sight but quickly sobered when he saw her father approaching with a look of fierce determination.

"I'm sorry about yer father, Luther, but I cannae allow ye to back out of our agreement. A deal is a deal, even if it must be honored from the grave," Fergus said when the two men were face to face.

"I was not consulted about this deal. I have no wish to marry, especially one such as she," he said standing taller than Fergus, even at his young age of eight and ten.

"I know the lass is a wee rough about the edges but ..." Fergus tried to say before he was cut off.

"Rough? Why, she is a little hellion always pulling my hair and spitting at me. I want no part of her," Luther boldly stated.

"Listen laddie, she is young, and I'll admit that she's wild but give her time. It's not with the first stroke that the tree falls. These things take a firm, guiding hand. She'll make ye a fine wife when she settles down, mark me," Fergus argued.

"I'm afraid there isn't enough time in the world to tame that little ... child," Luther protested with obvious disgust.

It was hardly lost on Fergus that his daughter was unmanageable, but it had been more than he could endure after her mother, along with her brothers had been taken by the fever that had spread throughout the land a few years back. In his grief, he had ignored the girl, allowing her to run with the stable master's lad as he was the only living child about to keep her occupied. Consequently, she had quickly cast aside her skirts for breeches and her dolls for horses. Soon, she had mastered all manner of weaponry too while he wasted away with drunken grief. There had been no one to guide her in those times and now, well, her ways seemed truly cemented. What was a man to do?

"I will not marry her and that is final," Luther stated then turned toward his horse.

Luther wanted to put all this madness behind him so he could go back to London to catch up with his friends. He needed some time to get over his father's passing so he could accept his new lot in life. He was the Marquess of Huntley now and though his roots were in Scotland, England was his home. The last thing he wanted to do was to settle down here with these people who were little more than savages – and that girl? No way would he take her to wife.

If, and it was a very big 'if', he ever married, he would have a woman with curves, beauty and charm. One who would be skilled in the arts of pleasing a husband, not some wild creature that fancied herself a boy. No, this would never do; he had to stick to his principles in this, contract or no.

"I would remind ye that there be a contract," Fergus stated with anger brewing in his tone.

"Damn the contract and damn you sir if you think to trap me into this madness," Luther said, mounting his horse.

"Ye've ten years Luther, ten years to think about doing the right thing. I willnae hold yer feet to the fire just yet as ye are grieving the loss of yer father, may he rest in peace, but marry the lass ye will or so help me, I'll hunt ye down and make ye see the error of yer ways," Fergus threatened.

Luther ignored this, exhaling the breath he hadn't realized he had been holding as he turned, urging his horse away from his father's best friend. He didn't want to hear any more about contracts of marriage. He had a new life to settle into and London was calling.

Chapter One

1813
London

"Just go away Luther! Why must you always be underfoot? Haven't you anything else to do besides pester me like some bored, school-aged lad?" Jasper Townley, the Earl of Pembrook, raged at his long time friend.

The two men had been continuously cooped up together since the accident that had left Jasper seriously injured nearly a year before when he was testing one of his inventions. The rocket-propelled flying machine that he had put himself in had flipped, end over end, several times before coming to a crashing stop. By some miracle, he hadn't been killed, but his injuries had been so severe that they had all been certain that he may never regain the full use of his legs. Luther, being the only available party as well as Jasper's closest friend, had been designated his caretaker, remaining by his side from the beginning. Jasper's current state of well-being served as a true testament to Luther's loyalty, as without his care, they would have had to put him in an institution as he had no living relatives to turn to.

Jasper had amazed them all, however, recovering quite nicely to the point that he was even able, though with no small amount of struggle, to navigate the stairs to his apartments on the second floor on his own. Walking with the assistance of a cane had initially been a huge challenge, but he had mastered it, which gave him much more independence.

Now, truthfully, there was no more need for Luther's constant presence. Jasper always enjoyed having him around, but now it was time for them to part. Jasper needed to be alone, but Luther was like a dog with a bone, never allowing him a moment's peace.

"You know I'm not supposed to leave you alone Jasper," Luther countered.

"I am fine now with barely a limp. Just go back to your own town house and leave me be, man," Jasper fairly shouted.

Luther stood looking sorely dejected, but there was nothing to be done for it as Jasper had received an urgent summons from the home office requiring his special talents, and no one, not even his friends knew of his work for the crown as it was a closely guarded secret.

"I know! Why don't we go see the twins?" Luther offered with obvious excitement at the prospect.

Jasper knew what must be done. He would have to risk hurting his best friend in order to honor his obligations to his majesty, the king. The summons hinted at some kind of assassination plot though the details were somewhat sketchy. He only knew that it was of the utmost importance; therefore, he would have to make this sacrifice in order to meet with the Bow Street agent at the designated hour mentioned in the summons.

"I don't want to see the twins, and I don't want to see you. Go home, Luther, for God's sake, just go home. I grow more weary of you with every passing moment," Jasper said with exasperation that he could not allow himself to regret.

"Fine, you arse; to hell with you then," Luther said in frustration as he stormed out of the library of Jasper's home.

He wouldn't stay where he wasn't wanted. He would just go see the twins on his own. "If Jasper wants to be alone so be it, the more fun to be had for me," he grumbled as he stomped down the hall and out the front door, slamming it behind him as he went.

Luther was in a fine huff as he marched down the street on his way back to his own town house. Things used to be wonderful before the accident that nearly crippled his best friend. Well, if he were to be honest with himself, things hadn't been good much longer than that. Before two of his other friends had married, the four men had been a force to be reckoned with. All young and virile men, carousing about London getting into all manner of mischief, they had always been quite content to spend their nights in drunken debauchery, but now it was just Jasper and himself.

Luther was growing more restless in days of late, feeling that there must be something more to do than sit around watching Jasper tinker around with his projects. Luther craved the attention of females, but it seemed that lately Jasper had lost his lust for life, preferring to hermit himself away in his apartments like some old decrepit man.

Luther had never pursued the ladies without his friends around to bolster his confidence. He was rather shy and somewhat awkward when it came to the fairer sex unless he was in his cups and part of a pack of bachelors. If left to his own devices, he wasn't sure he would even know how to go about it. He had always relied heaviest on Jasper's guidance as he had always been closest to Jasper though if he had to analyze the reason why, he couldn't truly say.

Jasper was broadly considered brilliant, whereas everyone viewed himself as though he were somewhat dense. He fit the role he supposed, considering he was the youngest of the group as well as the largest, but he knew in his heart that he was an intelligent man. Next to Jasper, anyone would seem dense, but within their circle it was his role to be the younger brother, the one everyone poked fun at ... the lack-wit. He didn't mind it really because he loved his brothers, and when they were together, the world was at their feet or had been. Now everything had changed, leaving him more to his own counsel.

Realizing he had reached his town house, he did his best to shake off his discord with Jasper. As if his arrival had been expected, he was met by his butler, Mr. Jakes in his usual professional rigidity.

"It's good to have you home, my lord," the elderly man stated formally.

Luther grunted his greeting as he made his way inside before going up to his apartments. He wanted only to get a bath so he could go out to find some mischief to get into. Perhaps what he needed was a new set of friends; he didn't want to get leg shackled as the others had, and following Jasper around wasn't stimulating anymore. Perhaps he could embrace this unexpected solitude by forging his own way, make his own mark upon the ton.

"Good evening my Lord," his valet Mr. Pitts greeted him just outside his room.

"Good evening, Mr. Pitts, I think I shall require your services this evening. I think I should like a haircut and a shave as I am thinking that a change would do me good. What say you?" Luther asked him.

"Very good my Lord, tis past time to reign in

those unruly locks if I may say so," his valet said with an approving smile.

"It is quite a mess Mr. Pitts; therefore, I shall rely on your good counsel in this matter," Luther told him.

In truth, he didn't know why he made the request but it was done now so he would just follow where it led. Maybe it was just the thing to set him off on his new course. He needed to command respect from his peers without his friends' esteemed presence overshadowing his own attributes. He was a marquess, after all, not some lackey stooge.

His unfashionably long, untamed hair had always been a source for amusement among his set, sparking all manner of quips and jibes issued at his expense. Until recently, he enjoyed the attention that it brought but now ... things would be different. It was past time for him to take control of his life, to set his own course by making his own mark in society and that was exactly what he planned to do. No more trailing behind his friends, existing on their scraps of infamy.

The thought of actually being alone briefly gave him pause. Can I do it? He sat in the chair under the direction of his valet, flinching when he heard the first snip as the man set about his task. No going back now, it would have to serve.

****

Luther hardly recognized himself as he stood looking at his own reflection in the mirror. As he turned his head this way and that, inspecting the handiwork of his talented valet, he noted that a very handsome man had lain hidden beneath all that hair. One thing that caught Luther's notice straight away was how much darker his hair appeared to be at this length. Gone were the sun-bleached curls, replaced by a more manly, darker shade of reddish blond; nearly brown but not quite. He wondered then why he had never thought to sheer himself before as he had always found the color of his hair to be unpleasant, but this ... this was wonderful.

The style was of medium length with a tuft of curls resting just so on his forehead giving him the look of a man with great confidence. Mr. Pitts was a clever man to have left him with some very generous sideburns that were sure to catch the eye of many a fair lady. The overall transformation was quite debonair actually.

"I say Mr. Pitts, a splendid job, my good man," Luther said with clear pride in the outcome.

"I daresay the ladies will swoon at your feet, my lord," Mr. Pitts said beaming.

"We shall see about that as I have plans to go out this evening," Luther told him.

"Are you in search of a bride, my Lord?" Mr.

Pitts ventured.

"Absolutely not, I simply wanted a change is all," Luther said scoffing at the notion.

"Forgive my impertinence my Lord, it's just that I thought perhaps since so many of your friends have married that you would naturally follow suit. You are of an age, my Lord, and you must consider the future of your title," Mr. Pitts boldly suggested.

"Bugger my title Mr. Pitts. I am still young and have no plans in the near future to imprison myself in such a way," Luther said in a tone brooking no further discussion on the matter.

"Very good, my Lord. Will you require anything further?" Mr. Pitts asked.

"That will be all, Mr. Pitts, you may retire to your reading," Luther told him.

In truth, Luther had considered marriage recently, but the woman had married his friend Dylan instead. He had not been in love with her in the true sense of the word, but he had and still did love her dearly. He had imagined himself quite happy in the marital state with Claire by his side, but it was not meant to be as her heart had belonged to Dylan.

It was just as well really because Dylan was so much better off now as Claire had chased away all his demons and that was worth the price of loss he may have suffered by not winning the girl for himself. He wasn't sure if any other woman could spark such a reaction in him as she had done, so the idea of marrying anytime soon was moot. It would have to be a special woman to capture him in such a way. Indeed, he had been betrothed as a younger man, but he had escaped that noose by refusing to honor the agreement his father had made when he was a young man to a wild hellion of a child by the name of Roslyn.

Now and again he had wondered whatever became of the girl but not enough to ever inquire. He was sure that by now she had married some poor unsuspecting soul. Poor man, whoever he may be, Luther lamented. His memories of the child had been of frustration and annoyance. The child had been so unruly that even five minutes in her presence had seemed like an eternity of turmoil.

After the reading of his father's will, he had been so angry about the revelation of the betrothal contract that he never properly grieved his passing. Instead, he had been relieved that he was no longer obligated to spend eternity with that loathsome brat. Good riddance!

Luther gathered his coin purse, tucking it in his coat pocket, then took one last look at himself in the mirror. Yes, the future would start now, he mused as he admired the outcome of his decision. People would hardly know him now as the alteration was so great. He imagined that he could walk right past his group of friends, and they wouldn't even give him a single look of familiarity.

The notion made him smile, then the smile was lost when the thought truly sank in. He would miss his brothers, but most of all, he would miss Jasper or rather his place at Jasper's side. Gone were those days as now he would forge ahead … alone. He shook off the melancholy as he turned away from his image. He wouldn't look back.

****

"Shh, there he be, I'd recognize his sorry arse anywhere, Trapper," the woman whispered to her partner.

"Ye dinnae tell me he was so big," the man whispered in return.

"Aye, he be big, but there be two of us. Just follow the plan," she commanded as she was clearly the leader.

The woman jumped down from the carriage quietly following the target, the carriage creeping along at a safe distance behind. The man didn't seem to notice he was being stalked as he made his way up the darkened street. Upon reaching the darkest spot on the street, the carriage pulled up ahead, stopping in front of the man just as the woman reached him, placing her pistol in the small of his back.

"Turn around," she commanded.

The man stopped in his tracks, taking a deep sigh before turning around to meet his assailant.

"It's a little early for cutthroats," he stated with a measure of boredom in his tone.

"Shut yer trap and hand over yer coin," the woman sniped as she waved the pistol in front of him to show that she meant business.

Luther stood assessing the creature before him. Though it was the voice of a woman, the person before him appeared to be a man, a slightly larger than average size man. Luther himself was nearly six and a half feet tall, towering over everyone he had ever encountered, including this person too though the crown of his head reached his own shoulder.

Luther had a moment of amusement when he considered that the man before him had the voice of a woman and smiled. He was just a youth; therefore, Luther felt certain he could escape this situation with relative ease.

"Ye just wipe that smile off yer face if ye know what's good for ye," his assailant commanded.

"You're nothing more than a young pup, why

ever should I be frightened of one such as you?"
Luther taunted.

The person before him nervously looked past
him then poked him in the chest with the pistol.
Luther gave pause to the wisdom of taunting the
youth further as he seemed unwavering in his
course. Young though he may be, he was armed
with a deadly weapon, after all.

"It's time for ye to come home, Luther
Rollins."

Luther's eyes went wide with surprise, but he
didn't have time to make sense of the words before
he was felled by a powerful blow to the back of the
head, rendering him unconscious.

"Let's load him up Trapper so we can make
away before someone sees us," the woman
commanded.

****

"He should've come round by now Trapper.
Ye dinnae have to clout him so hard," Roslyn said
as she wiped at Luther's brow.

"Aye, it's been hours now," Trapper conceded.

"Ye don't suppose he'll die do ye?" she asked
with fear cracking in her voice.

She hadn't wanted to harm Luther, only gain control of him so she could spirit him away from London quickly without being seen. She didn't have time to plead her case with him as she knew he would refuse to willingly go with her. Her birthday was only days away, and if she couldn't convince him to marry her by then, her father would give her to that no good Magnus McCarty.

Magnus McCarty Laird of Clan McCarty, Duke of Monblenneth had become her tormentor in recent months as he coveted her lands that bordered his own. He wanted to unite the clans, MacClarent and McCarty, where he would be laird of them all, gaining access to the rich mineral deposits that lay beneath her estate.

She had heard tales about mining in other parts of the country, she just simply couldn't allow it to happen to her home. It sounded like such a ghastly practice with the peasants always suffering consequently. She loved her people, indeed she took her future role as laird to heart. It was her duty to protect them from all manner of harm.

Reasoning with her father about that no good Magnus had proved to be futile as he hadn't been himself in a good while. Declining with old age, her father's mind was not as sharp as it once was. It was up to her to set things right, to make sure that no harm could come to her clan. She would bring Luther back to Scotland then force him to marry her over the anvil if that's what it took to save her lands and her people. She had to make him understand that it was his duty to protect the people of the region from harm as his estate bordered her own, as well.

If Magnus managed to obtain her land through marriage, then there would be no stopping him from wreaking havoc everywhere, even on Luther's lands. Luther hadn't been to his estate since the passing of his father, letting it fall to near ruin with only a caretaker, may he rest in peace, a steward and a few servants remaining to watch over the place. It was rumored that Luther's steward was in cahoots with Magnus in a plot to steal Luther's land, so it was vital that she made him see reason. Lives and fortune were at stake.

She looked at Luther with a flutter in her belly as she was struck by how handsome he had become in manhood. The last time she had seen him he'd been a lad, but now he was a man fully grown. She remembered him being tall, lean, awkward in his skin with reddish blond locks of hair that reminded her of writhing snakes jostling for prime real estate upon his head. How she had enjoyed tormenting him by tugging at those locks then dashing out of his reach before he could retaliate.

Too, she remembered fondly, though she hated to admit to any fondness, his big green eyes that she had imagined were magical emeralds bestowed upon him by the great mythical gods of her ancestors, and those dimples? There had been times that he had actually smiled at her, making those dimples cave in upon his cheeks, giving him the face of a cherub.

She shivered as she cast aside the memories of the boy she had so long ago loved as she looked upon the man that lay before her now. Even as he lay wounded, she could sense his virility. Gone were his boyish charms, replaced now with strong, hard lines of masculinity. He was just what she would need to stand by her side as she assumed her role as the leader of her clan.

Considering that he had virtually ignored his own responsibilities, she supposed he would be malleable. He wouldn't stand in her way or cause her to stand aside while he ruled in her stead. Nay, he didn't even want her, so it was possible that once she forced him to marry her, he would run back to London to continue his life of debauchery. That would be fine with her as all she really needed him for was a certificate of marriage with their name upon it, which would put her out of that awful man's reach for good.

She had heard how Luther and his friends went through the ton chasing skirts, drinking, gambling while committing all manner of lascivious acts. She knew that he could never find her desirable as she wasn't at all a typical female. She had led a hard life since the passing of her mother and brothers, learning early on what was to be expected of her. She had learned to hunt, shoot, wield a sword and ride a horse as well as any man.

Too, she had managed the estate quite well, physical labors included, since her father had been afflicted. She didn't need a man to protect her other than give her his name to secure her lands. Who better than Luther? It's better to dance with the devil, who will give you the least trouble, she reasoned.

"Let's 'ave a look to see if he needs stitchin," Trapper suggested breaking into her musings.

"We dinnae have anythin to stitch him up with. Best just to clean him up and let him sleep it off," she countered.

The abandoned shack offered nothing in the way of supplies, but they had managed to scrape up enough blankets for bedding. They hadn't planned for injuries, so they were at a loss on how to offer him aid.

"Ye don't suppose he's pretendin' to sleep do ye?" Trapper asked suspiciously as he watched Roslyn wipe away the dried blood from Luther's face.

It had been many hours since they had abducted Luther, aside from a few moans when they removed him from the coach, there hadn't been so much as a peep out of him. It was worrisome to be true, but what could she do? Neither she nor her lifelong friend Trapper had skills in the arts of healing; they were on the road with at least two more days journey before they reached Scotland, so there was little that could be done. She couldn't seek out a surgeon as they had abducted Luther and would surely be thrown in the gaol when the truth was learned.

"Quit pinchin' him," she hissed.

"I just wanted to see," Trapper defended.

"Just leave him to sleep. Make yerself useful and go take care of the horses; make sure the carriage is out of sight while ye're at it," she commanded.

Trapper slunk away mumbling as he went to perform his tasks. She looked again at Luther, deciding that worrying would serve no purpose, so she would just seek her pallet and see how things were in the light of day. Morning would come soon; she was exhausted, but before she would be able to truly rest easy she would tie a rope around Luther's ankle and secure it to her own so she would be awakened if he tried to get up.

With that done, she settled down beside him trying to shake off the long day and night, but having him so near was a bit disconcerting. She wasn't sure how he would react when he came around, but she knew one thing was possible, he could be sorely angry, probably even fit for a fight.

Trapper was right! He was a very big man. She wasn't sure that she nor Trapper could hold him off if he took them unawares. Best to be ready for anything she mused as she settled down with her pistol nestled at her side, patting it for comfort as she closed her eyes. Moments later, Trapper came back in and sought out his own pallet. She could tell he was brooding by the slump of his shoulders and the stern set of his square jaws.

"Go on then, what be the matter with ye, man?" she inquired.

"I tell ye again, I dinnae like this," he grumbled.

"What's done is done," she countered.

"I dinnae see why it has to be him ye marry. Why can't we marry? I could offer ye protection as well as he, and I've known ye yer entire life," he told her.

"I love ye like a brother Trapper, tis why we cannae marry," she told him with frustration hinting in her tone.

"Ye know I would do anything for ye, but when ye marry him, I'll be done followin' ye around," he told her.

"Aye, it wouldn't be proper, I suppose," she

said sadly.

"Let's just leave him here and go to the blacksmith in Gretna Green. I would make ye a good husband," he tried once again.

"Don't ye see this is the only way to save our people. Ye cannae go up against a Duke; ye've no title or fortune with which to fight. It has to be Luther. I dinnae like it any more than ye, but it's the way it has to be. Now hush yerself and go to sleep dear brother," she said, putting emphasis on the word brother to make her point stick.

Trapper said no more on the matter, for which she was relieved. They'd had this argument many times on their way to London, and she was getting irritated with him for constantly bringing it up. There had never been a hint of anything romantic between them before so why did he keep harping at her now? The idea was absurd.

True enough, he was a handsome specimen, but the idea of marrying him would never serve. Besides, she knew full well that he was as randy a knave as every other man in the village as he never lacked for female company; how could he possibly make a good husband? He was little more than a boy, besides.

Often times, when she had need of him, she found him holed up with one serving wench or another at the old tavern inn. It had never bothered her to find him there because she had always known that she came first in his heart as she was like his sister.

Even when they had bathed in the loch naked as the day they were born, they would wrestle and frolic, but he never did anything untoward with her. Nay, he was her brother, not a potential husband. She shook off the thought, rolling over on her side to watch Luther as he slumbered.

Would she have to bed him? She had never considered herself in such a position with any man, but she would be married to him in just a few days, so she couldn't help but wonder at the prospect.

The only man she had ever seen naked was Trapper, he was nowhere near as large as Luther. Trapper was only nine and ten, but Luther was near ten years his senior. The thought caused her to wonder if he was as well endowed with his manly parts as Trapper.

The notion made her shiver with a feeling of dread. She couldn't imagine herself in the scenarios she had seen Trapper and his many women in. She didn't imagine she would like it much either because the women were always shouting and crying out as though they were in pain. However, they must have liked the act because they always chased him around afterward, flaunting themselves in his face with invitations for assignations.

She yawned widely as the thought rested in her mind, her eyelids becoming heavy from her long day. Soon after, all such thoughts drifted away as much-needed sleep quickly overtook her.

Chapter Two

"Where the hell am I?" he grumbled.

Roslyn sat up, quickly looking around in a panic before remembering where she was, then relaxed a bit. She looked at the window as she yawned in an attempt to shake off the sleepy feeling, noticing that the sun had already risen, but it was still very early; she couldn't have been asleep for more than two hours at best. She trained her focus on Luther seeing that his eyes were still closed, but she was sure that she had heard him speak, causing her to awake so abruptly.

She inched closer to him on her hands and knees, touching his forehead to see if he had a fever, noting that he felt cool to the touch, which was a good sign. Suddenly, without warning, she found her wrist encased in his firm grip as she was brought nose to nose with the man, the very angry man.

"Where am I?" he growled.

Roslyn's heart was pounding frantically as she tried to rally her sluggish brain into quick thinking order.

"Shh L-Luther, ye are safe," she stammered.

"Who are you?" he asked with a puzzled expression.

She pried his fingers away from her wrist then quickly positioned herself apart from him. He didn't resist but continued to look upon her as though she were a strange specter.

"I'm thirsty," he rasped out.

"Hold still, ye are injured. I'll go and fetch ye some water," she told him as soothingly as she could manage.

Her body quaked with fear at the realization that he had nearly overpowered her, but she thanked her lucky stars that he seemed weak and unable to cause too much trouble, allowing her to escape his hold as easily as she had. Quickly, she removed the tether from her ankle then retrieved her pouch of water to bring it back to his pallet. She hunkered down beside him, trying to assess whether or not he was truly awake; his eyes were closed again so she was unsure if she should proceed.

"Are you going to give me the water, lad?" he asked, opening one eye.

Startled into action, she put the pouch to his lips, watching as he quickly took the liquid down his throat. She watched with fascination as the muscles in his throat, now covered with stubble, moved back and forth as he drank. After a spellbinding moment, he took his fill then thrust the pouch back at her, bringing her back to her senses.

"I need to piss," he grumbled.

Before she knew what he was about he had pushed her aside as he tried to rise to his feet. He didn't get far though before he spun around, landing squarely on his backside, sending her into a high pealed screech as she rushed to his side.

"I told ye that ye are injured," she admonished.

She looked around the room for Trapper, distressed to find that he was not there. She didn't have time to wonder at it because the cursed man was trying to rise to his feet once again.

"Here, let me help ye to get to yer feet," she said, offering her strength to aid him.

She wrestled him into a standing position, draping his arm around her shoulder so she could guide him to the back door of the shack to relieve himself since there were no facilities to be had indoors.

"Thank you, lad," he grunted as she opened the door.

She halted then, unsure what to do next as she darted her eyes around looking for Trapper, but it was clear to her now that he had taken one of the horses and disappeared. She had no idea where he could have gone, but she sorely needed his assistance now. How was she to help Luther with this task? Perhaps he went in search of food, she briefly mused, cheering slightly at the prospect.

"Steady as ye go, now," she said trying to extricate herself from his grip so she could allow him privacy.

"Don't leave me just yet lad, I don't think I'm able to stand up alone," Luther stated with frustration.

He urgently began to fumble with the flap on his breeches, then quickly drew his member out to relieve himself. She gasped at the sight, then forced her eyes tightly closed to avoid seeing what she had already seen. Lord, the man is as big as a stallion, she inwardly groaned. Of course, her reaction was not lost on the blasted devil as he began to chuckle at her distress.

"What's the matter lad? Have you never seen a real man's cock?" he asked as he continued to relieve himself.

She said nothing to this, only kept her eyes tightly clamped shut; a greater mortification, she could hardly fathom.

"You are a big enough lad, I imagine when your bollocks drop you'll be about the same size," he further taunted.

She continued her silence, praying that this humiliation would come to a quick conclusion, but he seemed to have a river backed into his pipes as the seemingly endless stream went on unhindered. While enduring the ordeal, she became hotly aware of his arm clutching to her waist; thankful for her heavy leather jacket so he wouldn't feel her curves. She was content to have him think she was a young boy for the time being as she was alone with him now and had heard many tales of his prowess with the ladies.

Sometimes, God is merciful, but not so much as to spoil a person as after what had seemed a small eternity he was finally finished, for which she drew a mighty breath of relief before the unthinkable happened.

"Lad, I will need your assistance to button my breeches," he said.

"W-what? Surely ye can't be serious," she blurted out.

"I can't exactly do this with one hand now can I?" he asked with irritation ringing in his tone.

Though she hated to admit it, there was logic in it. True enough, the man had fallen when he was left to stand up alone. She knew there was no hope for it, yet she would rather eat a mud pie than submit to such a request. With a heavy sigh of resignation, she turned to position herself in front of him, careful to make sure she kept her shoulders available for support, then set about the embarrassing task. She closed her eyes again when she realized that his sex was still visible. Before taking hold of the thing, she took a deep breath as though she were about to swim a mile underwater, then before she could lose her nerve, she grabbed hold of it to tuck it away.

"Careful boy!" he shouted.

She froze in place, remaining there with her eyes tightly shut with a firm hold on the offending appendage while her heartbeat thundered through her ears. Sweat began to bead upon her forehead, but she didn't dare move a muscle; she didn't dare breathe.

"God's bones, are you addled?" he asked as he removed the tight grip of her hand.

After a hair-raising moment, much to her relief, she realized that he had taken the matter of tucking himself into his breeches into his own hand. Slowly, ever so slowly, she let out the breath she'd been holding in, then bravely opened one eye to allow a peek to assess the situation. Praise be to the saints, the thing was finally put away.

"Now then, please button my breeches," he said with strained calm.

With trembling hands, she made short work of it, then quickly darted back to his side so she could guide him inside the shack. Her heart was still thundering in her ears, but with great effort she reigned in her nerves, content that the humiliating matter was now behind her. She managed to lead him back to the pallet where with considerable effort she assisted him down. After relieving herself of the burden, she stepped back from him, grateful for the distance, small though it was.

"Now then, who are you?" he demanded.

Her heart fell into her stomach at the question, not having fully prepared for this moment. She knew that it would come, but she had hoped that Trapper would be here to help her if he became violent. She walked away, stalling for time to think about how best to handle this new development. She knew that she had best be careful how she answered him, or she could find herself in the gaol or worse.

"It's not so hard a question," he prodded.

She quickly turned back to face him with her shoulders squared and her chin slightly lifted. The idea that he could so completely forget her was somewhat painful, but she would not let him see that it bothered her.

"Do ye not remember me?" she hedged.

He looked her over from head to toe before rubbing his forehead as though deep in thought.

"Truth lad, I have no memory of you or how I came to be injured. Perhaps you can fill in the blanks," he said with clear confusion in his voice.

She really wished that Trapper was here right now. She knew this could quickly escalate beyond her control. She had to tell him something or did she? She had a weapon or she did. She cast a look around until her eyes landed on her pallet with the pistol she had all but forgotten lying there. His eyes followed hers then curse me for a fool, he saw the pistol too. With speed she wouldn't have thought he possessed in his current condition, he lunged for the weapon, taking control of it where it now rested in his lap, mocking her for her mistake.

"Yours?" he asked patting the weapon.

She cringed when she realized that the tables had turned. How could she have been so stupid as to have left her weapon there?

"How about filling in those blanks now. With the truth," he said patting the pistol once again for effect.

She wasn't a stupid girl. She knew the moment of truth had arrived, she would just have to deal with it head on. Boldly, she lifted her arms above her head to remove the long braid of hair she had neatly tucked inside her collar. The long length of brown rope landed just above her waist when brought forward. She removed the tie that bound it at the end then slowly began running her fingers through the weave to unfurl it, noticing that she had his rapt attention then. Once she had her long brown hair unbound she removed her jacket to reveal the thin lawn shirt she wore beneath.

"Do ye recognize me now?" she asked in a husky voice.

Luther sat there transfixed at the sight before him. The creature standing there was no lad, of that there was no denying. He had wondered at it before but had cast the thought aside because truly, she was the tallest female he had ever encountered. She had to be at least five foot, eleven inches tall, maybe more, which would have easily put her taller than the average sized male. Lord, she is a giant, but a beautiful giant, he realized.

Her hair was a glorious crown of sun-streaked brown and her eyes were a dazzling shade of hazel, her skin seemed to be made of the sweetest honey. Too, he could tell that she was well endowed with a luscious bosom, visible through the thin material of her shirt, and wondered how he had not noticed her shapely form before, even though she had worn the heavy leather coat.

Indeed, the woman was a buxom specimen of

femininity now that he'd had a good at her, not at all hard to look upon, though try as he might, he could not place her. He shook his head 'no' in mindless answer to her question as he continued to drink in the sight before him.

"I am Roslyn MacClarent, yer betrothed," she told him.

Well, that was like a bucket of cold water to his face. Betrothed? He wasn't betrothed! Why, I am ... I am ... he couldn't remember. Suddenly, he went rigid with fear as his mind tried desperately to make sense of things. Something was wrong! He closed his eyes tight, trying to capture a shred of anything that would explain this madness, but there was nothing, nothing! He opened his eyes and looked about the room searching for something, anything that he recognized, but there was absolutely nothing.

"I don't have a betrothed, I'm sure of it," he mumbled dazedly.

Luther! He remembered that she had called him Luther when he had first awakened. But Luther, who? He dredged the depths of his mind trying to come up with his last name, but the more he tried to figure it out, the more his head began to pound in answer to the question. Feeling a bit dizzy, he shook his head trying to remain focused.

"Dinnae ye remember me?" she asked clearly

insulted that he could so easily forget her.

Something isn't right here. How could he forget his own name? How could he forget this beautiful woman who claimed to be his betrothed, and how did they come to be here in this dank, dreary shack with an injury to his head? His head answered his questions with a tremendous booming. He felt weakened by the pain of it, realizing that he was in danger of swooning.

"Lass, in truth, I don't even remember who I am. How am I supposed to remember you? Tis all very vexing. My head is aching, and I can't seem to think. Perhaps, I need to lie down," he slurred the last part as he leaned back on his pallet.

He had to figure this out, but it was no use, his body demanded rest. He closed his eyes, trying to fight off the pain, but the darkness threatening to claim him overwhelmingly engulfed him.

****

Roslyn wasted no time when Luther swooned, quickly rushing forward to reclaim her pistol where it lay across his legs, then tucked it in the back of her breeches for safe keeping. She breathed a sigh of relief though she began pacing as she tried to sort out all that had occurred. Clearly, the injury to his head was great as he seemed to have no memory; this could be bad, real bad.

Where in the name of all that is holy has Trapper gone? Stomping to the door, she opened it to have a look around, seeing nothing but rolling hills of the English countryside to give her comfort. She knew that they were about an hour's ride from the nearest posting inn, so perhaps he had ridden there to obtain food. Roslyn hoped that was the case because she was mightily hungry, having been nearly a full day since she had eaten last. As she was closing the door, her stomach growled as if to lodge its own protest to her thoughts.

One thing she was sure of; Luther needed a surgeon. She couldn't in good conscience allow him to languish unaided with such an injury. If she took him to a surgeon, there would be questions, but if Luther really had no memory, perhaps things could work to her advantage. She sat down on her pallet beside Luther, drawing her knees close to her chest while she continued to mull things over. She laid her cheek upon her knee then closed her eyes trying to find serenity in hopes that an answer would soon come to her.

Her mind began to drift back to that embarrassing scene earlier, causing a warm sensation of blush to roll along the length of her body in response. Lord he is a handsome man. In her wildest dreams, she never could have imagined him so from her scant, precious memories of him.

Too, she remembered the look on his handsome face when she revealed herself to be a woman and not the lad he had thought her to be. His expression had been one of a primal, hungry nature as his eyes traversed her body from one end to the other. The feeling that it had given her allowed her to imagine that he had actually found her beautiful. The notion evoked a silent giggle; the idea that he could actually want her was intoxicating. These were the last conscience thoughts flitting through her mind as she drifted off to sleep with a contented smile upon her face.

****

Roslyn was startled awake once again, this time by the sound of the front door slamming shut though she was soon relieved to see Trapper standing there. Unsure whether to pummel him or hug him, she quickly jumped up to greet him.

"Just where have ye been?" she demanded.

"We needed food dinnae we?" Trapper responded, demonstrating the packages he held.

"I'm fair hungry, yes, but ye dinnae tell me ye were leavin' now did ye? While ye were gone, he woke up and I had need of ye," she admonished.

Though she was irritated with her friend and co-conspirator, Roslyn's ire began to settle when her mouth started to water as the aroma of the food reached her nose. Without further thought to her anger at him for disappearing, she followed Trapper to the old table watching eagerly as he set about opening the packages.

"Tell me what happened then," he commanded as he busied himself.

"Och Trapper, it was awful," she said darting a glance in Luther's direction, noting that he was still sleeping. She lowered her voice then began to tell him her tale. Trapper listened quietly until she finished telling him all, making a whistling sound indicating his surprise as he looked at Luther to confirm that he was still sleeping.

"Amnesia? Could work to yer advantage, aye?" he asked.

"Do ye really think he has amnesia?" she asked with what sounded like fear mixed with guilt.

"Dinnae fash yerself Roz, he be a stout man, and I'm sure he will come back to his senses soon enough, but in the meantime ye need to convince him to marry ye," he told her.

His comment made her draw pause just before she was about to bite into a hunk of bread.

"Why Trapper, just last night ye were tryin' to convince me to leave him here and marry ye. Why the change of heart?" she asked before biting off a piece of bread and chewing it with gusto.

Trapper's shoulders tensed in the way they often did when he felt like he was being challenged.

"Well, now Roz, I know ye are determined in yer course and I did all I could to try and change yer mind. I suppose I see the logic in it so I willnae try and stop ye," he said with the tension releasing from his posture.

Roslyn looked at his face as if for the first time realizing that there was beauty in the young man's countenance. Until this moment, she'd never really seen him as a man, only Trapper, her lifelong companion. He was handsome standing there with his long blond hair with waves like ripples on a pond accentuated by his blue eyes, clear as the sky on a spring morning.

Too, that dimple just off the corner of the right side of his mouth always seeming to laugh at you when he smiled. Truly, he was a beautiful man, but he lacked the virility of Luther ... She shook off the unwanted thought then darted another look over at her betrothed, confirming that he was resting peacefully.

"Ye dinnae want to marry me anyway, but I thank ye for trying to save me from marrying a stranger or that dreadful Magnus," she said wistfully.

"Tis true my bonny Roz, I would do anything for ye, even if it means to just stand aside," he told her giving her a brotherly hug about her shoulder.

She sank into his side taking the comfort he offered; really, she didn't know what she would do without Trapper. He had been her devoted friend her entire life, now she would have to leave the comfort of his familiarity to forge a bond with a virtual stranger to save her land and her people. The thought was overwhelming, prompting tears to slip free from her eyes.

"What's this?" a stern voice spoke from behind them.

The two jumped apart, turning in unison to the direction of the interrupting voice, like the two guilty culprits they must surely appear to be. Luther was awake, on his feet, looking as fierce as a highland warrior as he took in the scene before him.

"Luther, yer awake!" she blurted out as she wiped away the tears that had escaped her eyes.

"Aye, and apparently none too soon. Am I interrupting?" he asked with sarcasm dripping from his voice.

"Ho, brother, stay yer horses. This is not what it seems," Trapper said, holding his hand out in placation.

"Brother?" Luther asked perplexedly.

"Och, tis true then, ye have amnesia," Trapper hedged.

Roslyn wasn't sure what Trapper was about but took the wise course of silence to see where it led. If Luther indeed had amnesia, then they may have an easier time of it. She watched as Luther placed his hand upon his forehead rubbing it as though it ached but said nothing else.

"I was only offering comfort to yer betrothed as she is so very worried about yer condition. She tells me that ye cannae remember who she is or even yer own name. So it's true then? Ye cannae even remember yer own brother?" Trapper prodded further.

Roslyn gasped at his last comment but held her tongue. She had no idea why Trapper would be claiming to be Luther's brother.

"God's truth, I can't remember anything," Luther said with a shake of his head.

"Why don't we all have a seat and eat some of this fine food I fetched while I'll tell ye all about it," Trapper suggested motioning to the old table.

Roslyn took Luther by the elbow, leading him to one of the rickety old chairs at the table. She hoped it wouldn't collapse under his massive bulk or hers for that matter. Though she wasn't overly plump, she was large in stature, and the chairs didn't look quite up to the task. Luther gingerly took his seat followed by her and Trapper. The chairs squeaked in protest but held allowing her to breathe a sigh of relief.

"Let's dig in shall we?" she suggested.

Each of them pulled at the roast chicken and bread, eating with their hands as there were no plates or utensils to be had; as hungry as they all were it hardly mattered that they were using such ill manners. After a few moments of tense silence, Luther finally spoke.

"I'll have that explanation now if you please," his tone laced with suspicion.

Trapper was bold, plunging ahead.

"We were on the road to Gretna Green so ye and Roz here could elope as ye had planned, when we were set upon by highwaymen. After they made off with our possessions, ye jumped on yer horse to give chase but ye were thrown when yer horse decided it dinnae want to cross the stream and ye struck yer head on a stone. Dinnae ye remember any of this?" Trapper asked with mock concern.

Luther digested this information but still he had absolutely no memory of any of it. He looked at the boy before him, then at Roslyn. They seemed to be honest; try as he might, he couldn't imagine why they would contrive such a tale, but still it didn't feel quite right. Why had Roslyn been dressed in male clothing and why had she felt the need to keep a pistol to be safe from her fiance? He looked at his own clothing noting that his were of fine tailoring while they were dressed as … well, as highwaymen.

"Why is she dressed as a man?" he found himself asking.

"Well now, that's easy enough to explain though ye may not like the answer," Trapper said with a look of concern.

"Out with it," Luther barked.

"Well, if yer sure ..." Trapper hedged.

"Yes yes, out with it man," Luther commanded with annoyance.

Trapper looked at Roslyn with a look of pity before launching into his explanation.

"Ye see, we had been on the road for quite some time, and when we came to a nice spot off the road near the water, Roslyn said she wanted to bathe. Well, of course, we cannae deny a lady's request in such a matter so we accommodated her by allowing her the privacy that she needed. That's when the bandits showed up and one of them took it in his head to have a little sport with her, stealin' her pile of clothes as they lay on the bank. Of course, since they left us with very little we had to scrape together some clothes from my bag for her to wear. It was luck that they didn't find my bag or poor Roz here would have had to go all the way to Scotland without a stitch of clothing," he explained with a chuckle.

Roslyn was mortified as she sat speechless, feeling the burn of blush as it coursed across her skin. The idea that she would have been naked in a stream, accosted by bandits was embarrassing whether it had actually happened or not. Luther looked at her with concern etched on his face.

"Did they hurt you?" he asked her.

With her hand covering her mouth, she shook her head vigorously but found she could not form the words as her embarrassment was too great. She would kill Trapper for this later, but for now she knew that she had better remain quiet. The lies being told by Trapper were too much for her. How would she ever be able to look Luther in the eye when he found out the truth?

"Why did you feel that you needed a pistol against your betrothed?" was his next question.

The question took Roslyn by surprise as she had completely forgotten about the pistol. With eyes wide open, she nervously looked at Trapper for the answer but now it seemed he was at a loss for explanations. Now, of all times, the liar was speechless?

"Y-ye were acting strange," she blurted with a stammer.

"Aye, after such an ordeal it's no wonder she was jumpy," Trapper quickly put in.

That seemed to mollify Luther as he nodded his head that he understood. She found herself sinking down in the chair as she began to relax now that all the lying seemed to be finished. Trapper too appeared at ease as he resumed eating with gusto. Luther remained quiet though, this she couldn't help but wonder at. What could be going through the poor man's mind?

"Why were we eloping?" he asked after a few moments of awkward silence.

"Well now, that's another tale, and I dinnae want to tax ye too much," Trapper dodged.

"Yes, ye need the rest Luther, we can speak of it later," Roslyn added, realizing that Trapper was buying time to come up with a rational explanation.

"I find that I am of a mind to have the answers now if you please," Luther insisted.

Trapper drew a breath to tell the tale, "Ye see Luther, ye have been gone for quite some time, and in yer absence, ole Magnus McCarty took a liking to the lass and wanted her for himself. As yer brother, I cannae allow this so me and Roz came to fetch ye after we received word from ye that ye would honor the contract that her father and yers made between ye and Roz to be married by her eighteenth birthday," he explained.

Roslyn was glad that he was partially sticking to the truth, relaxing slightly until Luther's next question.

"Why did you have to come and uh ... fetch me, as you say? Why did I not make the journey on my own if I was of a mind to honor this so-called contract?"

Trapper was briefly stumped, but once again proved to be a fairly artful liar as he continued with ease.

"Well now, when we received yer missive, she decided that she had to have one of them fancy weddin' dresses made by one of them French seamstresses that are so popular in London, so we wrote back to ye that we'd be coming to London so ye could ride back with us," he said, clearly proud of himself for his quick thinking.

"You traveled alone with my betrothed?" Luther asked again with suspicion.

Roslyn quaked with nerves as the layers upon layers of lies seemed to be endless. At this point, she hoped he never recovered his memory. How could she ever unravel this web of deceit?

"Ah, well ye see brother, and this part ye may not like either, but I suppose I have the task of tellin' ye all of it. I'm yer bastard brother, and I was raised as the stable master's lad on Roslyn's estate. Truly, I am more like her brother than yers as I grew up with the lass while ye were away at Eton then went on to live a bachelor's paradise in London. The fever that raged through the village years ago killed her mother and brothers as well as most of the children, so Roz and I naturally formed a bond as we were of an age," he said with what sounded almost like contempt laced in his tone.

Roslyn sat astounded at this masterful tale of truth mixed with fiction. She looked at the two men, realizing that there was indeed a strong resemblance though she knew it was only a coincidence that was not lost on Trapper, one that he chose to use to their advantage. The tale was quite believable really, and though she detested the lies, Roslyn began to warm to it. Everyone fell silent as Luther sat digesting the information for a moment.

"And our father, what of him?" he asked.

"He died about ten years' past," Trapper stated without emotion.

Luther mulled all the information over in his mind, trying to grasp hold of the flickering images that danced to and fro in his memory. The story sounded somewhat familiar, but he couldn't quite grasp the full knowledge that he so desperately sought. It was there, dancing at the edge of his mind, teasing him through a foggy veil of confusion, preventing him from seeing the full story.

If he were indeed this girl's betrothed, even with a contract stating so, then he saw no choice but to marry her; he had quite compromised her after all by allowing her to see his cock with that embarrassing ordeal earlier. The idea of marrying her didn't cause anxiety really but being unable to recall anything about her or himself did.

"You say there was a contract?" he found himself asking.

"Aye, there be a contract, and it so happens that we brought it with us to present to the smithy in Gretna Green so we would have no problems with the marriage," Trapper said, reaching into his coat pocket retrieving the document.

Trapper handed it to Luther, who quickly unrolled it to read it.

"I am Luther Rollins, Marquess of Huntley. I am a lord?" he asked a bit perplexed.

The idea that he could be a man of nobility hadn't yet occurred to him. He searched his mind again for information but found nothing to lend credence to this new development though he did note that his speech would certainly indicate that he had received a fine education.

"Aye, ye be a lord and Roslyn be a lady, future laird of the Clan MacClarent," Trapper said with challenge laced in his tone.

"And this McCarty, who is he?" he asked.

Roslyn found her voice then.

"A despicable man that would force me to marry him to have access to my land so he can plunder it of its riches," she said with a spit to the floor indicating her true feelings about the man.

"Aye, Magnus McCarty, Laird of Clan McCarty, Duke of Monblenneth has been promised Roslyn if ye dinnae come back to seal the contract by her eighteenth birthday, which is only a few days away. So ye see brother, we no have time to waste. Tis why ye and she were to elope," Trapper put in.

"Why should I care about the Clan MacClarent and the land it hails over?" he asked.

"Because brother, yer land borders it, and if ye are no careful, he will snatch that away from ye too. Ye have been negligent in yer duties and yer clan's people have all left and been absorbed by either the Clan McCarty or Clan MacClarent for protection.

Yer estates have fallen to near ruin in yer absence, so ye must come back and claim what's yers, man," Trapper shouted with passion.

Luther was stunned by the vehemence in the young man's tone. Was all this true? If it was, then there were surely wrongs to be put to right. He wished he could remember something, but try as he might, nothing of substance would come to him.

Roslyn was a beautiful woman; any man would be lucky to have such as she for a wife, but what if this was all some sort of ruse? It didn't make sense that they would concoct such a story with no proof. The contract was proof of a promise to wed, but was he really Luther Rollins? He needed real proof of that before he could fully consent to marry a stranger.

"I would have more proof before I honor this contract," he told them.

"What sort of proof?" Roslyn asked.

She wasn't sure what more she could produce to prove that he was her betrothed and felt slightly offended by this demand.

"I would like to see this land first and speak with Roslyn's father before I take yer word for all this," he said with sure determination.

Luther decided that he could find it all easier to

believe if he were actually in the setting where all of this was said to be taking place. Taking the word of two strangers when he could not even remember his own identity seemed a risky prospect, all things considered.

"We no have time for that. It will take another week to make it there if the weather holds, and that's a very big if," Trapper told him.

"Well, that's the way it has to be or there will be no marriage," Luther said, slamming his fist on the table.

Trapper shook his head in frustration before continuing.

"I know ye are having trouble believing all of this, but brother we simply cannae take the risk of going there first when her father has declared that if ye dinnae marry her by her birthday that he will give her to Magnus. Old Fergus is getting on in his years, and his mind isnae what it used to be. The only way to protect yer interests as well as protect Roz is to marry her in Gretna Green as ye planned to do. Surely ye must see this the only way," Trapper said with his temper flaring.

Luther was starting to feel stifled, and his head was beginning to pound again. He couldn't think clearly in this condition, but somehow he felt that he had no choice but to believe them. The idea that he could possibly disgrace the girl by refusing to wed her didn't set well with him, nor did the idea that he had been a derelict lord. If what his brother said was true, then time was critical.

Though he could remember nothing to confirm or disprove what he learned here today, there was a strong possibility that he could recover his memory in a matter of days. His injury had been serious enough to cause a painful lump with some bleeding and swelling, yet it didn't seem so severe that he could suffer permanently, as a result.

In all likelihood, they were telling him the truth, then once his memory returned he would be perfectly content to be married to this woman. Still, there was the slim chance that they could be some kind of schemers with nefarious plans that he couldn't quite fathom just yet, so prudence would dictate caution.

"I will compromise with you. If I don't have my memory back by the time we reach Gretna Green, I will marry the girl, but there will be no consummation of the marriage until I have proof that all you have told me is true. That way if it comes to pass that you two are a couple of charlatans, I can get an annulment with no harm done," he said with finality.

Roslyn and Trapper exchanged looks with each other, then Roslyn nodded her head in agreement.

"It will be as ye say brother, but mind ye, if ye

dishonor our bonny Roz in any way, so help me God, I'll kill ye," Trapper threatened.

"Why do you not marry her yourself? You obviously love her," Luther retorted, remembering the scene he had interrupted earlier.

Trapper stood, knocking over his chair as he did, then leaned forward across the table placing himself nose to nose with Luther.

"Because she deserves better than a poor bastard!" he growled, shoving himself away from the table before storming out of the shack, slamming the door behind him as he went.

Luther was stunned by his brother's emotional outburst as he made his declaration. So much passion had been put behind it that Luther was certain the duo were genuine, making it difficult to continue an argument against marrying the girl.

Chapter Three

Alone with Luther after Trapper's performance, Roslyn was somewhat perplexed by all that had occurred. If she didn't know better, she would have believed everything that Trapper had said, even the part about being set upon by highwaymen. That part she had inwardly laughed about as he told the tale, but the part about him being Luther's bastard brother was very disturbing. What could have possessed him to say such things? And with such passion?

She looked toward the door that he had fled through, wondering if she should go after him to speak with him about it. Surely he knew that sooner or later the lie would come back to roost, causing all manner of problems when Luther got his memory back.

"You should go after him," Luther said as if reading her thoughts.

She shot him a startled look. Did the devil read minds?

"He loves you, it seems," he stated softly.

Her shoulders sagged under his words as Trapper's behavior just now certainly seemed to imply deep feelings for her, love even. Still it wasn't that kind of love, so there was nothing for Luther to be concerned about.

"Aye, but not as ye think. Me and Trapper have been mates since we were in leading strings," she said with her chin up in defiance.

She left the table to go over to the window to see if he had left her alone with Luther again. She relaxed when she saw him sitting on the ground with his knees drawn up, his elbows propped on them as he held his head low as if in deep thought. Perhaps she should go to him if only to discuss the lies he told. She didn't like lying to Luther because he was to be her husband soon and marrying a stranger was hard enough without lies hanging about between them to muddy up the waters.

"Go and ease his mind Lass, I find I am in need of more sleep, and the quiet will do me good," Luther prodded.

She cast him a questioning look before opening the door, then reassured by his nod of consent she walked to where Trapper was and sat down beside him in much the same posture.

"Yer a fair actor, Trapper," she said after a moment.

"Aye," was his response.

She could see that he was still riled up from his

conflict with Luther, so after a few moments of silence she ventured cautiously.

"What do we do when he gets his memory back then?" she asked.

"It will sort itself out my bonny Roz," he said as he draped his arm around her in the brotherly fashion that she was so accustomed to.

"Do ye think he will really marry me then?" she asked.

"Oh, I think he will, even if he gets his memory back before we get there. I saw the look in his eyes when he saw my arm around ye," he said with a snicker as he knocked against her knee with his own.

She was pleased that he had put away his anger but still she wanted to remind him just how serious this was.

"Everything is so funny to ye, but what if he gets his memory back and refuses because of all the lies ye told him?" she countered.

"Would it be so terrible?" he asked with seriousness in his eyes.

"Ye know it would," she hissed.

"This is the last time I will mention it, but ye

should marry me instead," he said solemnly.

Roslyn shook her head as tears welled up in her eyes. She couldn't help but wonder if she were making a mistake by insisting on a marriage with Luther. He had never shown any interest in her or his people. What if he never did? What if he abandoned her and she were forced to deal with Magnus on her own?

"I thank ye for caring for me Trapper, but the course is set. It must be followed through if we are to save our people and our land. Ye know what a horrible man Magnus is. It will take power that neither ye nor I have to stop him. Luther is nearly his equal in rank and fortune ..."

"Damn titles and fortune," Trapper said cutting her off as he stood up.

"I'm sick and tired of hearing about titles and fortune. We don't need either to fight him, just yer marriage to another," he said in frustration.

"Yer forgetting that my father would never allow a marriage between us even if I were of a mind to have ye," Roz said equally frustrated with his persistence.

Trapper kicked at the ground, unearthing a clod of mud. She could see that he seemed genuinely hurt by her rejection, but there was nothing for it. This was the way it had to be. The idea of marriage between them was completely out of the question.

"Listen to me Trapper and listen well. I cannae have ye fer a husband. Besides ye are just a boy and have many years left before ye should be thinking about finding a wife. Ye dinnae really want me in that way, now do ye? No, if ye did, ye never showed it before so I will hear no more about it. Just rest yer mind on the matter and let me do what I know is best."

"What does a wee lass know about what's best?" he asked with a sarcastic chuckle.

"I know Magnus would eat ye fer breakfast and feed yer bones to the dogs," she countered.

"He may at that," was his dark response.

After a moment of silence between them, Roslyn yawned wide as she felt exhaustion begin to seep into her bones.

"Ye need to get some more rest before we get back on the road," he told her.

"And ye?" she asked.

"Aye and me," he said with his own yawn.

"Ye won't be disappearing again?" she asked.

"I told ye I would help ye to secure yer

husband, and I will. Just go inside, and I'll be behind ye in a little while. I need a little time to myself," he said with a bit of sadness in his voice.

****

Luther watched the exchange from the window as the two argued. He could see that his brother had feelings for the girl, but something in him told him that she really was meant for himself. He struggled to try and put the flashes of pictures together in his mind to form coherent memories, but they remained just out of his reach.

Images of a young girl running about with wild abandon, laughing joyously flashed through his mind that felt like a memory, but the meaning evaded him. He sighed and walked away from the window as it appeared that they had settled their differences now, whatever they may have been. Were they telling him the truth? He sensed that they were, and the urge to take her in his arms to protect her was strong within him.

Aye, she would be a perfect fit for him as she was nearly his equal in stature. Other women ... other women? Hmm, there was something there. More pictures flashed through his mind of women, many women, twins, in particular. Who were they? He shook his head as if to clear the fog away, but again, there was nothing of substance.

Did he have more family? What of his mother? Did he have sisters, twins perhaps? Again, he tried to reach for something, anything that he could grasp hold of, but again nothing but a pounding in his head to remind him of his injury.

Roslyn was a fair beauty to be sure. Even though she was dressed as a man, he could easily envision her dressed in a lovely frock that would enhance her abundant womanly assets, the image making him stir within. Though she was so very young, she was wizened beyond her years, convincing him that she would have no trouble transitioning from his brother's childhood companion to his own wife under the proper tutelage.

If the story had been true, then she had been forced to grow up fast without a woman's guidance to encourage her in the arts of decorum, which would explain her seemingly rough manners. He had watched her when his brother had been relaying their tale and had inwardly chuckled when she spat after her damning words about this Magnus fellow. Not the kind of thing a lady of proper breeding would do, he was sure, but he had found it somewhat endearing, nonetheless.

He could see she was a woman of great passion with honest character, which compelled him to believe what he had been told. Perhaps he should quit struggling so hard to remember and just follow his instincts and marry the girl without a fuss. He wasn't sure about his own age, but he sensed that he was at least ten years her senior, which would make him the perfect guiding hand to help her into womanhood. She would make a beautiful bride; with the loyalty she displayed for her people, he felt that she would make a good wife and mother, one that he could be proud of.

But still, what if there was another woman somewhere? He didn't really know, and that was the part that bothered him. What if he already had a wife, children even?

He looked at his left hand, noting with relief that there was no ring nor a mark indicating prolonged wear of one. The only jewelry he wore was a signet ring with a ruby stone and the letter H in the center on the small finger of his right hand. He went to remove it, finding that he had to give it a good twist to get it off, leaving behind a deep indention which did seem to indicate that he had worn it for a good period of time. He could believe that he had worn the ring for a decade even as the skin beneath was pale compared to the honey color of the rest of his hand.

Huntley, the Marquess of Huntley, that was what the contract had said his name was, and the 'H' seemed to lend credibility to their story. Luther Rollins, Marquess of Huntley. He rolled the name around in his mind, hoping that it would spark something, but still there was nothing. The name did feel comfortable to him, he realized as he began a search of his coat pockets for anything else that may help identify him.

What's this? He pulled a rather heavy pouch out of a pocket on the inside of his jacket, it too emblazoned with an 'H'. Opening the drawstring, he was startled at the contents as there had to have been at least thirty guineas within, amazing considering that they had been set upon by highwaymen. Apparently, they had been novices to miss such a prize, and what of his horse?

The sudden thought prompted him to walk to the back of the shack; opening the door, he noticed two horses, but they were apparently meant for the carriage that was outfitted to accommodate them both. Where was his horse? He needed to find out because he was sure that any horse of his had to be worth a small fortune as apparently he was a man of means and could certainly afford better than the two tied to the post.

"Ye need to rest yerself for the journey," came a stern female voice from behind him.

Luther turned toward Roslyn and smiled at the vision before him. There she was with her hands fisted at her hips as though she were a schoolmarm and he a naughty student that she was about to take to task. He closed the door then slowly walked toward her, stopping just a few inches away so he could have a good look at her. God's teeth, she's a beauty, he noted with clear concurrence from his loins.

"What of my horse?" he asked.

"Horse?" she asked blinking her eyes at the question.

"Aye, my brother said I was thrown from my horse when I went after the bandits," he said with a raised eyebrow.

"Och, of course, I nearly forgot about yer horse," she said with a shake of her head.

She turned away from him taking several steps to put distance between them as though she were wary of him. He wondered at the change in her demeanor, going from schoolmarm to the frightened child she must be, again the urge to wrap his arm around her to protect her ran strong within him. Strange that! She was a stranger to him, yet he felt drawn to her as though they belonged together somehow.

He found himself moving toward her without conscious thought to do so, stopping just in front of her as he reached for her hand then brought it to his mouth. After a brief savoring pause, he ever so softly placed a gentle kiss upon her knuckles, noting that her hands seemed somewhat roughened as though she spent hours toiling away in hard labor. A woman of class should not have such hands he thought as he turned it over to examine her palm. The act seemed to offend her as she pulled her hand out of his grasp with a gasp.

"Why do you have the hands of a servant?" he asked.

"I work hard for my people," she said with a squaring of her shoulders as if she were preparing to defend herself.

"I don't understand. What do you do for your people that servants could be better employed to do?" he asked, realizing he sounded accusing as he spoke the words.

"My father has no sons," was her reply as if that were the answer to any further questions.

She turned from him again, this time seeking her pallet, clearly dismissing any further inquiries that he might have. Perhaps it was best to allow her to escape what was obviously a sore subject. He stood there a moment watching as she nestled herself into her blanket, turning onto her side, presenting him with her back.

"I meant no insult, I only wondered why such a beautiful woman, one of nobility, would have such roughened skin," he said as he too went to seek his pallet.

"Ye had better rest before we get back on the road. We've a long journey ahead, and I'm exhausted. While ye slept for hours, I sat awake worrying over yer health," she said, ignoring his attempt to make amends.

"What of Trapper?" he asked as he lie down beside her.

"Hush yerself now, and go to sleep."

Within mere moments of her command, he realized that she was fast asleep. He realized too that she had avoided answering his question about his horse. Women are curious creatures, he mused with a wide yawn. Listening to her rhythmic breathing felt soothing to him, and it wasn't long before he found that he could no longer deny the sleep that was threatening to overtake him.

****

"Quit following me around brat," the young man barked at the girl who was the bane of his existence.

"Ha!" she shouted with a laugh as she bounced just out of his reach.

"Come Luther, let us see how the twins fair, shall we?" the tall, lean man beckoned him.

"Your mother died from complications of a fever, lad." The old man told him with a pat of sympathy on his head.

"Quit pulling my hair you insufferable

creature," he shouted as he started to spiral into a pit of darkness.

"Where's Dylan?" he asked as he was tossed about in the vortex.

"Jasper!" he cried as he began to panic. Where is everyone?

"Hawk!" he cried in horror when at last he landed in a desolate field. Where am I?

"Wake up man, yer thrashin' about as though the Devil were at yer heels," Trapper said with a kick to Luther's leg.

Luther sat up quickly, his breathing harsh and rasping. He looked around the room through what felt like a fog as he tried to reconcile the images that had been racing through his mind with his current reality. What did it all mean, and who were all those people?

"It's time to set about our trip to Gretna Green. Refresh yerself then meet with us at the carriage," Roslyn instructed.

Luther looked up to see her as she towered over him. Still dressed as a man, she was a sight to behold, lovely in ways he couldn't have conjured even in his most erotic of dreams. He shook off the thought, yawning loud as he scratched his head vigorously like a dog scratching fleas, causing a loud outburst of laughter from his betrothed.

"Fleas, have ye?" she snorted, then walked away.

He hoped he didn't have fleas, but he suspected he might after laying about in this filthy hovel. Good riddance, he thought as he rose to his feet, pleased to find that there was no dizziness as he did. The sooner they got on the road, the better. He wasn't sure how much time had passed since he'd laid down to rest but suspected that it had only been a couple of hours as the atmosphere in the shack gave the impression of late morning nearing the noon hour.

He felt renewed, stronger even as the pounding in his head had subsided. That was a blessing he would embrace, but that dream had been unsettling. Who were all those people? Were they memories? They must have been because they had seemed so real.

He stepped out the back door of the shack to relieve himself, noting that the carriage was gone, presumably it was out front awaiting him. Once relieved, he went back into the now empty shack, realizing that they were indeed ready to leave and quickened to have a look around to make sure he wasn't leaving anything behind. Once assured that he had everything, he went out the front door to find Trapper atop the carriage and Roslyn tucked away inside.

"Where's my horse?" he asked Trapper after assessing that it was nowhere around.

"We couldnae catch it when ye took yer fall," he grunted.

Well, that explained the absence. No sense worrying about the beast now. It was probably already in the hands of someone else, the bandits perhaps, he reasoned as he walked toward the driver's bench and leaped up beside his brother.

"Ye dinnae want to ride with yer lady?" Trapper asked.

"It wouldn't be proper," Luther simply stated.

"Aye, I suppose yer right," Trapper said snapping the reigns.

"Besides, you seem to have all the answers I seek. Perhaps you can continue to enlighten me as Roslyn seems to prefer to remain uh ... mysterious," Luther told him.

"Dinnae fash yerself, ye will get yer memory back soon enough, I wager," Trapper said evasively.

Luther could see that Trapper was in no mood to entertain him, but he had so many questions, and his brother seemed to be a wealth of information.

"You said my father passed away, but what of my mother?" Luther asked undauntedly.

"The same fever that took everyone else took her too," Trapper told him with real sadness.

"Did I have other brothers? Sisters?" Luther asked.

"Just yers truly," Trapper said with a cheeky grin.

Luther mulled this information over in his mind. It felt right somehow, but his dreams had indicated a close bond with others, others that felt like family.

"I dreamed of three men that I had some kind of attachment to," he spoke the thought aloud.

"I hope ye ain't one of them perverted sorts," Trapper snickered.

Luther elbowed him in response, nearly unseating him from the bench.

"Relax brother, I was just having a little sport with ye," Trapper said as he rubbed his shoulder where Luther had undoubtedly left a mark.

"They felt like family," Luther said to himself more than to Trapper.

"Perhaps it was some of the lads ye went to Eton with. We heard tales about ye and yer pack of bachelors runnin' all the ladies to ground in London," Trapper observed.

"Do you know their names?" Luther asked him.

"No, but Roz probably knows, she kept an ear to the ground about ye all these years while ye were away," Trapper said as he adjusted his position on the bench to allow more space between them.

Luther noted that Trapper seemed tense and wondered at it.

"Tell me about her," Luther said after a moment.

Trapper was silent as though deep in thought then started speaking softly as though he were lost in a vision.

"Aye, she be the most beautiful woman in all of Scotland. She doesn't know it though as she is the most humble, hardworking person ye could ever meet. She never thinks about herself, nay, only her people. She wakes up every day before dawn and sets out to make her rounds in the village dispensing medicine to the sick and food to our clans people. Two years back, I saw her work herself to near death to make sure ole widow McShan had a good roof for winter and plenty of wood to keep her old bones warm and dry. She never stopped until she had her safely set for one of the hardest winters we ever had. Somehow, she knew what was comin' as she has a way about her like that. She watches the land and the animals behavior and follows their lead. Her instincts are a spot on never leavin' us unprepared," he told him before going silent again.

Luther remembered her roughened skin with a gulp of something that felt like pride or maybe it was shame, he wasn't sure. The idea that such a young girl had to work so hard was humbling.

"Ye see brother, our bonny Roz could have anyone she wanted, but she wants ye fer some unknown reason. I've seen her turn away countless suitors, always tellin' them she's betrothed to the Marquess of Huntley, never waverin' from her faith that one day ye would come back. People laughed at her devotion, but she always remained steadfast. She loved ye even as a wee lass, and ye always tellin' her to leave ye alone. It broke my heart to see her bounce around ye tryin' desperately to get yer attention, but ye never had time to give it. Now, here ye are, and ye can't even remember her. I tell ye brother, it makes me want to wring yer neck," Trapper said, shaking his head.

Luther smiled as he remembered the images of the little girl taunting him. So it had been Roslyn! He smiled content with the knowledge that his impression of her was accurate. She would make a devoted wife and a good mother, but was he worthy? Apparently, he had abandoned her when she had needed him most. He turned his head in embarrassment to look about the countryside, he felt ashamed. How could he redeem himself?

"If ye hurt her, I'll kill ye brother, mark my words," Trapper said almost inaudibly.

Luther snapped his head in his brother's direction.

"I've had enough of your threats brother. I've no intentions of hurting the girl. I realize I've been negligent, but if all you have told me bears out, then I will do my duty," Luther said, feeling the rise of dignity he knew he didn't really own.

Who am I? He asked himself with disdain. He must surely be the worst person imaginable to have shirked his duties all these years.

"Duty! I'm sick of the word," Trapper said spitting off the side of the carriage.

"Aye, duty!" Luther said though he wondered why he obviously never cared before.

"Tell me, why did I run away?" he found himself asking.

"That's the way of it with yer kind. Ye think the world belongs to ye, and ye can have yer way about it. Ye dinnae want to be bothered after yer father passed. All ye wanted was yer friends and yer women. Ye should go back," Trapper said with venom in his tone.

"You would like that, wouldn't you? You want her for yourself," Luther challenged.

"Aye, but she'll no have me, it's ye she wants, her knight in shinin' armor," he said with a sardonic grunt of laughter.

Luther grew silent now. He couldn't feel any less of a toad if he tried, he had no defense for what was obvious. He didn't remember who he was, but it was clear that he was the lowest of the low, abandoning his people to waste his life away indulging in debauchery. Roslyn clearly deserved better, but was he the man to deliver?

He wasn't sure how he would feel when his memory came back if ever it did, but right now he wanted redemption. His brother's clear disdain seemed warranted, and he knew in his gut that he would have to do right by the girl and his people, he had much to account for, it seemed.

"There be a postin' inn just up the road, perhaps we can find ye a horse," Trapper said breaking into his thoughts.

The message was clear. Rejection. Even his own brother didn't want to be near him. Could he blame him?

Chapter Four

"I do," Luther said, surprised by how proudly he spoke the words.

The trip to Gretna Green had been rather quick after they had stopped at the posting inn to rid themselves of the carriage. Roslyn and Trapper had reclaimed their mounts while he had purchased one for himself. After they dined, Luther had offered to purchase some clothing for Roslyn, but she declined his offer saying that she was quite comfortable in the clothes she was wearing.

He was starting to sense that she was far more comfortable in male attire than she would be in ladies' clothing, so he didn't push the issue with her. It would probably be safer as they traveled for her to give the appearance of being a man at any rate. The smithy looked her over before he started the ceremony, clearly confused by her choice of garb.

"I now pronounce ye man and wife, ye may kiss yer bride," he concluded with a raising of his eyebrow.

Awkwardly, Luther moved closer to deliver said kiss as Roslyn backed away in avoidance. Luther was at a loss and looked at the smithy for guidance. He shrugged in response then slammed his hammer on the anvil. It was done; they were man and wife. Luther's head snapped around at the slamming of the door behind him. Trapper was gone. Roslyn started to go after him then quickly stopped herself, looking at Luther for permission.

"Go," he said with defeat.

He watched as she went running for the door, flinging it open, then fleeing through it without so much as a backward glance in his direction. He shook his head in exasperation, the whole scene not going unnoticed by the smithy.

"If I were ye, I would go see what yer lady wife and that young lad are up to," he said with a nod in the direction of the door.

Luther shrugged his shoulders as he took the marriage certificate in hand but did take the man's wise advice. Once outside, he saw that Roslyn and Trapper were locked in a fierce embrace, her crying like a child losing something precious and dear. Trapper with his face buried in her neck finally looked up when he realized they were being watched. Trapper's eyes blazed fiercely at Luther, giving him a moment of concern, truly, if looks could kill, then he would surely drop dead on the very spot where he stood. Trapper shoved away from Roslyn, pointing an accusing finger at him.

"Remember what I told ye," he shouted, then quickly turned away, mounted his horse then sped off as if the fires of hell were about to scorch him to ashes.

Roslyn stood there with her back to Luther, watching as Trapper disappeared from view. He could clearly see that she was crying from the motion of her shoulders, making him feel as though he had intruded on something sacred and very private. He wasn't sure if he should go to her to comfort her or go to her demanding answers about such a scene.

Without intent or memory of the movement, he found himself standing behind her; without consent from his brain, his hands reached out to gently massage her shoulders. What else could he do? He was her husband now, it was his duty to protect her in all things ... even a broken heart?

"He loves you," he spoke the words softly.

He felt her body go rigid in response to the words as he turned her toward him.

"Aye, and I love him but only as a brother so ye can put yer mind to rest dear husband," she told him.

"What just happened here, Roslyn?" he asked her.

"He wanted me to marry him. I refused, of course, I refused. He told me when I married ye he would be done followin' me around so it seems in order to gain a husband I had to lose a brother," she said and then began to sob anew.

Luther felt her loss. He pulled her into his arms, allowing her to cry as he rubbed her back to comfort her.

"I imagine he just needs space to cool his heels. Give it a little time, then we will both have our brother back," he assured her.

She cried harder then as though it could never come to pass, making him feel completely useless; he was truly at a loss. He had to think of something, anything that would comfort her.

"Come, let us go have an ale in celebration of our union. You can tell me all about our brother. I have missed out on a lot it seems," he suggested.

She bobbed her head, seeming to cheer slightly at the suggestion, following along without fuss as he guided her down the path to the inn near the smithy's shop. As he led her along, he became aware that people were staring at them, no doubt wondering why such an emotional outburst had been had between men. Summoning what he imagined would be his fiercest look, one by one, the people went about their business as he ushered her along.

****

Luther couldn't help but chuckle at his young bride. She had gotten well and truly sauced while having a wonderful time regaling him with tales of her childhood with Trapper at her side. He couldn't help but feel a little envious of his brother and wondered why he himself had not taken the time to enjoy her good company.

She was fascinating with her tales; though at times he could see so much sadness triumphed by an overwhelming spirit to succeed, even though life continued to kick her in the teeth. His bride was a marvel causing him to wonder if he would ever be the man she deserved, which brought his mind around to the reality that this was their wedding day. In most cases there should be a wedding night, but it would not be the case for them as he had vowed to postpone consummation of the marriage until he had his proof; however, at this moment, the need for proof seemed ever increasingly moot.

He knew everything he had been told was true and found that he had no regrets whatsoever. Still, he would wait to claim his bride until the time was right because she, or rather, they both needed time to get to know one another. It could wait, and he would relish in the waiting.

He shook off the thought, bringing his attention back to her as she swallowed the last dregs of her ale. Clearly, she was unfit to continue traveling; with the hour growing late, he realized he would have to procure rooms. Without further thought to the matter, he excused himself from the table and went to the innkeeper to inquire about their lodgings.

"I only have one room available my Lord," the man informed him.

It would have to serve. He placed his coin in the innkeeper's hand then accepted the key to the room. They had already bedded down together before so this wouldn't be any different, really. At least they were married so he wouldn't be putting her in an uncompromising situation, he thought as he made his way back to their table.

"Come, I have secured a room so we may rest before we get back on the road. The hour is late, and you my dear, are quite inebriated," he said with a big dimpled grin.

"I always loved yer dimples, Luther Rollins," she told him with a giggle.

"Come, my lady, let us retire," he said offering his hand.

She staggered to her feet at which point she nearly fell but was spared the humiliation of it by his quick action of support. He led his wife to their room, opening the door with one hand while keeping her upright with the other. It was a nice room, the bed being big enough to accommodate them both, but he wondered if he should request more blankets so he could sleep on the floor.

She pulled away from him to remove her coat then her boots, before he realized what she was about. Much to his surprise, she had removed all her clothes down to her undergarments then unceremoniously plopped herself in the middle of the bed. His wife had no shame, it seemed. He chuckled as he began to remove his own clothing, keeping in mind his vow to postpone the consummation, he kept his breeches on for the sake of prudence.

A moment passed as she lay so perfectly still with her face buried in the pillow that he began to suspect that she may be sleeping. While she lay in such a posture, with her buttocks slightly lifted drawing his notice, he couldn't help but admire her very shapely figure, he was a man, after all. With a pulse in his loins, he realized that he was in much need of distraction. Forcing his eyes away from her beautiful backside, he looked around the room, pleased to see spare blankets on a rack in the corner, at least he wouldn't freeze to death on the floor.

Just as he resigned himself to a long, frustrating night, his wife rolled over then sat up. The muscles in his chest rippled with excitement as her eyes drank him in. Did I say some foolish nonsense about no consummation, he wondered.

"It's a comfortable bed," she said patting it in

invitation then began unfurling her hair from its plait.

Luther's throat went dry making it nearly impossible to swallow. God's teeth, she is a vixen. How am I to resist so lovely a sight? Searching his mind to find some way to gain the upper hand in his dilemma, he began to wonder if he should take his leave, immediately, instead of trying to ride out the entire night, struggling with his manly urges.

"Uh, I had not planned to bed down with you," he said awkwardly.

"Oh, that's right, ye need yer proof. Suit yerself, tis no bother to me," she said before laying back on the pillows seductively.

"I'll just enjoy this bed and its fine comfort alone," she said with a crooked smile before closing her eyes then issuing a sigh as though she were resting on a cloud sent from heaven.

The wench! How was he to ignore such a tempting invitation, her with the nipple on her right breast peeking at him as if daring him to look away? Aware of the heat flooding his loins, certain that there was now a raging erection tenting below his breeches, he turned away from the bed, raking his hand through his hair in frustration. Torment, that's what this is!   Stomping over to the rack, mumbling nonsensically as he went, he snatched a blanket away then placed it in front of himself to cover the proof of his desire before moving back toward the bed where she lay.

"You should cover yourself," he advised.

Slowly, she opened her eyes, looking him over with clear mischief on her mind. Had he the good sense that God gave the common dog, he would have kept distance between them to prevent her from grabbing the blanket away from him, but no, he was completely mindless.

"Thank ye, but what will ye use?" she asked innocently.

Following the motion of her eyes as they traversed the length of his body, he watched as she turned the most beautiful shade of red when her examination came to a halt on the evidence of his desire for her. Her eyes went wide with a mixture of fear, fascination and curiosity, but mostly fear, so he quickly sat down on the side of the bed turning his back to her, embarrassed for them both.

"I had planned to use that blanket," he mumbled, softly.

A peel of laughter barely warned him what she planned to do, for the next thing he knew, with speed and agility that quite surprised him, she had wrestled him onto his back, whereby he found himself trapped beneath her. Positioning herself just so, she straddled him as though he were a stallion between her legs, grinning as though she had captured a grand prize.

He wasn't sure if she was aware of this, but having her heat next to his was utterly mind-bending. He wasn't sure what to do now; was he always this awkward when it came to females? He didn't know, but right now, he seemed like a green lad, she a skilled seductress making him fear that any minute now he would humiliate himself.

"Why did ye cut all yer hair off, Luther Rollins?" she asked breathlessly with her hands placed palms down upon his chest.

The rise and fall of her breasts as she breathed left him captivated. He could see their perfection, globes round, firm, begging for his attention. He could barely focus on the question she asked as blood, hot and pulsing, forced its way through his body, making him desperate to unleash his manhood so he could plunge it hard and heavy into her young tender flesh. She laughed, causing those luscious orbs to quiver. She-devil!

"Yer hair?" she asked with a thrust of her hips to get his attention.

Sweet agony.

"Lass, if you don't stop this now, you will find yourself giving away more than you bargain for," he told her a bit desperately.

She looked into his eyes but didn't move from her perch. A moment went by before he found that he was helpless to stop his hand as he reached up to stroke her beckoning breast. She slowly closed her eyes as if his touch pleased her, the action emboldening him to squeeze ever so slightly. She sighed softly as she ground herself against his angry sex.

"Please lass, you have no idea what you are doing to me," he told her, closing his eyes to the sweet torment.

"Ye are my husband, Luther Rollins, take what is yers," she said in invitation.

Luther was torn between wanting to succumb to her bold invitation and knowing that he had vowed to keep the marriage chaste until such time as he had the proof that all he had been told was true. As he battled with his desire to give way to abandon, to immerse himself within her warmth, he tried desperately to reason with himself.

Why was she trying to seduce him? Clearly, it was her intention to get him to consummate their union as quickly as possible, but why, when he had made it plain that he wanted to wait? Did she have a motive that was not yet clear to him? Could she already be with child, trying to dupe him into accepting another man's offspring as his own? Could there be more to the relationship between her and his brother?

This last thought brought clarity to the moment, allowing him the resolve he needed to push her away so he could extricate himself from such a dangerous predicament.

"Lass, perhaps you should rest," he said, clearing his throat in an effort to keep his composure. "It has been a long day, and you must be very tired," he continued as he removed himself from the bed.

He quickly stood up and set about making a pallet on the floor, not looking back at her as if by doing so he could remove her from the room entirely.

"Go on then, ye coward," she huffed.

Luther stiffened his back against her insult but said nothing to encourage further discourse. He was a man after all and should be able to command his body's responses in any situation, even one so tempting as his beautiful young bride's attempts at seduction.

Young! He had best remember that she was indeed very young but was she already skilled in the arts of lovemaking? Had she and Trapper been lovers? The idea needled him now that it had taken root in his mind.

Laying down on his pallet, he continued to mull the thought over in his head. Perhaps they had been lovers. Clearly Trapper loved her but observation of the couple had led him to believe that it was purely innocent, at least on Roslyn's part. She seemed oblivious to the fact that Trapper desired her as she seemed to regard him as a sister would a brother.

He sighed as he purged the thought from his head; he refused to believe it. Everything about Roslyn seemed genuine, with a true and honest character. No, they were not, nor had they ever been lovers. Perhaps she had simply had too much ale, causing her to lose her inhibitions; that seemed more likely to be the case. Remembering her drunken playfulness made him smile; perhaps, when the proper time came to consummate their marriage, he would ply her with wine as he rather liked this side of her.

After several moments of the sound of her rhythmic breathing, he realized that she was asleep. Relieved, he went over to the bed to assure himself that she was comfortably tucked away, chuckling softly at the picture she made, sprawled out in the middle of the bed with her breast still exposed. He gently tugged the blanket out from under her then placed it upon her to ensure that she wouldn't get a chill. With her tempting assets well covered, he kissed her on the forehead.

"Good night Roslyn" he whispered.

Her reply was a soft snore, proving his theory that she had simply been inebriated with no idea of the game she had been playing. Feeling better about the whole scene that had transpired, he blew out the lamp by the bedside and made his way back to his pallet.

****

"Luther, come back" came the cry of a woman from far away.

Luther woke with a start, fragmented images scattering through his head fast and furious before disappearing to the far reaches of his mind, making him feel as though he must have been on the verge of remembering something important. He rubbed his forehead, trying to recapture the images, but they were gone, making him wonder if he would ever remember anything at all about his life before waking up in that cursed shack.

The lighting in the room indicated that it was nearly dawn so with reluctance he pulled himself up from the warmth of his pallet to dress for the day ahead. While dressing, he observed that his wife was still sleeping but looked as though she had been twisting and turning fitfully in her sleep as the covers were tangled in her legs.

"Please, dinnae leave me," she whimpered.

Luther realized that it must have been her cries that caused him to wake so abruptly then felt compelled to go to her to comfort her. He couldn't help but notice how beautiful she was in slumber as he sat on the edge of the bed before gently sweeping her hair away from her face. What could she be dreaming?

Considering her plea, someone must have been leaving her, but who? Was she upset that Trapper had gone? Perhaps. The notion that she could have been dreaming of another man caused a spark of jealousy that made his stomach clench in protest. Why had he left her all those years ago allowing his brother to step in to fill the void? He would like the answer to that and so many other questions, but it seemed that he would have to wait.

"Roslyn, wake up," he spoke soothingly to her.

She slowly opened her eyes, smiling as she did, but the smile was quickly replaced with a severe scowl as she shoved his hand away from her face before propping herself up on her elbows. The look on her face told Luther that she was angry at him, but he chuckled anyway. She was a beauty even scowling at him in such a way, like some angry fish-wife.

"It's time to get up so we can continue our journey to Dunheath," he told her with a smile.

"What are ye doin' in my room?" she asked

with furrowed brows.

He touched the end of her nose with the tip of his finger. "Our room," he simply stated. "Now up with you. We need to get an early start. I will await you in the dining room below," he instructed as he removed himself from his seat.

****

Roslyn watched as her husband left the room. "The man is insufferable. I'll not be lettin' him order me about," she grumbled aloud to the empty room as she plopped back down sinking defiantly into her pillow.

That's when she remembered; Lord, what did I do last night? As fast as lightning, she jumped up from the bed to examine the sheets. No blood! Thank goodness, but where are my clothes? Her mind raced as she frantically searched the room locating various pieces of her clothing, noting that they were strewn about as though she had no care for them at all.

After a quick glance at her body, much to her relief, she realized she was still wearing her drawers and chemise. Taking a deep calming breath, she sat on the edge of the bed as she went over the events from the night before. She had been completely out of her head with drink! She had tried to seduce him! He hadn't wanted her!

"Saints preserve me, what shall I do?" she cried to the empty room.

Moments of mortified embarrassment passed while she contemplated her situation. True, she had been drunk, but she was sure that she had done everything right. She had removed her clothes and invited him to partake of her body, the thought causing a slight shiver. Why hadn't he succumbed?

On the way to fetch Luther, she had asked Trapper what to expect on her wedding night. At first, he hadn't wanted to discuss it, growing angry as she continued to pester him on the issue until finally he told her not to worry about that because no man could resist a willing female. He went on to tell her that all she had to do was present herself to him, and he would do the rest. So where had she gone wrong? She had certainly presented herself, though not quite the way she had imagined when Trapper had spoken of it. Perhaps, he had been repulsed by her drunken behavior, perhaps he found her lacking somehow.

Reluctantly, she began to dress herself as she continued to mull it all over. Whatever the reason, he had rejected her, she wouldn't allow him the chance to humiliate her again. If he didn't want her, so be it! She only needed the marriage certificate so she would be off limits to Magnus. Well, I have it! She didn't need him hanging about telling her what to do! No! This suited her perfectly.

After dressing herself, she sat back on the bed not really feeling the bravado she had moments before. Luther doesn't want me, whether he remembers me or not, she thought with slumping shoulders.

Chapter Five

A trip to the highlands on horseback is not the best way to become acquainted with one's new bride, Luther mused as he watched the rigid form of his wife's back as she silently led the way for what must have been many hours now. When she had met with him in the dining room earlier that morning, she had seemed cold, indifferent even, with her shoulders squared, her hair once again tightly braided, giving her the appearance of a very rigid young man.

Clearly she was in a temper about something but he had no idea what it could be as he had been courteous and kind to her even in the face of her sniping remarks at the beginning of their journey. He had made multiple attempts at congenial conversation when they had first set out, but she had set the tone of the journey by urging her horse ahead refusing discourse of any kind. Whatever the problem was, he had decided it was best to let it run its course, allowing her the space she obviously wanted in hopes that sooner or later she would come around.

It would take roughly seven days at the speed they were traveling to reach Dunheath; the idea that it would be spent in silence annoyed him. Perhaps when they stopped to rest for the night, he could break the ice that seemed to have formed between them. Remembering the scene between her and

Trapper, he began to wonder if she was still upset over his abrupt departure the day before; the thought needled him to near distraction.

How does one woo a wife that is heartbroken over the loss of another man? Of course, if he had his memories intact, he would be better armed for such a mission, but everything still eluded him. Throughout the day, he had wondered why he had left Scotland, preferring to reside in dreary old London. It was truly a beautiful place with grass as green as any emerald carpeting hills that gently rolled along for miles until they lazily flowed into patches of forests, painted in various shades from the richest of red to the most glorious of gold from God's own palette.

Occasionally the landscape offered the mind sustenance to ponder such as crumbling old castle ruins, breathtaking water features including majestic waterfalls, ancient bridges left behind by the Romans, spanning the width of rippling streams or the many small lochs that quenched the thirst of the many herds of sheep grazing upon the luscious flora that was to be had so abundantly.

The countryside along the road seemed familiar somehow as though he had made the journey before. He was even fairly certain that there was a village up ahead that would offer food and shelter. Perhaps they would find a number of shops where he could purchase a set of clothes and other supplies to make the trip more comfortable for them both.

The idea struck him that it might be a good conversation starter to inquire with Roslyn, so with that in mind, he urged his horse into a faster trot, allowing him to quickly catch up with her.

"I say Roslyn, I feel certain that there must be a village up ahead," he ventured.

With an even more rigid posture than she already had, she cast her eyes forward with her chin up but otherwise did not acknowledge his statement; he continued undauntedly.

"I thought I would buy a new set of clothes as these are hardly roadworthy. Perhaps a few supplies wouldn't be unreasonable in the event that we find ourselves unable to find a posting inn further into our journey. It wouldn't serve to be caught without proper provisions if the weather were to turn," he said.

He thought he noticed her shoulders relax ever so slightly, but still she remained mute. Women! Still he needed to break through this barrier, so he continued.

"Surely you would like to get out of those clothes," he suggested.

Luther flinched in response as she snapped her head in his direction casting him a scathing glare. If her eyes were daggers, he would have fallen from his horse a very dead man, indeed.

"Ye'll not be getting me out of my clothes again," she sniped.

Luther didn't know why, but this struck him as the funniest thing he had ever heard, promptly bursting into a fit of laughter. The idea that he had gotten her out of her clothes was absurd. However, after noting that his bout of hysterical laughter had gained him nothing but more of her ire he tried to recover himself. Clearing his throat he ventured.

"Madam, I dare say that it is not my intention to get you out of your clothes, only to provide a clean set. I'm sure it has not escaped you that we both have taken on a fairly musty scent over the last few days, not to mention there is blood spattered upon my coat." There, that was true; how could she argue?

"Now ye insult me?" she challenged.

"Nay my lady, I meant no offense. I only wish to provide a measure of comfort for us both," he said with his hands up in surrender.

She seemed to consider this for a moment but said nothing further.

Luther could take no more. "God's teeth woman, whatever is the matter? Please, tell me how I can mend this bridge between us?" he pleaded.

"Ye, sir, are a pig!" she shouted.

"A pig?" he asked, blinking in confusion.

"Aye, a pig, worse than a scurvy dog," she grumbled before resuming her rigid posture from earlier.

Luther thought about her harsh words for a moment; clearly she was angry at him; she wasn't missing her friend Trapper as he had suspected. No, she was definitely angry at him. He must have unknowingly delivered some hurt upon her; now he was at a loss. He searched his memory from the night before trying to find a clue. Ah ... there it was. He had rebuffed her attempts at seduction. Now he understood, but how to proceed? He wondered if he wasn't a master in the art of relationships with the fairer sex. This was obviously out of his realm of experience. How does one reign in a woman's temper to make her more yielding to an attempt at peace?

The silence between them was loud and booming, but he was optimistic that all was not lost as she continued to ride at his side instead of racing up ahead of him as she had done when they first set out. Perhaps her lingering presence was an invitation to apologize.

"Obviously I have insulted you in some way and for that I offer my most humble apology. If you are angry about last night, I meant only to protect you because .... well, you were in a rather drunken state, and it wouldn't have been right to take advantage of you. We hardly know one another after all, and I thought only to allow time to do so before we engage in intimacy." There that was the truth, it would have to serve.

It seemed to mollify her as once again her posture relaxed.

"Ye need yer proof," she finally mumbled.

"Truth Roslyn, the need for proof is not so important as it was the day I learned of all this. I am your husband now, and though I find you rather alluring, we are strangers still and mind you, there is still the issue of my memory. I don't even know who I am. What if I find out that I am a horrible person? A person unworthy of you? We need time, do we not?" he asked with hope showing in his eyes.

"I know who ye be, Luther Rollins," was her swift reply.

"Perhaps you could help me by telling me about myself as I feel lost and confused. This is very difficult for me. Will you help me find myself?" he asked eagerly.

Moments stretched out uncomfortably as Roslyn seemed to be struggling with what to say.

Finally she broke, "What do ye want to know?"

"How do you remember me?" he asked after a brief moment of consideration.

She was his lifeline now, the one with the answers he so desperately needed. Perhaps he could learn of his character through her childhood memories of him.

"Ye were a gangly lad with wild unruly hair that dropped down beneath yer shoulders. Och, how I loved to tease ye about it because it was the only way to get yer attention. Ye were always too busy to notice me, so I took pleasure in taunting ye whenever I could. Ye were handsome in yer tartan too, but ye seemed loathe to wear it, perhaps because too much of yer skinny legs were exposed, I dinnae know. Ye were born of the land, but ye were never really at home there, always with yer mind in England. Ye had dreams and aspirations of a more refined lifestyle," she said with a mock air of indifference.

"Ye dinnae fit in," she continued. "It was well known that ye argued with yer father, swearin' that ye would never take the role of chieftain. Ye thought we were a barbaric people and insisted on goin' away to Eton where ye could get a fine education among yer real peers. No doubt, it was yer mother's influence as she was English born, she herself never wanted the life of a highlander. It's a hard life to be sure, so it was understandable that she never adapted," she relayed.

She went silent again, and Luther took the time to absorb her words.

"What was my mother's name?" he found himself asking.

"Lucinda Belmont was her name, a woman of nobility. They tell me she was a beautiful woman, broadly considered the catch of her season. Her dowry was very rich and yer father, though much older than she, snatched her up so he could prop up his coffers. In the beginning, he used her dowry to make improvements to the manor, but when she died, yer father took to women and drink, never really caring about continuing the efforts. Some say he did not treat yer mother well. Once she had given him an heir, he had cast her aside in favor of tavern wenches."

She paused there as if something struck her before continuing, "I'm not sure what else there be to tell ye about her," she concluded.

That would explain Trapper's parentage, he surmised. As she had been speaking of his mother, he felt a sense of familiarity but could not form any recognizable images of what his mother may have looked like. He shook his head, dispelling the frustration.

"I keep having images flash through my

dreams, very confusing. It seems as though I had some kind of bond with several gentlemen, a brotherly bond," he was quick to clarify. "I can't remember anything about them, only that I felt an attachment somehow," he said the last more to himself than to her.

"Perhaps ye are rememberin' yer friends from Eton," she offered.

"What can you tell me of them?" he asked, his tone laced with hope.

"A bunch of rogues, the lot of ye," she grumbled with obvious disdain.

"Rogues?" he pressed.

"Aye, ye and yer pack of bachelors; all ye cared about was seein' who could out-do the other in yer sports of debauchery," again with clear disdain, she answered him.

Luther could see that she was loathed to speak of this subject, but he felt like he needed to hear the full of it.

"Please continue. Names, I need names if you could provide them," he prompted.

She sulked for a moment but began to relay what she knew. "I know there be a duke, a couple of earls I think. I'm no sure exactly, but there be a man they called Hawk, he be a duke. Gabriel, aye, that be his name, but I cannae remember the rest of it. Then there be a man called Jasper and one by the name of, let's see, what is it ... oh, Dylan. Aye, yer 'pack of bachelors' as the gossip papers called them," she finished.

"Gossip papers?" he asked somewhat concerned.

"Aye, tales of yer exploits reached all the way to Dunheath. Ye and yer fine friends," she said before spitting.

"I wish you would quit doing that," he chastised.

"Quit doing what?" she demanded.

"Quit spitting. It's hardly ladylike," he explained.

The amiable conversation between them quickly deteriorated into a quarrel, but Luther would not back down in this as her manners were simply deplorable. Her lessons in ladylike decorum would start now. However, it seemed that his wife would seek to teach him some lessons as well.

"And just who do ye think ye are tellin' me how to behave?" she challenged with her shoulders squared for battle.

Luther puffed his chest up for effect so that she could see that his authority as her husband would prevail in the matter then proceeded to instruct her accordingly.

"I would remind you that I am your husband, and it is my wish that you behave with a little more decorum, madam," he said with a raised brow.

Luther's attempt at dominance was quickly quelled when she glared at him with such hostility as to make one fear for their safety then proceeded to blast him for his efforts.

"No man will ever tell me what to do, Luther Rollins, husband or no," she said before spurring her horse forward, leaving him behind.

Luther watched her disappear from view as a trail of dust encompassed him, sputtering as it reached his nose and mouth.

"Good show old boy," he grumbled aloud.

Luther knew that he would not get any more information from her now that he had set her temper up, so he allowed her escape without pursuit. She wouldn't get far, so he wasn't concerned, but damn the dust.

Sneezing his way forward as he went, he was grateful when the dust began to die down, allowing him to see that she was up ahead at a safe distance.

He would allow her the space for a spell so she could properly sulk. His wife liked to sulk, it seemed.

He smiled as he watched her ride up ahead; his wife, such a determined creature. The more discourse he had with her, the more he was certain that she would never behave submissively nor dress in womanly refinements; he was fairly certain that breeches and boots were her normal garb.

The realization triggered a memory from the conversation about how she came to be dressed in such a way. According to Trapper, her clothing had been stolen, and she was wearing his clothes. Was that a lie? If so, to what end? It seemed so trivial a thing to lie about so he couldn't imagine why it was necessary to do it.

Whatever the reason, there were bigger issues to sort out, so he filed it away for future consideration as he urged his horse to close the gap she had set between them. He wasn't sure why, but he felt the need to be closer to her.

Though the rolling lilt of her Scottish brogue soothed him, he would allow the silence; if she wanted to remain quiet for now so be it but having her so far away made him feel bereft. Once he closed the gap, he was relieved when she allowed the close proximity, but as he suspected, she was still brooding over their exchange.

****

Roslyn cursed herself as she rode silently with Luther at her heels. Why do I let him get under my skin so? Embarrassment from the night before still stung her pride, but just as she began to forgive him for the insult he insulted her again. First, he told her that she smelled bad, and then he told her she was unladylike. How dare he!

Still, she couldn't help but feel sorry for him, unable to imagine what it must be like to lose your memory; of course, there was the fact that she was responsible for his memory loss. She truly hoped he never figured that part out, but she had never been so lucky as that. One day it would be time to pay that piper, but until then she would just bide her time, hoping for the best outcome when the truth was learned.

When he had asked her to help him remember things, she had felt honored, and as she spoke to him she began to rekindle her childhood feelings about him. Damn, but I loved him then and double damn but I love him still, but why? He had never before cared one whit about her, yet she had waited all these years for his return until finally she realized she would have to take drastic measures by dragging him back, possibly kicking and screaming all the way. It had been worth the risk, she wouldn't undo it if she could, but when he learned of it ...

Telling him about her part in his memory loss would certainly ensure that he would revert back to his former attitude where he would no doubt treat her as the nuisance he deemed her as a child. She had to tell him though, didn't she? He has the right to know who he is, of course he does. Would he run from her again when he regained his memories? She tried to tell herself that it didn't matter, but she knew in her heart that it did. Roslyn had wanted this, this marriage to Luther her whole life. Often she had dreamed of it when she slept and continued daydreaming of it while she toiled away her waking hours.

Somehow over the last few months the dream had begun to fade with the fast approach of her eighteenth birthday. When the harsh reality that he would never return to claim her had fully set in, she began to lose hope, but when her father had promised her to Magnus, she had become angry at Luther, bitter too that he hadn't wanted her after she had pined away for him for so many years. He had forgotten her, the notion stung mightily.

The knowledge that she had to go after him to force him to honor the contract to save herself as well as her people sat in her soul like a festering thorn. On the journey to fetch him, she counseled herself to remember that he didn't want her, that this would only be a marriage of necessity, then once she had secured herself, she could set him free to go back to London to do as he pleased. Now with his memory loss, the tables had turned. The plan had gone awry with his injuries and subsequent lies laid between them so that she wasn't sure how to go forward from here.

Strange, that he seemed to be so willing a participant in the marriage; however, she knew that if he had his memory, he would have thrown her in the gaol by now. At times, it seemed that he was actually pleased to be married, they hadn't had to hold a pistol to his head, after all, as she had imagined the scenario would be. He had proudly said the words to the smithy and had been pleasant to the point that she could believe that someday they would be happy together. Could they be happy together? Perhaps she should take his words of advice to heart and try to behave in a more ladylike fashion, but she didn't have a clue how to go about it. She had never had the guidance of a female in such things, only Trapper.

She sighed deeply at the loss of Trapper, she would miss him dearly. She wished he was here now to help her through this, but she knew in her heart that it was best to go it alone.

Having Trapper near would only serve as an aggravation as he seemed so adept at lying; she had never realized that he possessed such a talent. Clearly he hadn't wanted her to go through with the marriage to Luther, but she couldn't fathom that he had actually wanted her for himself. She would miss him, but this was how it had to be. She was pulled out of her brooding when she heard Luther whistling an obnoxious tune.

"Would ye please cease yer racket?" she sniped.

She knew she was being harsh, but damn the man, she didn't want anything to do with him right now.

"You do not enjoy music?" he inquired with mock injury to his feelings in his tone.

"Is that what ye call it? Then no, I dinnae enjoy music," she said turning her face away to hide the smile she could not stop from forming.

"I thought only to woo you from your ruminations. I'm starving, and I believe we are approaching a village," he pointed ahead of them as he spoke.

Thanks be to the saints, a diversion from the cursed road. Roslyn's spirit soared with the sight up ahead. They had been traveling since dawn, and it was well into the early evening hour, the need to seek shelter and sustenance was dire as her stomach had been growling for hours now. She knew Luther had been right when he pointed out that they needed to get provisions for the road, she was ashamed that she hadn't thought of it herself. Some leader she would make for her people when she couldn't even plan to bring proper provisions for a journey such as this.

Without much thought behind the action, she jabbed her horse in its sides with her boots, shooting forward shouting, "Last one there pays for our supper."

****

The couple secured their lodging for the night then set out to some of the local shops to procure what they could for their travels. They were lucky to find a small shop still open at that time in the evening offering a fairly abundant selection in second-hand clothing. They were quite pleased to be able to purchase some fairly decent items for them both.

Roslyn had refused a nice riding habit in favor of more breeches, shirts and the like, which she said would be far more comfortable on the road. Luther didn't argue as he had already surmised that she would make such a choice, deciding to let the matter stand unchallenged. Once they had secured decent clothing, they found another shop that offered blankets and other supplies for traveling, ensuring a comfortable journey at least.

Later they ate their dinner in companionable silence, sprinkled with pleasant though reserved discourse. Luther had tried to encourage her to have ale with her meal, but she flatly refused with what seemed like embarrassment at the memory from the night before. Luther didn't press her, noting that she seemed relieved, especially since they were again to share a room. She seemed to want to keep her wits about her, presumably to fend off any advances he might wish to make.

Luther was amused at the thought that he would make advances when clearly she had been the instigator before. However, he was a bit deflated as he had thought to offer ale to her in hopes that she might lose her inhibitions once again because the idea of intimacy was starting to entice him more and more.

As he watched her consume her meal, he couldn't help but think about her lovely lips pressed against his own as their bodies meshed together in a shared heat. He remembered how perfectly her breasts had felt in his hands, their lush bounty an offering to satisfy a great hunger within him. Her body was well rounded where it mattered …
"That's why ye'll be sleepin' in the stables."

Luther blinked his eyes rapidly at the rude awakening from his wayward thoughts. What was she saying?

"The stables?" he questioned.

"Aye, the stables, ye lecherous dog. I see ye oglin' me like some kind of starvin' animal!" she hissed.

Her tone was like a dousing of cold water to his

face, all he could do was sit there in confusion trying to understand what he had done to cause such an outburst.

"Madam, I was not ogling you as you say, I was simply … er … that is to say, I was … I was lost in thought," he stammered in defense of her accusation.

"Aye, I know what ye were thinkin' and that's why ye'll not be beddin' down in the same room with me," she said as she stood to leave him there alone at the table.

He watched her stomp away and briefly considered going after her. He was sure that giving chase would only serve to cause a scene that he wished to avoid, so he simply sat back in his chair letting his shoulders slump in defeat. I married a shrew, he thought, looking at the ceiling as if rescue from his dilemma resided in the rafters of the rickety old inn.

Chapter Six

Trapper rode long and hard for several days to put as much distance between him and the newlyweds as he could, barely stopping long enough to rest his horse to keep the poor beast from collapsing under the fierce demand he had placed him under. Watching Roslyn marry his brother had been more than he could stomach. In truth, it had been the hardest thing he had ever done, knowing that it would probably be the last time he ever laid eyes upon her, it had nearly ripped his heart in two.

Gone now were the days filled with her carefree laughter as the two of them got into all manner of mischief, replaced with what was sure to be a bleak, icy solitude without her. Never again could he entertain the notion that someday she could be his wife as now she belonged to another, his own brother, no less.

Thinking about that day at the shack when he had introduced himself as Luther's brother, Roslyn had thought him to be a fine actor. He didn't know why he had never told her before that Luther was his half-brother, but he never had. It had never really mattered much to him, but he had always been told by his adopted father to keep quiet about it, so he had.

He never held any secrets from Roslyn, save that one. His motive for revealing it then and there was that he knew that their time together was coming to an end, he wanted her to know who he really was. He wanted her to know that he could have been worthy of her, that only a cruel twist of fate kept them apart. Now, the man who loved her with all his heart had to, by an accident of birth, give her up to the man that ran from her, staying hidden away these long ten years while never once giving a care for her welfare in his absence. Tis truly cruel beyond measure.

Everyone, even Roslyn herself knew that Luther had abandoned her as well as his estates so the idea that their marriage would never come to pass had been generally accepted. That is to say, until lately when Magnus started to pester her father to give Roslyn to him. She nor he would ever stand for that, it had to be prevented at all costs as Magnus was a devil of the worst sort. No doubt, he would have made her miserable as a husband, not to mention what he would have done to her lands and her people. That was why he had first consented to help Roslyn make her way to London so that she could plead her case to Luther, in hopes that he would agree to honor the betrothal contract set by their fathers. He really was the only person that could save them from such a catastrophe.

The day before they were to leave for London, hope sprang in Trapper's heart when Magnus with his silver tongue had approached him with a deal to get Luther out of the way. Magnus had told him that if he would kill Luther, which would have allowed him to inherit his property as Luther had no heirs and Magnus was next in line, he would stand down and allow Trapper to marry her in his stead. He didn't really want the girl, he had told him, he only wanted access to the rich minerals that lay beneath Dunheath. Trapper had given it thought, concluding that it would be the only way he would ever be able to have Roslyn for himself, so he and Magnus had struck a bargain. Trapper would kill Luther, get the girl and a cut in the profits if he were to allow Magnus to mine the land unfettered.

He didn't know his brother, so the idea of killing him had seemed like an easy thing. He had grown up hating him for what he had done to Roslyn, so with a little help from Magnus he had convinced himself that killing him would be an heroic act. Of course, Magnus had played that angle up to entice him to agree, but it hadn't really been that hard to convince him.

It had actually been Magnus who had the idea to have Roslyn abduct Luther then bring him back to Scotland to force his hand in marriage. Roslyn being the adventurer that she was, naturally, agreed to the plan when Trapper had in turn suggested it to her. During the abduction, it would then be Trapper's role to strike him very hard upon the back of his head with a cudgel with the intended result being Luther's tragic and unfortunate death on the mean streets of London.

Now he was ashamed of himself that he had

even considered it, but he was further ashamed that he had actually tried to do it. He counted himself a very lucky man that he hadn't actually succeeded, for it would have surely been a devastating blow to Roslyn to have had a hand in Luther's death; a point he hadn't considered when the idea had been conceived.

However, he had double-crossed the Devil by helping Roslyn actually marry Luther. Perhaps it was an act of contrition, he wasn't sure, but he was fairly certain that he would be a marked man. He didn't care about that as he planned to leave Scotland after he returned home to collect his things and tell his father goodbye. There was nothing left for him there, in Dunheath, only memories of a life with the woman who was never meant for him.

He had loved Roslyn his whole life, even dared to dream that one day they would marry, living out the rest of their lives happily together forever, but he knew the reality of that now; it could never have happened. He was a bastard, she a lady, a future clan laird no less, a position necessitating a marriage to a nobleman to secure her lands and position. He knew this but knowing it didn't make it any easier to abide.

Trapper was grateful to God that he had been given a chance to do the right thing by helping her secure her husband, but he knew when Roslyn learned of his treachery she would surely hate him, that was the real reason he wanted to flee. How would he ever face her after she learned that he had schemed with Magnus to take her for himself while helping the evil bastard pillage her land and enslave her people?

Roslyn was safe with his brother, forever out of reach of Magnus with his ruthless ambitions. The knowledge of it would have to be a balm to his soul in the times to come when he would surely miss her dearly.   He would forever curse the fates that made him a poor bastard putting Roslyn so close yet just out of his reach. She was the most beautiful girl he had ever seen, she had been his best friend, his entire world since he was a wee pup of a lad. They had shared much together but sadly never so much as a simple kiss.

Aside from his dreams, he had never known a moment of passion with her beyond laughing, playing and fighting as children often do. When she started to take a woman's form, he found that his thoughts toward her had grown from innocent to lustful. They had bathed in the loch many times without a stitch of clothing on as children, but when she started to form breasts everything changed, forcing him to find other things to do rather than hang about with her at the loch. That's when he discovered that for the price of a coin, serving wenches could be very accommodating to a young man's needs, but they could never hold a candle to her. They only served to keep his lust tamed so he could behave honorably when he was with her.

The first time she had discovered him with one of the light skirts had been when they had gone to the village, he had taken the opportunity to slip away while she had gone inside one of the shops. The woman had beckoned him so naturally he had followed her around the corner into an alleyway. Apparently, Roslyn had seen them go then decided to follow, arriving just as he had gotten the woman's skirts up to commence. Her eyes had gone wide with shock; he being frustrated at being caught, had shouted at her to go away. Thankfully, she had, but she had questioned him later to no end about what they had been doing.

He had been embarrassed at the time, but she had caught him many times since in such situations as he seemed to be, according to her, a randy dog. After he had explained his needs to her, she seemed to accept it, never holding it against him even though he privately had hoped that someday she would show some sign of jealousy, but she never did. It was always Luther whom she loved.

Well, now she had him, her knight in shining armor; now there was no place in her life for a lovesick fool, the poor bastard brother of her husband hanging about so he had best move on. Perhaps he would go to sea or even to the colonies. He had a little money saved up, maybe just enough to gain passage on a ship with some left to hold him over until he secured employment somewhere.

Wherever he ended up, it wouldn't be far

enough away from his conscience, he knew this just as sure as he knew that he would never love a woman the way he loved Roslyn.

****

In the days that followed on their way to Dunheath, Roslyn and Luther made little progress toward marital bliss. Within a day and a half's ride to Dunheath, her nerves were wound tight. It was getting harder and harder to resist Luther as he was ceaseless in his kindness toward her. She had treated him deplorably, she knew, but it was only to shield herself from the inevitable. She knew he wanted her, she could see it in his eyes for he couldn't hide it as he seemed to be an open book.

She wanted him too, which was why she refused to bed down with him at any of the lodgings they had secured since their wedding night. Where there was only one room to be had, she would relegate him to the stables, or when a spare room was available, she would demand that she have her own room at every inn they had stopped at thus far and Luther, the consummate gentleman had accepted her dictates without argument night after night. Tonight, however, they would sleep beneath the stars as there would be no more inns until Dunheath.

The hour was growing late, the sun was starting to set. Soon, she would have to find a spot for them to camp; her stomach clenched at the notion. The idea that there would be no safe haven to flee if he made any advances toward her, advances she were likely to embrace, set her teeth to grinding. She just couldn't allow him that kind of intimacy knowing that when the truth came out he would shun her.

Several times along the way, she had thought to come clean, but every time she opened her mouth to form the words she would panic then quickly shut it to prevent her confession from escaping. Her husband probably thought the worst of her by now as she always sniped or growled at him about one thing or another.

He hadn't asked her to tell him anymore about himself, seeming more content to learn about her. Now and again, he would spot something along the road that seemed familiar to him, halting them so he could stare as if trying to sort it all out, otherwise he had very little to say about his memory loss. It seemed almost as if he were embracing this new start in his life with a degree of enthusiasm that quite impressed her. She marveled at the man that he could so easily accept the loss of so many years, moving forward, not knowing where he was going without any sense of trepidation. He seemed confident that he was on his true course, and with time, everything missing would fall into place.

He seemed like such a jovial man, always whistling a silly tune or trying to make her smile with playful antics. She wished she could smile, but the fear of losing him was constantly there, growing more menacing as they moved closer to Dunheath. Lies! How she hated lies, liars too, but now she was one herself.

Lies ate at one's soul like a savage beast, taking all that is decent and pure right out of you. She didn't know how much longer she would be able to hold it all in, but she knew she must, at least until they reached Dunheath so she could present her husband to her father in order to vanquish any notions that she would ever marry Magnus. Once that was done, she would come clean with Luther by telling him everything. Even if it meant losing him, she must cleanse her conscience if they were to ever have a real chance at happiness.

****

Luther hadn't mentioned this to Roslyn, but the closer they got to Dunheath, the more his memory seemed to be returning. The familiar old castle ruins on the hill with a small loch nestled nearby were the perfect location to make camp for the night. Off the main road, as it was, the location insured that they would be able to go undetected by any would-be highwaymen or other nefarious types that traveled the road leading to their destination. Everything here seemed so familiar that he knew he had been here before, many times perhaps.

Several times along the way he would recognize a set of hills or an old tree triggering images that had to have been from a childhood long forgotten. He was certain that he could have made the journey on his own with relative ease as the clarity of the visions were so comforting as if an internal compass had been set to guide him forward. Home, he was going home; he knew this without a doubt.

He remembered a woman, his mother, she had been so young and beautiful before the fever had taken her. He remembered the love in her eyes, a mother's love. He remembered his father; a giant of a man with wild flaming red hair with the booming voice of a living god, the chieftain of their clan. He remembered many things, he even remembered her. Roslyn, the young she-devil that took sheer delight in tormenting him at every opportunity. He smiled at the thought. Too, he remembered the sad little boy that always followed her around; his brother.

He lost the smile when he thought about Trapper. Had he known that the boy was his brother then? He couldn't really remember, but he suspected that he did. Perhaps that was why he had been angry with his father, he wasn't sure. The finer details were still elusive, but the memories were strong enough to comfort him. He had made the right decision in trusting Roslyn and Trapper. He had no regrets. It was frustrating to remember so many things, yet he still could not grab hold of memories from his life in London; strange that. Perhaps he wasn't really leaving anything behind worth remembering.

According to Trapper and his wife, he had been a derelict lord, choosing a life of debauchery over responsibility. He hated to think he had been such a self-absorbed cad while so many suffered in his absence. He had much to atone for, and whether or not he ever regained his full memory, he knew what he had to do. He had to become the man he had been sired to be, the Marquess of Huntley.

Luther sat with his back resting against a bolder watching as his wife gathered kindling to build a fire. He knew he should be doing it himself, but he was content to watch as the self-sufficient woman went about her task. She was in her element now; as he observed her, his admiration for her grew by leaps and bounds. It astounded him that such a young woman could go about the countryside in such deplorable conditions without issuing so much as a single complaint for her discomfort. He was certain that she was unique in every way that he could imagine.

Other females her age would surely be nestled comfortably in their homes at this hour, dressed in their evening frocks as they piddled around aimlessly with their stitching or some other mundane activity while they patiently awaited the call to dinner. Not his Roslyn, no, she was busy making preparations to sleep out of doors as though it were an everyday affair.

His heart had nearly turned upside down in his chest when she drew out the large blade that she had tucked inside her pack to begin hacking away at broken limbs, but he soon settled his nerves as he watched her wield the tool with complete efficiency. Though he suspected he would meet much resistance, he silently vowed that he would make her life easier, allowing her the free time to pursue more womanly arts. He chuckled at the notion.

"Just what do ye find so amusin'?" she snapped, jerking him out of his reverie.

"I was just imagining you adorned in a lovely evening gown while you toiled away your time perfecting your stitches," he replied with a chuckle.

Roslyn stopped hacking at the large limb and stared at him with what seemed like embarrassment in her eyes before returning to her task.

A moment later she looked up again, "Do I embarrass ye?" she asked.

Luther was hunkered down beside her in a blink of an eye, placing a staying hand atop hers.

"Nay my lady, I marvel at your magnificence. Please, allow me to take over this cumbersome task as I feel that it is I who should be doing it," he said as he gently removed the blade from her hand.

"I dinnae need yer help, Luther Rollins," she said but made no move to retrieve her weapon.

"Tis true my lady, I find that you are quite capable of handling any situation on your own, but I begin to feel useless, so please allow me an opportunity to reclaim my pride," he told her as he began to break up the limbs.

Roslyn laughed softly before standing up to stretch her legs. She stood there looking over the scenery in silent contemplation before saying, "I think I would like to wear an evenin' gown, but I'm no sure about the stitches."

Luther's heart clutched at the sadness in her voice. He snapped the last of the branch then stood, returning her blade to her. She took the thing from him then slipped it into her pack. He felt like he should say something but again he sensed that he had never been good with the ladies.

Not wanting the moment to pass he ventured, "You're beautiful as you are."

She turned away from him, but before she could make her escape, he reached for her hand to stay her. She didn't turn around as he had hoped that she would, but he knew this moment was crucial.

"Roslyn, don't you know how beautiful you are?" he asked her.

She dropped her head down, taking a deep

breath as though she were about to say something but then she stiffened her back as she tugged her hand out of his. All he could do was watch with an aching in his heart as she went to gather the reigns of the horses and began slowly walking the animals to the loch so they could drink. His wife was an enigma.

Curse me for I am a fool, Roslyn thought as she led the horses to the water's edge. She too had imagined herself dressed as a lady should, soft and delicate without calluses on her hands. Only in her vision, there had been children there in a room made cozy by a fire in a hearth. The children lost in rapture as their father regaled them with fanciful tales while she mended a torn piece of clothing or perhaps embroidered a handkerchief with her husband's initials.

In that lovely moment, that one precious moment, she had imagined herself completely content in such a scenario until the sad reality struck her that it would probably never come to pass. Tomorrow, she would put an end to such silly notions by telling him the truth. As soon as she presented him to her father as her husband, she would unload her conscience then see what developed.

In the days of their travels, she had begun to hope that he might be an understanding man, forgiving her for her transgression. She had even begun to believe that they could indeed find happiness, but as the hour of confession grew near, her crimes seemed to loom increasingly larger, overwhelming her with dread.

Tonight she would have no protection against his charms. There was no room to flee to, no stables to send him. It would be just she and Luther alone in the open countryside, in the dark, by a fire ... what am I to do?

She could fall back on her charms, of course, the shrew she knew that she seemed to be. She could continue to snipe or snap at his every comment or she could do as she longed to do. She could allow herself this one night, here with him under the stars. She could allow herself to be whisked away by the fantasy that they were in love. She could encourage him to consummate their marriage. What would it hurt? She continued to reason with herself as she stood there along the shore of the loch, not realizing that Luther had quietly slipped up behind her.

When she felt his arms slide around her hips she closed her eyes stilling herself, not daring to breathe, here it was; the time of reckoning. She could rebuff his attempts at intimacy only to risk never knowing what it was like to be wrapped in his strong arms again. Or she could ... the breath she had been holding slowly left her lungs with a shudder when she felt his lips on her neck.

"This is a beautiful spot, is it not?" he asked as

he continued to nuzzle her neck.

She dared to open her eyes, the sight before her was breathtaking. The sun was setting, and the sky was painted in the most brilliant shades of lavender, orange and pink, the colors dancing on the loch in a shimmering spray of majesty.

"Aye, tis most beautiful here this time of year," she purred her agreement.

Luther kissed her along the line of her jaw, she could feel her body yielding to his gentle command.

"I meant this spot, just here," he said as he gently nipped her neck just below her earlobe.

Her knees buckled slightly then as she was lost to the moment, but Luther held her firm while he continued to intoxicate her with his sensual ministrations. Never in her wildest dreams had she ever imagined this moment, this feeling, this warmth that radiated throughout her body relaxing her muscles and bones, making them feel as though they were made of soft baker's dough.

All the tension that she had felt before began to seep from her body as she seemed to be floating on a cloud of euphoria. She let her head fall back upon his chest as he boldly began to explore her curves with his deft hands. Soon those hands had begun to loosen the string on her shirt, allowing him access within, but she didn't stop him; no, she purred her pleasure, encouraging him to take even more liberties. He did, and without her realizing it, he had removed her jacket then ever so slowly began to remove her shirt.

"Turn around," he gently commanded.

She was mindless now, turning to face him, she had no reserves about her nudity. She stood hungry and wanting as he began to unbutton his own shirt, exposing his massive chest for her perusal. She drank in the sight of him, noting that he was built like a prized bull with solid muscles, perfectly sculpted. She couldn't help herself, she reached out to caress him, shivering when she saw the skin around his nipple tighten in response to her touch.

"Take off your boots," he commanded.

Slowly as though under a spell, she looked down, noting that his feet were bare while doing his bidding, kicking them off, first one, then the other. When her boots were removed, he reached out, tugging her forward by the waist of her breeches, hushing her gasp with a punishing kiss. With a primal growl of dominance, his kiss demanded her submission as he furiously shoved her breeches down below her hips. Reaching around to take the mounds of her backside fully into his hands, he growled again in appreciation of the generous bounty he had discovered there, kneading and squeezing while he continued to ravish her mouth.

She was bereft when he pushed away from her but only for a moment until she realized that he was coming out of his own breeches with an urgency as if the garment were a deep offense upon his person. Finally, they stood face to face, naked as the day they were born, with their chests heaving with exhilaration.

"Perfection," he spoke softly under a labored breath.

The simple word seemed to break the spell she had been under, for she covered her bosom with her arms then turned her head away from him. Then, as if she had suddenly gone mad, she started laughing uncontrollably. Unable to recover from her laughter to explain herself, she continued laughing until Luther, confused, looked in the direction of her apparent amusement. Then he saw it, his horse, his poor pitiful horse, bobbing his head to and fro in an hilarious attempt to remove Luther's breeches from his face.

Luther grumbled as he went to rescue the beast from his pitiful plight, stumbling over another discarded garment as he went. He nearly toppled over but was able to quickly recover before he made a total cake of himself.

This too seemed to strike his wife as amusing as she continued to cackle incessantly. He, nor the horse found it amusing, however. The poor animal seemed to be on the verge of panic as it began to rise up on his hind legs crying out woefully in his distress.

It was then that Luther realized that his man bits were dangling dangerously close to the wild animal's front hoof as he continued to dance around trying to remove the offending garment. He bent his body forward while thrusting his arse backward as far as he could, trying to put as much distance between his family jewels and the thrashing horse as he reached up to grab hold of the breeches. Again with the cackling! God's bones, does she not see the danger?

It seemed that one of the legs of the breeches had become entangled with the saddle so he had to reach for the bridle in an effort to still the animal as best he could. Finally, after considerable effort he managed to reign the animal in, which allowed him to remove his breeches; as he had hoped, the animal was grateful enough to quickly settle down.

Luther stroked the animal on the side of the face, making soft sounds of comfort while he brought his own nerves under control. Damn and blast! A perfect moment ruined by dumb luck. He should have been more careful where he had tossed his pants. He stood there a moment longer willing his heart rate to slow, becoming aware that his wife's laughter had ceased. Thank heavens! It had been most embarrassing, and now the moment of seduction was lost.

A moment later, his attention was diverted when he heard the sound of a gentle splash in the water behind him. He turned his attention to the loch but saw only a rippling circle in the water, perhaps a fish had caught a fly for his supper, but where had Roslyn gone?

He searched about but could not see her until, there she was, rising from the water like a magical mermaid from some old Scottish fable softly giggling at him with a seductive blush upon her cheeks. His body reacted instinctively to her wet, gleaming flesh with the top of her luscious bosom floating tantalizingly above the surface.

She stopped her laughter when her eyes fell on the evidence of his arousal, her features taking on a more serious expression. She lifted her arms out of the water then began loosening the plait of her hair, allowing him to see her perfectly peaked nipples while his feet, seemingly by some glorious spell, propelled him into the water to join her. He stopped inches from her, never breaking his eyes from hers; with breathless appreciation for her beauty, he managed, "Enchantress," before lunging for her mouth, slightly opened as though waiting to receive him.

This kiss, this wondrous kiss evoked within him a great, driving need to possess her completely. Their thrusting tongues sparred with one another for dominance until finally the perfect harmony had been achieved, and they became one with their passion. She, just as hungry for him as they delved deeper into one another as though trying to seek the other's very soul. Though he could not remember, he was sure he had never been moved so completely by a kiss, but this was more than a kiss, this was a profound joining, a recognition of what was, what would always be his true and singular purpose for existing. This woman, this spectacular woman could only be his soul mate.

Luther's joyous cry of rapture was muffled as he pressed deeper, deeper still into her mouth, pressing his hard muscled chest into the soft, pliant flesh of her bosom, pressing into him in return, both with seeking hands frantically claiming their territory. It was a claiming, a declaration that from this moment forward, they belonged to each other; this was the language their bodies commanded one another.

Desperate hunger drove them onward until she instinctively wrapped her legs around him in invitation; mindlessly, he accepted by inserting his shaft home with one swift thrust. She cried out at the intrusion, but he covered her cries with his furious kiss while he stilled himself within her to allow acceptance of his hard, stubborn appendage; he would not leave this spot, even if God in heaven commanded him to do so. This was where he belonged.

A torturous moment passed before he felt her buck against him, granting him permission to continue; he did, daring to remove his lips from hers he blazed a trail down her neck sucking, branding as he went until his hungry mouth landed on those luscious orbs. Why must there be two? A brief moment of madness made him ponder, greedy so he was, he couldn't make up his mind which one deserved the most attention. Never mind his stupid question, he would take them both as an offering from his goddess to sup upon them at his leisure.

First one, then the other, he tried to encompass them with his ravenous mouth but found their offering too bountiful so contented himself by sampling their full and wondrous circles of perfection, sucking and branding his way around as his shaft thrust to and fro within her. Heaven!

Without conscience thought, he began to move them out of the water onto the bank of the loch. Her distress at the interruption was made clear when she moaned her displeasure, her cries soon appeased when he shifted her just so, as he lay down on his back bringing her down atop him so he could encourage her to ride him. His wife instinctively knew what to do as she began to undulate her hips; he never wanted this to end, this pleasure, this sweet torture as she ground herself against him.

Moments later, he felt bereft when she stilled to look at him as if seeing him for the first time; a look unlike any he could imagine crossed her face. Was it fear? Was it regret? Not wanting the spell to be broken, he reached out, encompassing her face with his hands, bringing her forward, kissing her fervently as he bucked his protest beneath her.

Again, she pulled away from his kiss with that same unfathomable look in her eyes until a moment passed, then whatever she had been thinking passed with it, and mercifully she began to bump and grind against him once again with renewed vigor.

Afraid now, that he was about to pass his seed too soon, he wadded her hair into his fist, giving a commanding tug to still her; she thought to fight him in this, but he quickly flipped her onto her back so he could take command.

"Slowly lass, you will unman me," he cautioned as he pulled himself out of her.

She whimpered her distress, but he did not let that deter him in his course as he once again began to claim his territory with a slow sensual branding along the length of her torso until he was at the triangle of her sex. He nudged her thighs apart to gain him access, lifting one of her voluptuous thighs over his shoulder, he latched on the glorious flesh with his hungry, sucking mouth.

He knew he was leaving marks all over her body, but he didn't care because he was making clear to her, to all who would see that she was his, his woman. As though some primal wolf had always lain dormant within him, now suddenly brought to life; crazed and starved for what only she could provide for nourishment, he continued his hungry claiming.

Grabbing handfuls of his hair, she guided him to her center; he knew what she needed even if she didn't fully understand it herself, so with a growl of dominance he moved her other thigh aside then dove home with his ravenous mouth. She bucked and writhed under his assault, crying out something in her Gaelic tongue, a language that he had forsaken but silently vowed to learn again as it had been so incredibly arousing while he supped on her succulent flesh.

Just when his own discomfort had nearly conquered his need to satisfy her, she tensed, seeming to break apart as her body became fluid, then she collapsed beneath the weight of her orgasm. He took no mercy on her; lifting her rear off the ground, he slammed home just in time to encounter the pulsing and throbbing of her bliss. It didn't take long for him to find his own release after a few determined strokes, then finally with a feral growl as loud as thunder, he thrust violently home one last time until he too collapsed atop her, pouring his life giving essence into her.

He lay there a moment, still seated within her, wholly content with his head upon her breasts until like a slap to his face, he heard, "Ye are a savage beast! Ye loathsome animal, get off me," and then he found himself pushed out of heaven.

Chapter Seven

Roslyn was in a high temper as she donned her clothes by the banks of the loch. 'Bidh gaol agam ort fad mo bheatha, thusa 's gun duine eile', she had told him in her tongue. 'I will love you my whole life, you and no other.'

Now with a sickened heart, she could not believe what she had done. She was lost, truly lost in love with a man that would most likely leave her tomorrow. Their coupling had been so devastatingly wondrous, but now she damned herself for a fool because she would never know such wonders again. Looking over the marks he had left along the length of her body sent a shiver through her. He had branded her, there was no other word for it. He had marked her as his. Oh, how she had enjoyed it, but tomorrow, after he learned of her treachery, he would no doubt run for his life; it could be the last time she would ever see him.

Every mark he had left upon her body throbbed, demanding recognition for one simple fact, she belonged to him, she had been claimed. Oh, this is terrible! She had heard tales of such things, had even seen the evidence of the claiming on some of the village women. It was said that when a man was in love, he served notice to any and all who would seek his woman's comforts by leaving marks of his possession; she hadn't understood it then, but she did now.

Too, she had seen women with a broken heart after their man had abandoned them for another. They would waste away in solitude waiting for a man that had forgotten them. She had lived through that already but through the expectations of a child; she was a woman grown now, she understood the hurt that those women must have suffered. Roslyn couldn't allow this to happen, much was expected of her by her people. She had to protect herself; put up a shield. She would just have to make Luther believe that her interest in him was a trivial thing, that his presence in her life would be a thing of tolerance at best.

One thing she knew for sure, she could never, ever allow him to know how deeply in love she was with him. Their joining had changed her, altered her very soul. No one must ever know! She was the future laird of her clan; she must be strong or at least give the impression of strength. How could she lead her people otherwise? She couldn't afford to fall in love with a man who would leave her, causing her to waste away into obscurity. No! She simply couldn't allow this.

"Did I hurt you?" Luther's voice broke in.

"Just stay away from me, ye lecherous fool," she spat.

She stomped away from him, then set about

starting a fire, silently cursing that there was no place to escape him. I must have lost my mind to have behaved so irrationally, she inwardly grumbled. Of course, Luther was not heeding her warning, here now he came to sit beside her.

"If I hurt you, I am not sorry for it. I know I should be, but that was a very moving experience for me, one that I am certain I have never had before, and I had thought that you had been equally moved," he said as she struck at the flint to make sparks for the fire. She did her best to ignore him as he continued.

Relieved when at last she had gotten a small flame from her distracted efforts, she set about lighting the kindle she had gathered, pleased to see it rise to life. She added a few pieces of the limbs she had gathered earlier then sat staring into the flame wishing she were any place else but here, now, after what she had done.

"Roslyn, listen to me. This might sound strange, but I think I am home with you. It was the feeling I had when ... well ... when it was happening. I just knew that I was home. Did you not feel it?" he asked with hope in his tone.

Her shoulders sagged against the weight of his words. This was much worse than she had imagined, for she had felt it too.

"I dinnae know what ye be blatherin' about,"

she told him as coldly as she could.

She winced when she felt his hand around her forearm, not from physical pain but from pain of the heart as she knew she was being a horrible shrew, but it must be so.

"Look at me woman," he gently commanded.

She gulped hard in response, trying to fortify her convictions for what must be before looking into his eyes. What she saw there was nearly her undoing. Love. Saints protect me, but there is love in his eyes. No, she refused to believe it, he did not love her, he didn't even remember her and if he did, he would run as fast as his horse could take him right back to London. She had to remember this even if he didn't.

"Did you not feel the intensity of our union? Did you not feel it when our souls bonded, and we became one?" he asked her with a slight shake to get her attention, desperation pouring from his eyes.

Tears, she could see tears forming there in his beautiful green eyes. She hardened her resolve as she shrugged out of his grasp, "So ye think ye are in love, do ye?"

"I think I have always loved you," he said softly.

She laughed with sarcasm at the irony of it.

The fool thinks he loved me then and loves me now? If he only knew, she thought, shaking her head in disgust. She knew what must be done. She must deliver a blow so hard, so callused as to remove all doubt that they would ever be together in marital bliss. Summoning all the courage she possessed, she hardened her face, squaring her shoulders to project the strength she did not feel.

"Heed me Luther Rollins, for I willnae tell ye this again. We had carnal relations, that is all there was to it. I dinnae love ye, ye dinnae love me. It was ... how to say this ... aye, it was nice but it is past. Tomorrow, I will present ye to my father as my husband then I dinnae care what ye do after. Ye can go back to London and wallow in yer debauchery same as ye always have for all that I care. Ye think ye are the only man I have ever bed down with? Ye think I was moved do ye? Ye are a fool, ye are a means to an end, that is all," she said with finality as she stood to make her escape.

Roslyn's body quaked as she walked away from him, she didn't want to see the hurt she had intended to inflict. She had to get away, she had to find some place to go so she could shed the tears she felt burning her eyes. Her mission had been accomplished, she had put the barrier between them so he could never hurt her the way she knew that she had just hurt him.

****

Luther stared bewildered at the backside of his wife as she sauntered away from him. What did she mean that she had bedded down with other men? The evidence of her innocence had been plain. He had felt the resistance when he had smashed through it like a Viking warrior breaking down a castle wall. He knew without a doubt that she had been a virgin. He had felt the shuddering wracks of her pain as he held her until it eased. What game was she playing at?

He searched his mind, sorting through all that he could remember since he woke with amnesia, searching for anything that would make sense of what she had just said. He remembered what Trapper had told him, she had loved him all her life. Aye, she had waited for him to return, she had even turned away countless suitors waiting for him to come to claim her. Why then, would she say such things now?

The woman was a complete enigma to him, he was at a loss to understand what she had just done. It was as though she were trying to put up barriers, but why? Perhaps he had rushed her, maybe he should have given her more time before trying to consummate their union. It had been his intention, but she had called to him like a siren, he had been mindless to stop himself.

Perhaps she had been hurt by his aggression. He knew that he had behaved like an animal in his lust to have her. In fact, he had tried to consume her, perhaps it had frightened her. At first, he had felt a bit of pride at the marks of his branding, but now he could see that maybe he should feel ashamed, but how could he be ashamed by what had transpired between them. It had been raw, hungry desire, pure want and need, he had felt her reciprocation with equal intensity.

They had needed to come together as they had, he knew this instinctively. If he could do it again, he wouldn't hold himself back, not even a little. They had expressed their love in the most profound way two bodies could. He knew this, he had felt it, had reveled in it as it spurred him on. So why this?

He watched her disappear into the encroaching darkness wondering if he should follow, but he had not finished dressing when he had thought to speak with her, wishing only to calm her when he noticed her fit of temper.

Initially, he thought that perhaps he had hurt her, but now he just didn't know what to think. He knew that she would come back eventually as she had left everything behind. She probably just needed time to recompose herself. He saw no reason why he shouldn't allow it other than it was dark now, and there could be all manner of things out there in the darkness that could be a danger to her. His wife was a self-sufficient woman, but a woman, after all; still, he would give her a few moments, and if she didn't return he would seek her out to make sure she was safe.

He may not know what to do or say to her now, but one thing he knew with absolute certainty was that he would never leave her, he could never leave her, she was his life now. It didn't matter what he learned once his memories came back, he loved this woman now. That's when it struck him. Maybe she was worried that he would leave her when he got his memory back, that had to be it. He cheered slightly now that he had found a possible reason for her behavior, she was trying to protect herself from hurt. Poor lass! He would just have to show her that he was here forever.

In time, she would begin to relax, even embrace their love, but for now he would have to continue to woo her. She was a passionate woman, now that she had gotten a taste of the passion to be shared between them she would surely want more. He would just have to be patient, taking the abuse that she would, no doubt, continue to deliver until she understood that he wasn't going anywhere. He hunkered down before the fire, feeding more logs into the blaze; he would stoke it well to serve as a beacon of his love for her so she could find her way safely back to their camp.

Tomorrow they would go to Dunheath, and he would forever put her fears to rest. He would tell her that he had partially regained his memories, that he no longer felt any apprehensions about having a life here with her. In his heart, it felt as though he had always belonged with her, he had tried to tell her that when he told her that he thought he had always loved her, a recognition of souls he believed.

While they were making love, he had imagined that there must be a place in heaven where souls awaited to be born or perhaps reborn, a place where two spirits seeked and found one another so they could join in holy union then were granted a blessing whereby they would be returned to earth so they may reunite in the earthly realm where they were free to express physical love. That's what it had felt like for him, that's was what he had wanted to express to her before she had rebuked him.

Whatever else he found when his memories returned, he had found her, his soul mate; he would never, ever forsake her again. Perhaps he was a romantic, but he didn't sense that he had ever been with a woman who had made him feel the way he had with her. He closed his eyes, searching the depths of his mind, trying to find some shred, some sliver of memory that would confirm what he was feeling. There was nothing there, no one else there. Only her, the child that had danced around him, giving him no respite from her games of torment.

A smile broke across his face, he couldn't help it, this one memory of her proved that she had always been his, he had always been hers. This was what he would cling to as his armor in the upcoming war for his wife's affections.

Chapter Eight

London

"It is as we suspected, Luther may have been kidnapped. According to our man at Bow Street, there had been a scuffle just over a week ago that went noticed by a lady of the evening. She had observed Luther leave his town home then saw him accosted by two ruffians who tossed him into a carriage where he was quickly spirited away," Gabriel Hawkins, the Duke of Windhaven told his long time friend, Dylan Crenshaw, the Duke of Blackstone.

"What do you suppose they want with Luther?" Dylan asked with alarm.

"That is a point that perplexes me. There have been no demands for ransom, and he has no known enemies. Everyone that knows Luther regards him with the highest esteem. Tis most perplexing indeed," he said taking a sip of coffee.

The two men sat broodingly at White's while they turned the information over in their minds.

"We should tell Jasper, perhaps he will have answers for us," Dylan suggested.

"Ah well, as to that, Jasper is missing too. I went around to have a word with him before coming here, his butler said that he had not seen Jasper in a week. Something is afoot my friend, as to what, I have no clue."

"Perhaps Jasper pulled a prank on Luther, and they are together somewhere on a lark," Dylan suggested.

"No, I don't believe that is the case, though it would certainly seem possible considering those two, but Jasper's butler went on to inform me that they had quarreled, then Luther left in a huff. So naturally, I can only assume that Jasper is not involved as he had stayed the rest of the evening indoors, though he did depart rather early the next morning from which he has not been seen since. Luther's valet told our man that Luther had been in a rather peculiar mood when he returned from Jasper's place and requested a haircut saying that he was in need of a change. He went on to say that when he left the house, he had been carrying a rather sizable purse. Easy pickings for a couple of cutthroats," he said with unease apparent.

"What should we do? We cannot sit here and do nothing. Which direction had the carriage been heading when it left and did we get a description of it?" Dylan asked, charged with concern for his friend.

He wasn't so worried about Jasper as he was known for slipping away to Pembrook for solitude to work on one project or another, which was likely where he was now, but this thing with Luther, there was an eyewitness to his capture. Something more had to be done.

"Jackson, a detective with Bow Street, is expected here any moment with a report. He suspected that the thugs had taken him North and had sent a man to follow the trail. Ah, here he comes now," Gabriel said, standing to greet Mr. Jackson.

"Mr. Jackson, please have a seat," Gabriel told him.

Harold Jackson was a serious young man, stout and robust in stature and was reputed to be one of Bow Street's finest investigators, which, of course, was the reason Gabriel had called for him to assist in their search for Luther. Jackson took his seat, dispensing with pleasantries, choosing instead to get right to the meat of the issue at hand.

"Your grace, I have received word from my agent that a trio of men matching the description landed in an inn about a day and a half's ride north of London. They spent the night there then the following morning they traded the carriage for fresh mounts and continued north on horseback. My man is still following the trail, but I have not received another report as of yet," he told them.

"Horseback?" Dylan asked.

"Aye, tis most confusing as it seems that Luther had been a willing member of the traveling party as he was not bound in any way and could have escaped at any time. Another peculiar point is that one of the men in the group appeared not to be a man at all, but a young woman, and the other, a lad of about eight and ten years of age. It was said that when they had arrived Luther and the young man had been together on the driver's bench while the woman had been inside the carriage, further confusing us. Consider, if Luther had been the one kidnapped, would he not have been inside the carriage?" he asked with a rub of his chin.

"Another point worth mentioning, it appears that they are highlanders as their accents were rather thick with the Scottish brogue. It is my summation that they are traveling on to Scotland," he thought to add.

"Luther is from the highlands," Dylan pointed out.

"Yes, I believe you are onto something there my friend," Gabriel concurred.

"Perhaps a trip to Huntley is in order," Dylan suggested.

"We have already dispatched a man to trail them, should I send word to the Home Office to send another man on to Huntley?" Jackson asked.

"No, that will not be necessary, I will make the trip to Huntley myself," Gabriel put in.

"I will go with you, I can be ready in an hour or so," Dylan told him.

"Then it's all settled, we shall leave this afternoon just after luncheon. Come around after you have gathered your things, and we will depart immediately after," Gabriel instructed.

"Shall I travel along as well?" Jackson asked eagerly.

"It would not hurt to have an extra man along as we have no idea what we may be up against," Dylan advised.

"Of course, come around to my town home just after luncheon, and we will depart," Gabriel told him.

"Right you are, your grace; I shall go and inform the Home Office then prepare for our journey," he told them standing to take his leave.

"Oh, and Jackson, if we are to be working together, you may simply call me Gabriel. It would be wise to travel incognito, I would imagine. We wouldn't want to raise suspicions or draw unnecessary attention to ourselves by announcing to the world that we are two dukes accompanied by a detective from Bow Street," he told him.

"Yes, that would be wise, and I am Dylan," he put in.

Neither man had ever felt the need to exploit their rank, preferring instead to remain humble whenever possible, but, in this case, prudence would certainly dictate discretion. If Luther had been kidnapped and a ransom was to be made at some point, the kidnappers would certainly see an opportunity to raise the ante if they knew of the wealth that existed between two dukes. It would be far better to appear as though they were merely three nondescript men traveling the North Road.

After Mr. Jackson left for the Home Office, Dylan and Gabriel sat a moment longer in contemplation.

"Do you remember Luther once told us of a betrothal arranged by his father and his friend?" Dylan asked.

"Now that you mention it, yes. Do you think it could be connected?" Gabriel asked with interest.

"I seem to recall he said that he dissolved that contract upon his father's passing, so it is not likely, but I can't help but wonder given that the two abductors were suspected highlanders and our Luther is also a highlander. Wouldn't it be amusing if we get to Huntley only to find Luther has gotten himself leg shackled?" Dylan said with a grin.

"Let us hope it is as harmless as that my friend, let us hope," Gabriel grinned in response.

"I don't know that it could be considered harmless as I also seem to recall that Luther considered the girl a loathsome creature to the extent that he vowed to never return to Huntley for fear that he would be forced to honor the contract. He remarked that her father was a fearsome man that didn't particularly appreciate Luther's refusal to honor the agreement, vowing to make him submit when the child reached marriageable age," Dylan explained.

"I believe you may be onto something. Perhaps we had better hurry my friend; Luther may be in a serious situation if he proves to be stubborn in his refusal to take the girl to wife. Those Scots can be rather determined when honor is in the balance," Gabriel pointed out.

The two men rose with urgency from the table, making for their respective homes to make ready for their trip. Feeling confident that they were on the right path.

Chapter Nine

Roslyn's nerves were razor sharp by the time they had reached the outer border of Dunheath. Her temples felt bruised from keeping her jaw clenched so very tight in an attempt to hold in her confession. It had been so difficult to maintain a posture of indifference with Luther as he had continued to treat her with the utmost kindness and respect. Remaining steadfast in the face of her unyielding rigidity proved that he was a worthy man indeed. A man that would stand beside her no matter what? That was the question that burned in her mind as she rehearsed over and over what she would say to him in order to minimize the anger he was sure to feel when he learned the truth.

There was no easy way to tell your husband that you had kidnapped him in an effort to force him to marry you or because of that attempt he had lost his memory. Then there were the lies that Trapper had told while she sat quietly by as if in complete approval. Shame! She was ashamed of that, but most of all she was ashamed at how she had treated him last night.

When she returned to camp, she fought the need to nestle beside him in front of the fire, to hold him tenderly, but instead, she had dragged her pallet to the other side in an attempt to ignore him. He had lain awake for quite some time after her return, telling her how much he loved her, that he would always be a good and faithful husband, but she had pretended to be asleep, never once acknowledging his heartfelt words. Later though, she had silently wept when she heard the agonized sounds he made when he had finally fallen asleep; in his fitful sleep, he had wept too. What had he been dreaming? Had he been dreaming of her? Perhaps he had simply been lost in a vision from his fractured memory, she wasn't sure, she had been too cowardly to ask him when they woke.

When they broke camp for the last leg of their journey, she had watched Luther while he stood on the shore of the loch looking upon the water as the sun rose upon it. He had been deep in thought for many moments before turning to look at her with an unfathomable look in his eyes. That look had shaken her to the depths of her being, but she couldn't think about that now, she had to brace herself for what was coming.

****

Luther remembered almost all of his life up until he had awakened in that shack with Roslyn. His dreams last night had been fraught with all manner of images that had helped to guide him in putting all the pieces of the puzzle together, he remembered so much that his head had begun to ache. Decades slammed into his mind upon awakening so swiftly that the experience had been rather excruciating.

'It's time to come home' she had told him with a pistol pressed into his chest as she with the aid of his brother had kidnapped him! At first he had been angry but found that he couldn't cling to his ire as immediately, he understood why she had done it; desperation was a fearsome motivator. His first instinct had been to get on his horse to return to London but found that he was too deeply in love with this woman who had once been the bane of his existence to ever leave her now. Even knowing that she had lied to him, allowing him to believe that he had been agreeable to the match, he was still of a mind that he was where he belonged.

He had no regrets except to say that he had been such a selfish bastard, running away from his responsibility that some young slip of a girl and her hapless sidekick had to kidnap him then cosh him about the head to make him recognize his folly. He had been a fool; he had chosen to waste the last ten years of his life running with his friends as though he hadn't a care in the world while so many people suffered, as a result.

Though it was no excuse, he remembered why he had left in the first place. His father's deathbed confession confirming what he had already suspected, that Trapper was his bastard brother, had sparked rebellion within him. In his youthful arrogance, he had judged his father then found him lacking in character for dishonoring his mother by seeking refuge in the comforts of another woman, culminating in a child out of wedlock.

Add to that, the betrothal to a child whose sole mission it seemed, was to drive him utterly mad. Thus, his temper had boiled over, causing complete outrage. His father had no right to make that kind of decision for him when he had so clearly demonstrated his own poor judgment. So he had fled, never looking back, never once considering what his childish tantrum might cost others.

He was awake now, awake to the reality that was his own. He knew that it would be difficult to make right all the wrongs that had been perpetuated these long ten years. He had been angry at his father, yes, but he had used it as the excuse to escape a life he hadn't wanted; to become laird of a people that he had felt disconnected from in the first place. He had never believed that he was born to be a Scotsman. His mother had been so miserable in Scotland that she often sought to cheer herself by regaling him with tales of her homeland, England.

England had sounded like a far away kingdom of fantasy with stories of Robin Hood, King Arthur and Knights of the Round Table. These stories had fed his imagination, so that when his mother had insisted to his father that he get his education at Eton, he had leaped at the opportunity believing in his young mind that he would actually meet those legends of old. Silly to think such things, but these were the inner workings of a juvenile mind, and it was in that same spirit that he had fled his responsibilities. When he had been away at Eton, he had formed a family of sorts with his roommates. They had become his brothers, he had become completely absorbed by them, making it easy to forget where he had come from, he had become a young man of England.

Mere months into his education, however, he had received word that his mother had died; he had returned home to find that nearly half of the village people had perished by a ferocious fever. At the tender age of three and ten, his mother's passing had released him of any further connections he might have had to the land. He thought only to return to Eton to finish his education, where he had tried to forget his homeland entirely.

Five years had gone by taking with them any emotional attachments he might have had for his home, during which time he had graduated then quickly set about as a bachelor of nobility. He and his group had barely begun to take the ton by its tail when again, word would come that he must return home to his ailing father. It had taken many weeks for his father to depart this world, the duration that he had spent there in the interim had been a small eternity as he thought only to return to his brothers.

Of course, there had been the young girl always dancing about, taunting him in one fashion or another, further adding to his misery. The girl, the child of his father's best friend, had come to stay at Huntley while her father kept vigil during his friend's illness. It must have been during those days that Fergus and his father had hatched the scheme that their children would marry in an attempt to join the clans as their lands bordered one another, so the contract had been issued.

The marriage would have cemented a future for the two clans, he could see that now, but he had not cared at the time. He had only cared about himself, his own comforts; so he had fled his responsibilities as if by doing so they would cease to exist. He had forsaken Huntley entirely, choosing to view Willowbrook Manor as his true ancestral home. Willowbrook, being one of the Belmont estates that his mother had left to him upon her death had often been a sanctuary of sorts for Luther.

Every year, he would return there to invest his interests in the estate with enthusiasm, maintaining a profitable income while never giving a single thought to what his clan at Huntley had been enduring in his absence. Why had he done it? He would never fully comprehend his reasoning, but one thing he knew without a shadow of a doubt; he would rectify the situation as best he could.

He would show his people that their derelict lord had seen the error of his ways, that he would now serve them by making the necessary improvements to ensure that Huntley could once again be restored to its former glory as one of the wealthiest estates in the region. Thanks to the profits of Willowbrook, his fortune was vast. He could afford to invest in both Huntley and

Dunheath, never again giving clan members reason to flee their homes in order to survive the harsh winters that were so common in the region.

The notion bolstered his confidence. As soon as they reached Dunheath, after speaking with her father, he would make his plans clear to Roslyn. Perhaps once he made his announcement, this would bring him in good stead with his wary wife. Perhaps when she saw that he truly meant to repent by improving the lives of both their people she would begin to trust in him. He knew this would be a hard, difficult journey, but he would embrace, even relish in the task he had set himself.

****

As the rise of her ancestral home came into view, Roslyn's body began to tremor with anticipation. Though Dunheath was in good condition, it was certainly overdue for some much-needed modern improvements. Like so many ancient structures, this one too had taken on a growth of moss that had crept along over the centuries on its constant path toward the top in an attempt to return it back to nature. The overall effect allowed it to blend seamlessly into the lush landscape surrounding it, which lessened its once imposing impact to any would-be raiders as it protruded from the top of the hill that it was built upon. Roslyn loved to take walks about the parapets in the early morning hours to take in the breathtaking view of the valley below as it cradled her beloved village.

Their arrival had generated much interest by the villagers, their party of two growing substantially with a band of followers, mostly comprised of children and barking dogs. This was it; there was no turning back. Slowing her precession, she allowed Luther to come alongside her, not daring to look at him to gauge his reaction to her home for fear that she would see the disgust he had displayed in years past. Instead, she stiffened her back with a slight rise of her chin, in what was her best impression of a future clan leader. Confidence! She must appear confident amidst all the speculation that was surely running rampant through the village.

On the last leg of the journey, she had begun to reconcile her mind to the possibility that once he had been introduced to her father, with her confession made, Luther would quickly return to London. Over the last few hours, he had grown unusually quiet; what had he been thinking? Many times she had thought to inquire into his musings but would quickly cower, deciding that perhaps it was better to remain in the companionable quiet that seemed to hang comfortably between them.

Roslyn was fairly certain that by now her father would have word of her return, too, that he would be fit for battle as she had not asked his permission before making the journey. She had, however, left him a note detailing her plans, deciding that it was better to face his wrath upon her return with a husband at her side than to try to convince him that kidnapping him then forcing him to marry her had been a wise course of action.

Of course, he would never have allowed her to go on such a quest, but she knew what must be done, so she had taken the risk. It was his own fault that she had done it as he had become quite demanding that she ready herself to wed Magnus the day after her birthday.

Yesterday was her birthday though she had not told Luther of it. With the consummation of their union, the deadline had certainly been irrevocably met. Her father nor Magnus could undo what had been done before God and man. Would Luther hate her once he realized that he no longer had an avenue for annulment when he learned of her deceit? Her shoulders sagged slightly at the thought, but there was nothing to do now except move forward.

Chapter Ten

The halls of Dunheath reverberated with the roar of old Fergus's temper as he stormed down the stairs issuing a string of foul oaths in greeting to his wayward daughter. Luther moved near his wife to demonstrate that she was now under his protection, causing Fergus to stop in his tracks as he reached the bottom of the steps to take measure of the man before him, chest heaving from his exertions as he eyed Luther with suspicion.

Luther was taken aback by the transformation of the once fearsome, robust giant of a man that was the Fergus of his youth to the bedraggled old man before him now. The man seemed to have shrunken in stature as both he and Roslyn towered above him. Still, the man's wrath was an awesome thing to behold, no doubt he could quite possibly instill fear in a lesser man than Luther.

"Och Lassie! I see ye dredged the depths of hell and dragged the Devil to heel," he growled before turning to spit on the ground in indication that he was nay impressed. He then turned his hard, calculating eyes with their grizzled brows on Luther.

"We've no need of ye here Luther, ye may go. Magnus is in residence, and the wedding party has been awaiting the return of our Roslyn to commence with the ceremony," he said with another spit to the ground.

Luther had expected to be received with hostility by old Fergus for his behavior over the last decade, but he had not considered that Magnus would be here and had little time to soak the information in, when as if on cue, Magnus entered the vestibule flanked by a small band of armed men that appeared to be some sort of guard detail.

Magnus had always had a flair for the dramatics as Luther recalled, but this seemed somewhat ostentatious, even for him. Something was afoot though what, he could only speculate.

"Well now, I see my wayward bride has returned," Magnus said with all the confidence of a man who had won the spoils of victory ringing in his tone.

Magnus was average in stature, being about fifteen years Luther's senior. Though he was no match for Luther in size, he had always carried about him an aura of menace that he found disturbing. He remembered tales of his cruelty to those in his clan when their loyalty was in doubt and had never liked to be in his presence, as a result. Then there were the many bastard children he had scattered about the land that he claimed no responsibility for, which Luther had always considered offensive. Consequently, they had never developed a true rapport of kinship with one another.

It could not be said with any truth that Magnus was a handsome man, with his dark hair and black eyes set into hard, angular features accented by a beak-like nose that gave one the impression of an other-worldly bird of prey. Because Magnus was very rich, very powerful too, he had never been in short supply of adoring followers for which he took great joy in exploiting.

Luther stiffened his back, lending a more powerful display to his own towering height at the words the two men had spoken. He would not be cowered by their obvious attempts to dismiss him as inconsequential.

"I am pleased to inform you both that the wedding ceremony has already taken place. Roslyn is my wife; therefore, you sir may take your leave, unless, of course, you would prefer to stay on to help us with our celebrations," he told Magnus with assured confidence as he took Roslyn by the arm, drawing her near.

The atmosphere in the room turned more ominous at his words as the two men stood glaring at one another, Luther taking note that the men in Magnus's company had moved closer to take a battle stance beside their master. Each one with their hands ready to draw their weapons should the need arise. Luther realized then that he himself had no weapon, just as Roslyn pushed away from him drawing out the pistol that he had all but forgotten she possessed.

"Ye'll not be staying for celebrations!" Roslyn said as she aimed her pistol at Magnus.

As quick as lightning, the men drew their pistols, all but one trained their weapons upon Luther while the one closest to Magnus aimed his at Roslyn. Luther felt his heart drop into his stomach as the need to protect his wife seemed imminent.

Magnus, however, seemed to be enjoying the scene as without any concern evident, he moved closer to Luther, "And who might you be?" he asked.

"I am Luther Rollins, Marquess of Huntley, cousin, and you may tell your men to stand down. There is no need for violence here," he responded with his best effort of calm command.

Magnus laughed mockingly before saying, "The last time I saw my cousin, he was a skinny lad with wild unruly hair. I confess that much time has passed, but you sir, have no resemblance whatsoever to his visage. How do we know that you are who you say you are?"

Roslyn growled beside Luther, but it did nothing to mask the unmistakable sound of the cocking of her pistol or the subsequent cocking of pistols that the men held.

"Roslyn! Stand down!" he ordered her.

"I told ye Luther Rollins, that ye'll not be tellin' me what to do!" she shouted at him while keeping both her pistol and determined eyes trained on Magnus.

"Woman, this is no time for such a discussion. Stand down, I say!" he asserted.

The last thing he wanted was a blood bath, neither did he want to show weakness to these men who seemed content to kill him if need be. Not having a weapon was certainly a disadvantage exacerbated by his inability to bring his wife to heel in order to avoid the need for the blasted weapon in the first place.

"Having trouble controlling your woman?" Magnus asked with a satisfied chuckle.

"What I do with my wife is no concern of yours. Tell your men to lower their weapons," Luther ordered.

Luther's frustration mounted as neither his wife nor Magnus's men moved to do as he commanded.

"I believe there was the question of your identity. What proof do you have that you are Luther Rollins, Marquess of Huntley?" Magnus asked tauntingly.

Luther quickly searched his mind for a way to defuse the situation. Proof? What proof did he have? His signet ring? It would have to serve.

"I wear the Huntley signet," he said offering his right hand for inspection.

Fergus moved in to examine the ring as well. "Aye, it is the Huntley ring," he concurred.

"Of course, he be Luther Rollins! Do ye take me for a fool, father?" Roslyn asked him.

Luther cringed at the sound of his wife's affronted tone. Did the woman wish to include her father among her enemies as well? Just what had he walked into when he agreed to this union?

"Nay, ye be no fool daughter, but tis true, this man bears no resemblance to Luther," he returned.

"Just ye take a closer look, father! Tis Luther, I've no doubt," Roslyn argued.

Sensing that he had best distract his wife before she brought an apocalypse with her irrational behavior, he pulled her close to him to demonstrate his command as much to her as anyone else.

"In any event, she is my wife whether you remember me or not. There was a contract put in place by you and my father to be honored on or before her eighteenth birthday. The contract has been honored with a certificate of marriage as proof and the union has been well and indisputably consummated," Luther said as he offered the marriage certificate to Fergus.

Fergus snatched the certificate out of Luther's hand, examining it closely. Luther noted that Fergus's hands were shaking, too that his eyesight seemed to be somewhat impaired as he had to draw the paper very near to his face as he looked it over.

"Tis authentic!" he declared.

Magnus took the paper from Fergus, he too examined it closely. After a moment of close scrutiny, he returned the paper to Fergus, then with a sniff of annoyance he gave a silent command to his men to stand down. After a hair-raising moment, Roslyn too, lowered her pistol.

"I offer you my congratulations, cousin or perhaps, I should say condolences," he said with a sneer toward Roslyn. "She is a wild one and truly, I had not relished the idea of the taming. The honey may be sweet, but I've no wish to lick it off a briar. No doubt, it would have been a tiresome chore," he continued with an air of indifference.

Luther was not fooled, he could see his cousin seething below the surface. He was sure that this would not be the end of the matter as he could see the wheels in his cousin's calculating mind as they turned. Perhaps, he was even now contemplating some kind of strategy for mischief; it would not serve to lower his guard just yet. Luther tugged Roslyn even closer to his side; though he knew he would be poking the eye of a dragon, he found he could not help himself by responding to the taunt.

"Oh, I don't know cousin, I find that I prefer my women to have a high spirit, especially in times of the most intimate settings," he said with a wink.

As he expected she would, Roslyn elbowed him in the ribs, but he held her secure to his side with a firm squeeze at the side of her torso; gratefully, she stayed still. It would not serve to have Magnus witness a humiliating display of his wife's high temper set against him when he was trying to demonstrate dominance. He knew he would most likely pay for this concession later, but for now, he was content that his effort to nudge his cousin's ire had been effective.

"Well then, it would appear that you two will be most compatible," Magnus drawled.

"Perhaps ye two would like to go upstairs to freshen up before the celebrations," Fergus spoke up.

Clearly Fergus had taken measure of the situation between the rival males, deciding it would be wise to lay a distraction.

"We dinnae need celebrations father. It would

be best if ye send Magnus home now so ye can be reacquainted with yer son-in-law. Besides, I'm fair exhausted from our travels and wish to retire early," Roslyn retorted with annoyance.

"Child, the hour grows late, it wouldnae be hospitable to send our guest out into the night. Nay, Magnus is welcome to stay until morning after the wedding breakfast," Fergus argued.

Roslyn knew better than to argue with her father on the laws of hospitality, but she wanted Magnus gone, hospitality be damned. She didn't trust having him under the same roof for the night, especially considering he could be plotting some kind of mischief. He was a threat to her peace of mind, he had to go!

"Father, I'm sure that Magnus would agree that there ..." she tried but was cut off by Magnus himself.

"Fear not, fair Roslyn, I've no wish to remain," Magnus allowed as he bowed to Fergus, then to Luther before turning on his heels and exiting the hall without further ado.

Roslyn watched him depart with relief. She had not considered that Magnus would be here awaiting her or that her father would have allowed him to stay to wait for her return considering that she had left him a note detailing her plans. It was almost as if Magnus had expected her to return alone, or perhaps he just wanted to be here to take measure of the situation for himself.

He was a despicable man, there was simply no accounting of the depths for which he could be capable of malicious trickery. Why then, had he relented so easily? Puzzling, but she wouldn't look a gift horse in the mouth tonight. She was only too glad to be rid of his pestilent presence. After Magnus had cleared out of the hall, no longer in range of hearing them speak, she turned on Luther.

"How dare ye interfere!" she bellowed.

"Interfere? How dare I? Woman, are you truly daft? You nearly got us all killed with your rash behavior!" Luther retorted with disbelief.

"I didnae no such thing! If I hadnae been here to protect ye, he would have laid ye low, mark my words," she told him with a huff.

"You forget that I am your husband, and it is my duty to protect you, not the other way around. In the future, when it comes to such matters you had best remember that and keep your pistol put away. Your actions only served to put us in real danger as those men were a hair's breadth away from slaughtering us all to protect Magnus," he challenged.

Luther was angry now. How could his wife not see that she had escalated the tensions between them by drawing her weapon? It had been unnecessary and had nearly cost them dearly.

"Ye dinnae know the devil as I do. He was waiting here so he could kill ye. Ye had best start carryin' a weapon if ye want to survive yer stay here at Dunheath," was her response.

Luther remembered then that his wife didn't know that he had recovered his memory, that he was well aware of the nature of the devil that was his cousin. As a youth, he had often felt threatened by Magnus as he was next in line to inherit the title if Luther were to die without issue. Having already been a duke, it didn't seem that Magnus would covet the title of marquess, but Luther knew the title was the least of which he desired; he wanted the land. The Huntley territory was vast, bordering Roslyn's land; therefore, Luther knew without a doubt, with so much to be gained, Magnus could be capable of plotting until no end if it truly suited his purposes to do so.

As to his wife's ominous warning? Perhaps he should seek to purchase a weapon in the village tomorrow. He had seen the malice in his cousin's eyes. He suspected that he had not heard the last of him. Now that he was married, naturally an heir would soon follow, which could be a prime motivator for a person like Magnus to strike sooner rather than later if he were plotting his untimely demise. On that thought he looked to his wife; she was afraid, truly afraid of Magnus. What manner of intimidation had he been using on her these last few years to instill such fear?

"Madam, I must apologize," he said after a moment of contemplation. "I know not this man as you do, but I do know this much; he is not going to go quietly away without making further mischief, so with your wise counsel, I have decided that I had better obtain a weapon to carry at the ready in the event that the need should arise," he continued with conciliation.

"Och now! Enough with such talk. Ye two must be worn from yer travels! Magnus is no threat to any of ye!" Fergus cut in.

Just then, Roslyn turned on her father, "I dinnae know why ye are so stubborn, ye old fool! The man is a demon with a black heart, but ye refuse to see it! Ye would have blindly sent me to his bed like a lamb to be slaughtered, never believing fer a minute that he would have been cruel beyond words. Is it any wonder that I had to go to such extreme measures?" Roslyn finished abruptly with eyes wide as if she had not intended the last words to leave her mouth.

It was at that moment that he decided he would wait to reveal to her that he had recovered his memory. He wanted to see what she would say next. Would she be honest with him now? He waited with outward calm, but inside an explosion of questions that had not occurred to him before were bursting through his mind.

Did she hope that he would never recover his memory out of fear that he would know she had lied to him? How long did she plan to perpetuate the lie? What would she do when she learned that he remembered everything? Was the source of her shrew-like temper because of a guilty conscience? These were but a few of the questions.

"I believe I will go to bed now. Father will show ye to yer room," she said as she quickly fled up the stairs.

Luther watched her flee with what felt like a deflated heart. Why had she run away when now would have been the perfect time to tell him the truth?

"Well laddie, it looks as if yer wife has abandoned ye. What say ye, we go and have a few nips while ye tell me what took ye so long to come home," Fergus offered with a chuckle.

Chapter Eleven

Roslyn cursed herself for a coward. She had no answer for it except that she just couldn't bring herself to confess her crimes. The moment had presented itself perfectly, but she had choked on the words, making it impossible to cleanse her conscience. Now as she lay alone in her bed, she felt ashamed that she could have been so gutless, but she had. She balled her hands into fists at her sides in frustration. How can I be a leader for my people when I am so truly spineless?

True, she had been shaken to the core by the scene that had played out with Magnus and the subsequent quarrel with Luther, but she was no shrinking violet; she should have seized the moment to lay bare her crimes for all to see. Let come what may! But no, she had cowered, then fled like a frightened child. She was no coward; she had proved it when she had drawn her weapon to protect the man she loved. She would have given her life then and there to protect his. Why then, had a few simple words of confession been so absolutely terrifying?

Unable to settle down, she got up from her bed to set about pacing as she tried to sort it all out in her mind. That's when she heard the sound of men talking just outside below her window. She hurried over to the window, hunkering down out of sight to survey the dark night below.

It was Magnus; she was sure of it. Though she couldn't make out the words he was speaking to his men, she recognized his voice. A deep foreboding passed through her stomach at the notion that he would still be lurking about. What was he up to? Should she raise the alarm?

Unsure what to do, she continued to watch with intense interest, silently cursing her position making it impossible to hear the conversation. How many men did he have with him? She thought she remembered three, but there were four men there with him now. Who was the fourth man?

She barely had time to further examine the man before one of the other men delivered a fearsome blow to his stomach, which sent him to his knees. He was quickly jerked back to standing then encompassed by the other two men who began to lead him away out of view. Fear shot through her mind as she quickly began to dress herself; she had to go out there to see what was happening.

She hurried with her task but took the time to arm herself well with two of her pistols as well as her small yet most prized rapier that she strapped snug to her thigh. Assured that she was well armed, she silently opened her door then hurried down the hall.

She gave pause to listen for her father and Luther but found that they were nowhere in sight, so she began a silent descent of the stairs then out the front door. Once outside, she crept around the side of the keep staying as close to the walls as she could, using the cover of darkness the shadows offered, allowing her to go unseen while she made her way to the rear bailey where she had seen the men.

Her heart was racing in her chest making it difficult to breathe, but she knew she must continue. In position at the corner of the keep, she paused to listen, but all she heard was the sound of her own blood rushing past her ears making it hard to hear anything else.

Slowly, ever so slowly she leaned forward to have a peek around the corner to afford her the view of the courtyard below her bedroom. Nothing! They were gone, but where had they gone, who was that man they had dragged away with them? Was he one of Magnus's men being punished for some kind of insubordinate behavior? Was he a member of her clan? She had to know, but there was no sign of them now. They had vanished into the night as though they had never been there to begin with.

Since her father had begun his mental decline, he had relaxed the security around the keep stating that there was no need for it now that there was peace in the region. Tomorrow she would rectify that as well as try to seek out the identity of the man who had been taken by Magnus. Tonight, she could do nothing more than consider her own safety as the realization that she could be vulnerable to attack struck fear deep within her, prompting her to scurry back to safety within the keep.

As she rounded the last corner, she began to breathe a little easier when the front door came into view. She stopped there to regain her composure while taking one last look into the night in hopes that she could get another glimpse of the group of men, but it was much too dark.

Though she could see nothing, the hair on the back of her neck began to prickle as though she were being observed by unseen predatory eyes. She was sure there was someone out there watching, assessing, making plans of what she could only speculate with a feeling of dread.

"Aye, ye be out there, ye devil," she whispered before turning to go inside.

Once inside, she quickly dashed up the stairs, where at the top of the landing she slammed into a wall of flesh. Her husband!

"Hold lass!" he said, grasping her around the waist to still her.

The air left her lungs, nearly causing a swoon, but she managed to stay upright within the confines of his capable arms. She sagged with relief when she saw that it was he, not Magnus as she had briefly feared.

"What's this now? Have I married a reiver?" he asked with mock concern, indicating with a nod to her weaponry.

Roslyn was taken aback by the question as she truly had no way of explaining why she had been out in the night armed to the teeth, but she began to stammer a response.

"I-I w-was, that is to say ... och, get out of my way, man," she said as she pushed past him in an attempt to go to her room.

Luther was quick to grab hold of her arm, spinning her back toward him. His wife was up to something, he intended to find out just what it was.

"What's your hurry?" he asked drawing her into an embrace.

He could feel her body quaking as though she were a frightened rabbit. What was she afraid of?

"Come now Roslyn, tell your husband what is amiss, perhaps I could assist you," he urged.

It was time for Roslyn to face the fact that she was a married woman now. There was no need for her to continue to take the world upon her shoulders when she had a husband whom she should defer all of her concerns. She should not be going out into the night armed as she was for any reason regardless of what she believed.

He knew that it would take some time to impress upon her that she would need to give over some of her independence, but he would be patient. Now was the perfect time to demonstrate this to her, so with a gentle hand he rubbed his thumb along her jaw in a soothing manner in an attempt to gain her cooperation.

"What could be so important that you go out into the night on your own?" he asked with a soft soothing voice.

Slowly she closed her eyes, relishing the soothing caress, but said nothing.

"Roslyn please, how can I help?" he asked.

She was so beautiful standing there in the dimmed light that he couldn't help himself, he leaned forward placing a gentle kiss upon her lips. The contact seemed to have shocked her as instantly her eyes snapped open, then she began a struggle to release herself from his embrace, but he held her fast.

"Come now, I can remain so all night. I would have an answer if you please," he said gently but firmly.

Roslyn knew she was trapped, she had to give him something. But damn the man for trying to interfere with her business. She was the clan's protector! She would be leader when her father passed on from this world. He had no right to hold dominion over her or anyone else. Still, she knew he expected an answer, so with reluctance she offered him a bone, hoping that he would be pacified enough to allow her to escape back to her room.

"If ye must know, I thought I heard a noise coming from the stables, so I went down to make sure all was well," she told him.

Luther was suspicious of her answer, but out of respect he accepted it though continuing, "Lass, it unsettles me to think of my beautiful wife going out alone into the darkness for any reason. You should have come to me, and I could have gone with you to see that you came to no harm," he offered.

Perhaps she had gone to see about Trapper and didn't want to admit it out of fear that he would go into a jealous temper. True, the idea that she would go out for an assignation with another man was disconcerting, but he understood that she would want to speak with him after their last encounter. This once, he could let it pass, but he fully expected that she would not make a habit of it. But if that's all it was, why was she armed so heavily?

"Just ye listen to me, Luther Rollins! In this and all matters of Clan McClarent, it is my responsibility to protect the people, and I'll no have ye pokin' yer nose around tryin' to undermine me," she told him with a lift of her chin.

Luther inwardly laughed at the thought of his young wife's bravado though he would never have her believe that he found her passion for her people a humorous issue. It has become very clear that she took her role seriously, for that he admired her. But still, she was his wife, she must obey him in all things out of respect. He would never undermine her authority as clan leader, but he would like to share in her duties to lighten her burdens. Now that he was here, he could help her a great deal; she just had to accept the idea.

"I'm glad we have a chance to discuss such things. It is not my intention to undermine your authority as clan leader to the clan McClarent, I wish only to offer my assistance to lighten your burdens. Here me out!" he protested as she drew breath to blast him with her rebuttal.

"Now then, on our travels here some of my memories returned, and I happen to know that I am a very wealthy man. As your husband, I would like to lend my purse to the improvements of Dunheath, including security so my wife doesn't feel obliged to go out into the night when she should be resting comfortably in her bed. What if you are with child? Will you go rushing out into the night fat with our child armed to the teeth as you are now? What of the safety of the child?" he asked, but before she could answer he continued.

"Roslyn, as your husband, you should afford me a certain amount of respect. You should seek my counsel in the very least before you make decisions that could affect your well-being or that of our children. Do I make myself clear?"

Roslyn was stunned. How much of his memory had been recovered? And what did he mean that she could be with child? Children? The devil acts as if he plans to stay. She sighed deeply, she had not considered these things. At any rate, it was ridiculous to consider that she could be with child; they had only lain together once. The bigger issue at hand was that his memory was fast returning, and she had to know how much he remembered.

"Yer memories have come back?" she asked with a deep gulping swallow as she choked down her fears.

Luther could see the wheels in her mind turning, she was worried about what he might remember. Deciding it was best to toy with her a while to see if she would release her conscience, he said, "Some, but not all."

Her shoulders sagged with what must have been relief. He took advantage of the moment to hook his arm through hers then began leading her to her room. When they reached the door, he stopped, drawing her into an embrace. He couldn't help but notice that she tensed up in his arms, making him wonder if he should take mercy on her by telling her that he knew what she had done.

Instead, he placed her away from him, propping his forearms upon her shoulders as he looked into her eyes for a suspended moment. Yes, she was afraid, but she needn't be. He understood her motivations and found he could not blame her or his brother one whit.

"Listen to me Roslyn. I know that I have not given you reason to lay your trust in me, but I will make you this promise here and now. I am your husband; therefore, I will be in your life until death do us part. There is nothing you could ever say or do to change that because I will never abandon you to the likes of Magnus again. I am here to stay, and I plan to do whatever is in my power to make your life easier. No more worries about the welfare of the clan, no more calluses on your lovely hands. I want a happy home full of children with a secure future, but most of all, Roslyn, I want you," he told her before leaning in to place a kiss upon her forehead.

With eyes closed to the soothing words Luther spoke, Roslyn felt as though she were floating amongst the clouds in some wonderful dream. For so many years, she had dreamed of such a moment as this, of hearing such words from Luther. Now, here he was standing before her saying them with such genuine love; could this be only a dream?

Would she wake up tomorrow with her hands full of hot ashes where the beauty of this moment had once existed as purely a figment of her imagination? What a wondrous thing it would be to lose herself to his promise; to trust that he loved her unconditionally, enough to stay with her for a lifetime. Could it be so? Truly?

"Luther, I-I ... I am very tired," the coward told him before reaching behind herself to turn the door knob of her bedroom door. "Good night."

Luther stood there looking at the hard, cold door where his wife had stood a mere second ago. He hesitantly reached for the doorknob but stopped short with the clicking of the lock from within. She had locked him out.

Tomorrow. Tomorrow perhaps she would tell him her secrets.

Chapter Twelve

"Take the bastard below and secure him between the posts. I shall deal with him in a moment," Magnus instructed his men.

Trapper knew what that meant. He was about to be flayed alive for double-crossing Magnus. He was supposed to have killed Luther but instead, not only had he left him alive, he had aided, aye, even witnessed the marriage between him and Roslyn.

He should have ran when he had gotten word that Roslyn had returned with Luther in tow, but with Magnus in residence at Dunheath, he had been concerned for their safety and had sneaked out to the keep to make sure all was well when he had been captured by Magnus and his men. His only hope now was that his death would be quick and merciful, but he knew Magnus would make him suffer for his transgressions. At least he would die knowing that Roslyn was forever out of his reach. He nor her father could ever harass her to marry him again. That was worth any price he was about to pay.

Trapper grunted in pain from the rough handling he was receiving as the men went about their dastardly duties, hoisting him to his feet to chain his wrists to the posts. It was difficult to breathe with what he was sure was a broken rib, maybe even two. The blow they had dealt him outside of Roslyn's window had been heavy and sure as it found its mark.

"Ye shouldnae have come home, ye stupid lad," one of the men told him.

"Och, maybe he wanted to die because he lost the girl," the big one snickered.

"Ye know he means to kill ye?" the first one asked as he made sure the irons were secured.

Trapper ignored their comments. It was pointless to try to plead with these men for help. They were devoted servants to Magnus, who undoubtedly paid them well for their loyalty.

"What say ye, we warm him up a bit," the joker said as he squeezed Trapper's cheeks, giving his head a brutal shake with one of his giant hands.

Trapper couldn't help but remember that giant hand as it had been the one that sent him to his knees in sheer agony earlier. Those hands had probably killed many people. By the looks of him, the man clearly enjoyed his work, evidenced by the maniacal light that shone in his eyes.

"Nay, we had best save him for Magnus. He wants the pleasure of handlin' this himself," the other suggested.

"Aye, it will be a pleasure," Trapper heard the

ominous words as Magnus entered the chamber.

Trapper could see him now, shirtless, with his hair tied back as he sauntered closer, twirling his cat o' nine tails about in the air as though it were a child's toy and not the brutal weapon it truly was. The display sent a chill up Trapper's spine, making him shiver with dread.

"Cold?" Magnus asked brows pulled together in mock concern.

Trapper swallowed hard then looked down, closing his eyes in silent prayer, but he didn't bother to answer the question as it wasn't meant to be hospitable.

"Duncan, stoke the fires! We wouldn't want our guest to catch a chill," he instructed.

Trapper continued to pray to God and all the saints to deliver him from this evil, but he knew that he deserved to endure a small hell on this earth before he met his maker to explain why he had ever bargained with the Devil to begin with.

"Where did we go wrong, you and I?" Magnus asked after a moment.

Trapper did his best to ignore Magnus as he continued his prayers. This might be the last chance he had to speak with the Lord to repent for all his worldly sins; he wasn't going to allow Magnus to cut him short as he had much to account for. The beating would have to wait.

"Come now, young Trapper, we have much to discuss, and the hour grows late," Magnus snapped.

Trapper jerked his head up to meet Magnus standing just inches away. Dread! Utter dread filled Trapper's body. There was no hope for him now.

"The time for prayer has passed, young Trapper. It's time to give the Devil his due," he taunted with a wicked smile.

Magnus reached up to wipe a tuft of hair away from Trapper's brow before letting his cold hand caress his cheek.

"You have the look of your brother," Magnus said almost wistfully. "Tis a pity you will die so young," he continued as he began a slow walk around Trapper checking the restraints. "Not too tight I hope," he said with mock concern.

Magnus continued his perusal before stopping behind Trapper. He braced himself for what was surely about to come then closed his eyes one last time in prayer. Magnus wasn't about to allow more prayer; instead, he grabbed a handful of Trapper's hair then roughly yanked his head back, the action bringing them cheek to cheek.

"You should have killed him like I told you to.

Now I have to take care of the deed myself," he growled before thrusting Trapper's head forward, causing pain to spike down his spine.

Trapper jerked as he felt his shirt ripped away, Magnus growling with rage in his efforts to remove the offending garment.

"All you had to do was hit him in the head, but you couldn't do it, could you?" he asked as he made his way back in front of Trapper.

Trapper remained silent. There was no point to any of this. It only served to prolong the inevitable.

"Duncan, loosen Trapper's tongue," he instructed.

The big man with the big hands came forward, quickly delivering a solid blow to his gut followed by another to his jaw, breaking loose a tooth. Trapper spit the tooth to the ground between gasping breaths but said nothing.

"Why didn't you hit him on the head, hmm?" Magnus asked with strained patience.

Trapper's head was wringing from the savage blow to his face, rendering him dizzy, but still he refused to speak; instead, he dropped his head forward trying once again to pray to his maker. Trapper's knees buckled under another savage blow to his stomach, but still he didn't speak.

Magnus sighed with irritation. "Clearly, he needs more encouragement," he said.

Trapper knew it was about to commence. He had heard many tales about Magnus's fascination with the cat o' nine tails, relishing in the damage it could inflict.

"You know, I would never have allowed you to actually marry the girl," he said from behind him before delivering a stinging strike across Trapper's lower back with the whip.

The first strike sent a shock through Trapper's body; the pain, unlike anything he could ever have imagined, briefly giving him pause to consider telling Magnus something to prolong the next strike. He knew it was hopeless though as Magnus seemed hell-bent on issuing great punishment before he dealt the killing blow.

"No, you would have been arrested and ultimately hanged for killing your brother, and I would have married the girl in your stead," he told him with another strike, this one a little higher up.

"It was such a nice plan, really," he continued as he struck him again.

"But you had to muck it all up, didn't you?" again, another vicious blow.

The beating stopped for a moment as once again Trapper found his head jerked back, bringing him nearly mouth to mouth with Magnus. Trapper's body was stinging as though he had found his way into a hornets' nest, the pain was absolutely mind-numbing. He wasn't sure how long he could endure, but he refused to give Magnus any satisfaction.

"Don't worry young Trapper. Magnus will clean your mess up. First, I will kill Luther, then I will marry the girl, then I will kill her too but not before I have my fill of her. It was my plan all along. I just needed a scapegoat to take the fall for my cousin's untimely death. You know, I had it all worked out quite nicely; I had planned for Roslyn to die in a hunting accident. Of course, that can still work as those kinds of things happen when a woman places herself in a man's world," he told him, spittle making him slur his speech with foul, hard-panting breaths.

Trapper hadn't time to brace himself for the next blow after his head had been violently thrust forward again. He was sure that one had removed flesh from his back but found it hardly mattered when a series of savage strikes followed behind it. Trapper began to lose himself to the pain, finding a small comfort in the delirium that began to overtake him.

"How do you suppose I should kill him now?" he heard Magnus from far away.

More savage blows, one after another until Trapper began to float in and out of consciousness. As he began to drift away, his thoughts were of Roslyn. Magnus still intended to kill her, now he wouldn't be here to protect her. All of this was for nothing; she and Luther were going to be killed, and he wouldn't even be able to warn them. This would be his hell. He would suffer an eternity knowing that he had failed her.

Magnus realized that Trapper was no longer with him as his body, unresponsive to the blows, hung limply in the restraints. Continuing the beating would be futile as the dumb bastard was already dead.

"Get rid of this rubbish," he instructed his men before storming out of the chamber.

"Ye stay and clean up the mess, and I'll get rid of the body," Amos offered.

"Why do I have to clean up the mess?" Duncan asked.

"Because I did it last time," Amos told him.

Amos removed Trapper from the restraints then hoisted his body upon his shoulder, making his way to the exit that would take him to the trail that led to the river. He knew he had to move fast if he were going to make it back before dawn. This was the kind of thing that had to be done under the cover of darkness. He couldn't risk being seen by anyone.

Quickly he made his way down the trail that came out at the water's edge, where he had left a small boat the last time he had to perform such a task. Gently, he lay Trapper's limp body into the boat, careful to lay him on his side so his injuries could begin to heal while he made his journey downstream.

He covered him with a blanket to keep the birds from picking at his flesh, then climbed into the boat. He grabbed up the paddles and with slow, sure strokes he began taking the boat further downstream where the current was swift enough to carry the craft onward in his absence. With any luck, someone would discover the poor wretch before he died and restore him to health. It was his only hope.

Once satisfied that he had given the boy a chance to survive, he stood over him, "God speed, cousin, and may the saints preserve ye," he said before bailing out of the boat.

Chapter Thirteen

"Lady's maid?" Roslyn asked the young girl standing at the side of her bed.

"Aye, my lady. His lordship brought me up from the village just this morn to serve yer ladyship," the girl responded with a curtsey.

Roslyn could tell that it was well past noon by the light and shadows cast about her room. Though she had never been one to waste her day away in slumber, she must have been exhausted from her travels enough to have lost nearly an entire day. Apparently, this was not the case with her husband who seemed to have been rather busy. Just what has he been up to? Judging by the young girl's presence, he had been to the village to acquire servants, but what else had he done? Deciding she had better investigate, she made an attempt to dismiss the child.

"Tess, would ye please stop with the formalities, and I can assure ye that I've no need of a lady's maid. Ye just go on back to yer mother as I'm sure she has greater need of ye than I," Roslyn told her as she flung her blanket aside to get out of bed.

"I'm to help ye with yer bath so ye can be ready when the seamstress arrives," Tess told her.

That piece of information stopped Roslyn in her tracks. She glared at the girl as if she had gone daft as she reached for her clothes.

"Seamstress! What nonsense is this?" Roslyn asked as she attempted to don her buckskin breeches.

"Ye mustn't dress yerself," Tess said more loudly than was appropriate while grabbing the breeches out of Roslyn's hands.

Roslyn was in a high temper at the notion that her husband had been so meddlesome, hardly noticing the girl's indiscretion. Lady's maid indeed! The girl was barely more than a child, no more than four and ten. She reached out to reclaim her breeches, but the girl was quick, darting evasively across the room and before Roslyn could give chase, there was a knock on the door.

Standing there in her nightshirt, she gave pause before opening the door, but it was of no matter as Tess quickly answered it, allowing a small army of servants armed with buckets of water and an old copper tub to enter the room. Who were all these people?

"I dinnae know where all of ye've come from, but ye can just turn right around and go back. I've no need of servants," Roslyn shouted.

The servants ignored her, continuing with the task of filling the tub under the close supervision of her lady's maid. Roslyn couldn't help but note that the girl was perfectly suited for the position of lady's maid as she was quite commanding in giving her instructions to the other servants. Roslyn attempted again to be heard.

"Stop this now and remove yerselves from my chamber this instant!" she demanded.

"Hush yerself daughter," her father's voice came from the doorway.

She snapped her head around, glaring daggers at the man. Clearly he had knowledge of her husband's scheming.

"What do ye know of this?" she asked him.

Her father stood there with a satisfied gloat upon his face, quite proud, he seemed. His expression amplified her concerns, sending a ripple of anxiety through her where it settled in her gut, making her stomach roll with unease.

"I know it's time ye start acting like a lady of yer station. Ye'er a married woman now, a marchioness no less," he told her with a wink.

His words slapped Roslyn in the face, bringing her to her senses. Marchioness? It had not quite occurred to her that she would carry such a title, but she did. Aye, she was a marchioness. Things would be expected of her now that had never been expected of her before.

Roslyn walked to her bed as though she were under some kind of spell and unceremoniously plopped down on the side as she blankly stared at the copper tub. This was more than she had bargained for. What did she know of such things? She looked down at her hands as if seeing them for the first time, inspecting the calluses along with all the dirt under her terribly worn nails.

A marchioness wouldn't have such hands, but the laird of a people would. Aye, she was future laird of her clan, she didn't have time for such nonsense.

"Where's Luther?" she demanded.

"As to that, yer new husband is in the bailey givin' instructions to the new guards," he told her as if this information was mundane.

"Guards?" she questioned.

"Aye, he told me of yer escapades last night, and I agreed with him that such things should be left to those more, how did he put it? Oh aye, more suited for the occupation of security," he told her with a sniffling twitch of his nose.

Roslyn could feel her temper begin to boil at

her father's revelations. How dare Luther take such liberties!

"This is madness! We dinnae need guards! We dinnae need servants! Just what in the name of all that is holy does the man think he's doing? He cannae just come here and start givin' out orders. Ye are the laird here!" she said rising from her bed.

She stomped over to her window to have a look at the rear courtyard below. Sure enough, there was her husband with half a dozen armed men dressed in full clan regalia, holding their crude weaponry, listening raptly to his every word. Well, she wouldn't have it!

She turned away from the window without thought to her improper attire, then marched out of her bedroom, down the hall to the landing at the top of the stairs where she was met by a battalion of women carrying bundles of cloth and fashion plates, blocking her path down the stairs.

"Och my lady, tis an honor! Yer husband summoned me just this morn. I am to fit ye with a complete wardrobe. Naturally, he wants this done quickly, so I took it upon myself to gather a few assistants," she gushed as she swept Roslyn into the crowd, ushering her back to her room.

Roslyn was trapped. There was no way to extricate herself from her current position without possibly causing injury to herself or someone else, so she allowed herself to be whisked into the crowd.

"Of course, ye are a large lass, but I'm certain we can fit ye proper with the latest fashions. So ye know, just last month, I traveled to Inverness and purchased some fine new cloth that will be perfect fer ye," she told her proudly.

Roslyn listened to the rotund woman prattle on with strained calm as she was ushered back to her room. Upon her return the servants preparing her bath quickly departed, but she was surprised to see her father still there, staring out the window at the bailey below. She thought back to the brief conversation a moment ago, realizing that her father seemed quite content with the developments. Why was he not in agreement with her? He seemed to be taking Luther's dictates as though he expected him to become laird and not her. Could this be true? Was this what he wanted all along? Did he not believe his daughter capable of leadership?

On that thought, Roslyn became aware of the hush in the room, prompting her out of her woolgathering enough to survey the room. It seemed the women were waiting expectantly for something ... yes, they must expect her father to leave the room, right, he should, but first she would use the silence to make her feelings known and understood.

"There's been a misunderstandin', it seems. I'm in no need of servants or a new wardrobe so ye all may take yer leave this instant," she told them as politely as she could manage.

There was a gasp among the seamstress and her crew, but that was overshadowed by the thunderous retort of her father as he spun away from the window, turning his attention to her.

"Ye listen to me now lassie and heed me well. Ye will do as yer husband instructs ye as I have given my full blessin' in his decisions. This is why the contract was made between his father and myself. It was always the plan to merge the two clans under one laird through this marriage. Now this has been achieved, and he will be my heir as I have no sons. Yer days of gallivantin' around the countryside, behavin' as a man, doin' all manner of manly labors has come to an end. Ye are a woman of consequence now, and ye had best start acting like it," he told her with a hard brow of vehemence directed at her.

Roslyn's hackles raised with the admonishing words her father spoke as the full impact of it hit her. Without thought to rationality, she gave way to her ire.

"So it's true then, ye have lost yer mind completely? Ye have no care fer what happens to me? Ye would just turn our clan over to a stranger? Ye would just as easy give me to a man with a black heart or another man that never wanted any part of us then hid these last ten years alongside the Devil in his heathen dens just to avoid his responsibility to his people?" she retorted hotly.

Her feelings for her father were dangerously close to loathing with the impulse to thrash him, making her hands ache to throttle him. How could he do this thing to her?

"The right man has claimed ye, and that's all that matters to me now. Why do ye think I dinnae come after ye when I found yer note and allowed ye to make the journey to fetch him? Did ye think I really wanted ye to end up with Magnus? Ye had to have a husband didnae ye?" he argued.

Roslyn growled with frustration. This was not at all how things were supposed to be. If she had known that her father would have conspired with her husband to demote her in such a way, she would never have sought Luther out.

"No, I didnae have to have a husband! I only needed a document to keep Magnus at bay. I could be laird to our people! Why must it always be a man?" she wailed.

"Hush now before ye wake yer mother," he told her.

"My mother is dead," she screamed at him.

"Tis why ye need to be quiet then, isn't it?" he explained as though the idea were completely logical.

Roslyn wasn't sure if he were merely jesting or if her father was beginning to slip into one of his spells, but she lowered her tone nonetheless. Madness though this situation was, she needed to behave with a little more maturity.

"Father, please do not allow Luther to come here and push me aside, I beg ye. Let us just send him on his way back to London. I can manage Dunheath as I have these last few years. I can work as hard as any man. I can mend fences and repair roofs. I can make sure the seeds are planted in time, and I can oversee the harvest. I can see to the welfare of our people better than any man, and ye know this," she implored him with eyes burning with the threat of tears.

Her father's expression turned to one of softness as he addressed her next. Gone now was the urge to do violence, replaced by one of absolute futility, her shoulders sagged in defeat.
"Och Lassie! I know ye can, but ye dinnae have to now. Luther has come home to take his place beside ye, now ye can live a life of leisure while givin' him plenty of healthy bairns as ye should," he told her with a palm to her tear stained cheek.

She had always known that she would become the Countess of Dunheath upon her father's passing since her brothers had died, so naturally she assumed that he would in turn name her his heir as laird to their clan.

The idea that he would so quickly take to Luther and name him his heir stung her pride, to say the least, but if she were to be completely honest with herself, she could understand why he would make this choice. Was it really so awful a choice for him to make? Could a woman project the strength required to have a people follow her with confidence?

Aye, lately she had proved even to herself that she lacked the simplest of skills required for leadership. Too, just last night she had felt as vulnerable as she had never felt when confronted with the darkness and the possibility that Magnus lie in wait. Perhaps her father was right in wanting a man to assume the role of laird. The notion that she was unsuited for leadership was humiliating but understandable.

Looking at her father now, she saw something there in his eyes in that moment that gave her pause. A moment of pure love shown for her in his eyes that she found utterly humbling. He truly believed that this was the best thing for her, so it must be. Her father may not be the best father a girl could have, but in his way, he loved her true and strong. He wouldn't knowingly do anything to harm her.

In the last year, his spells had become more frequent, causing her to take more and more responsibility for her clan. Most days, he was completely lucid, in charge of his mind, but now and again there was a slip from reality that seemed to leave him hanging on some precipice between the past and the present. He often asked where her mother was or made some comment indicating that he thought she was still alive; it had always broken her heart to see the confusion in his eyes when she or someone else reminded him of her passing.

Now in this moment, he knew what he was saying, he firmly believed it was what was best for her. Was she wrong to reject the idea so completely? Hadn't she dreamed of such a scenario just days ago? Why was she so adverse to the notion now? Why did it rankle that Luther was finally doing his duty when she and so many others had persecuted him for his neglect?

It was all very confusing. She sidestepped her father so she could make her way to the window to observe the men at work below. Luther was standing there in the center of the men with a broadsword in his hands demonstrating defensive maneuvers. He had removed his shirt allowing her a pleasant view of his strong muscular build. A more impressive figure, she couldn't imagine, her husband was.

She stood transfixed as the sun glistened on his sweat-soaked skin. Remembering the last time she had seen him in such a state of undress, she shivered at the memory of their passionate joining. It had shaken her to her very soul until the fear had set in, then everything had been ruined. Any hope or dream she was foolish enough to have was quickly incinerated because Luther would leave her when he learned the truth of her deeds against him.

Now she would have to consider what telling him the truth could cost her father. Obviously, he was comforted in knowing that he had secured her the best possible husband, thus ensuring the future of their clans. Telling Luther the truth now could jeopardize her father's peace of mind if he were to leave. Perhaps Luther never need know.

Chapter Fourteen

Roslyn took her supper in her room later that evening after having endured the entire day allowing the seamstress to have her way with her. It had been a tiresome ordeal that had culminated in two simple, practical day gowns along with one dinner gown made this very day along with a promise that much more would follow in days to come, now that her measurements had been taken and the fabrics matched to the fashion plates.

Roslyn didn't know one fashion from the next, nor which fabric was best for this gown or that, so she had stood mute while the ladies had clucked and clattered making the decisions for her.

All throughout the day she had waffled from one mood to another as she mulled over her new lot in life. This was not what she had bargained for when she made the decision to fetch Luther so she could force him to marry her. In her mind, she had conjured a completely different outcome than the one she was faced with now.

One minute she was angry with her father for so quickly casting her aside, then she would lament over the thought of losing Luther when he got his memory back. Too, she had pondered that perhaps she could secure him to her side if she were to employ more womanly arts of decorum.

Thinking along those lines, she considered the pastel blue dinner gown that gave her a rather alluring appearance and found that she looked forward to seeing Luther's reaction when she wore it tomorrow at supper. Even though he had never seen her in womanly attire, he had made her feel beautiful with his attentions.

The seamstress, bless her heart, had tried in earnest to offer advice on womanly decorum as she fussed over Roslyn during her fittings, even so, she still felt cast adrift on a sea of confusion. How would she ever make a proper lady when she had lived her whole life like a man? How could she soften her manners, her words or even her hands to make them more pleasing to a man?

When the seamstress had shown her how to curtsey, she had nearly toppled over when she tried to mimic her. Even after several tries, the seemingly simple task was impossible to execute. How would she ever manage the transformation? Perhaps, I will need a tutor.

In the meantime, she was content to hide away in her room sulking alone while she tried to make peace with her situation. Even though she understood her father's reasoning, she felt like a cat hiding in a dark space nursing its wounds after a fight with the dog. It hurt her deeply to think that her father had no confidence in her ability to lead their people, preferring to hand over the position to a virtual stranger instead. All her life, she had sought to prove that she was as worthy as any man, but in these last days she had been made to see that she was only a woman.

A woman was born to care for hearth and home, to provide warmth and softness in an otherwise hostile world. A woman was born to bring the next generation into that world, nurturing and protecting until it was strong enough to stand on its own. That in itself made a woman very valuable; perhaps more so than a man? Aye, that was a thought to consider, for where would man be without women? But what do I know of such things?

When put into perspective it seemed clear that women truly must be the backbone of society. Without women, men would be savage brutes living slightly better than animals. Perhaps, it was not so demeaning to be a woman in a woman's position after all, but a place of honor to be revered. This epiphany made her feel somewhat better, but it didn't remove the hurt that her pride had been dealt.

Perhaps in time she could embrace this philosophy, but right now, she couldn't overcome the insult to her dignity though she must try as it mattered not to her father who seemed dead set in his decision. Try as she might, she couldn't reach within herself to find the same confidence in Luther's ability to lead a horse to water, let alone, lead an entire people.

Until he lost his memory, he had shown no interest in responsibility. He had hidden away those long years to avoid his birthright. He had done everything to prove he was unworthy, yet her father had thrown his trust behind him with absolute confidence. Yes, it stung her pride, even made her feel bitter.

She let out a deep breath of defeat before turning out her bedside lamp. Tomorrow, she would consider how to go forward, but tonight she was much too tired to contemplate it further. She nestled into her covers just as there was a soft knock upon her door. Quickly, she sat up.

"Who's there?" she called from the safety of her bed though she already knew who it was.

"Tis I?" came the soft masculine reply of her husband.

"What do ye want?" she called to him.

"I would like to have a word with you," he replied.

She sat there a moment, annoyed yet strangely excited by his presence behind her door. She didn't really want to see him, yet the sound of his voice called to her in a way that made her body ripple with desire. Damn the man for having such an effect on her, and damn her body's betrayal of her better sense.

"It is late. We can speak tomorrow," she told him firmly.

The bold devil turned her doorknob to enter her sanctuary. Her heart thundered in her chest, prompting her to quickly pull the covers to her neck like a child afraid of the dark. Roslyn wasn't really afraid of him; she was afraid of her vulnerability for him. She wanted to hate him, but she knew that she couldn't. Her heart, body and soul worked against her determination to prove to him, nay prove to herself that she was impervious to the effect he had on her.

Time seemed to slow down as he opened the door, allowing her a moment of appreciation for his masculine figure as he stood in the doorway, his large silhouette invoking a shiver of anticipation. Of course, she didn't want him to see her desire as her wounds were simply too fresh.

"Whatever ye have to say can wait until morn," she weakly admonished.

He didn't listen; instead, he advanced into the room, making a direct path for her bed, for her. Roslyn couldn't believe it was possible that her heart could beat any harder within her chest than a moment before, but it did. It felt as though it were going to burst out in a desperate attempt to flee his presence.

"I missed you at supper," he told her softly as he sat on the side of her bed gazing upon her. She didn't like the way his beautiful green eyes were adoring her, it made her uncomfortable. It left her with a feeling a wanting, awful need.

"I was tired," she responded defensively.

"The seamstress said you might be as you had a very productive day with your fittings. I hope you were pleased," he said, hope ringing in his tone.

She had always been impulsive, her temper quick and scathing. She knew this, but she had never been able to control it, even now when she knew that she should.

"Ye had no right to send a seamstress," she snapped.

She hadn't meant to sound quite so harsh about it, but she had; she could tell that his feelings were hurt. Even if she wanted to take the words back, they were out now so there was nothing for it but to forge ahead with her current adversarial position.

"I had hoped it would please you to have some new clothing. I thought only to make you happy," he told her.

"If I wanted new clothin' I would've called for the seamstress myself," she told him with annoyance clear in her tone.

Luther sat dejectedly on the side of her bed, causing her a brief moment of regret for her behavior, but she couldn't seem to allow herself to be pleasant. He had to know that she wouldn't be cowed in such a way as to allow a man to make all of her decisions for her.

"Consider it a wedding gift," he mumbled, looking away from her.

Maybe she was merely angry for allowing him to touch her heart so tenderly, she didn't know. Maybe she just wanted him to hate her so he would return to England so she could go back to the way things were, she didn't know that either, but she was unable to stop the horrible words that flew from her mouth next.

"If ye be thinkin' to change me into one of yer London hoors, ye can just forget it. I'll not dress like a trollop to please ye," she huffed.

The shrew within her relished in her triumph for after having said such a thing it was clear he had taken offense. He jumped up from the bed as if it were made of hot coals, turning toward her with cold fire in his eyes.

"Woman, have you gone mad?" he thundered.

This is what she wanted, a fight, a full on brawl; this she could deal with. Those other tangled emotions only served to keep her confused, off balance. Now she was on familiar turf; now she was in control.

"Aye, maybe I have for thinkin' it a good idea to marry one such as ye," she said, warming up to her ire.

"One such as me? What is that supposed to mean?" he asked.

"Oh, that's right, ye have amnesia. Ye cannae remember that ye're a loathsome heathen that prefers to wallow in a life of debauchery," she said, coming out of her bed to stand before him.

Luther too seemed to be warming to his own ire as they continued to quarrel.

"I have told you that my memory is mostly recovered, I know full well who I am. Don't think that you can continue to beat me over the head with my past. I have come to terms with my shameful behavior with respect to you and our people and have pledged to make right those wrongs that I have committed," he retorted firmly.

"Ye can never right all the wrongs, Luther Rollins. Just ye go on back to yer pack of bachelors and continue where ye left off. No one here will care one whit, I can assure ye," she postured.

Luther stood staring at his wife as if she had

gone mad. She was striking out at him like a venomous snake, hell-bent on destroying him, trying to destroy any chance at happiness that they could find with one another. Why? What was really going on here?

"What is going on here, Roslyn?" he said, putting voice to the thought.

"I dinnae know what ye mean," she spat.

Luther pressed his hand to his forehead, trying to soothe the ache that was now threatening to grow stronger. Taking a few restorative breaths, he ventured on.

"Why are you trying to quarrel with me? What has set you off?" he asked.

"If ye must know, Luther Rollins, I dinnae appreciate the way ye have come here tryin' to take over. First, sending a seamstress, then setting up a guard. There is no need for such things here at Dunheath. Then ye take advantage of my father's addled mind, convincing him to name ye as his heir. Ye have no right," she shouted, stamping her foot.

The last part brought Luther up short. What was she saying? He had done nothing of the sort. There had been no such discussion with her father. He truly had no idea what she was carrying on about.

"As to the seamstress, aye, I thought to make a gift to you. As for the guard, I thought only to protect you, and as far as this other nonsense for which you speak, I haven't a clue what you are referring to. I can assure you that there have been no discussions with your father of such a nature. Please enlighten me further so that I may properly defend myself against this allegation," he implored her.

Luther could see that his wife was beyond reason, but he had to know just exactly what was going on to cause such behavior.

"He told me how ye told him of yer plans and that he was in complete agreement. He told me that he had no more need of me now that he had ye, his heir," she said on a sob, turning away from him.

Luther was at a loss. Clearly, something had been said by her father to leave her in such a state, but truly, he had no hand in it.

"Roslyn, please listen to me. I will speak to your father about this. It is not my intention to come here and take over as you have accused. I have told you that I would only serve to support you. I will never do anything to hurt you; this I swear. Please believe me."

Roslyn stiffened her back but refused to face him. She knew that she had hurled ugly accusations at him. She knew there was no truth in her words, but her hurt feelings were raw and unfettered. She could no more reign herself in now than she could grasp hold of the moon and draw it to her bosom. She only wanted Luther away from her so she could continue to nurse her wounded pride in private.

"Just leave me be. I wish only to go to sleep," she told him.

Luther reached for her but stopped short of touching her as he knew there was really nothing he could do to assuage her pain.

"I love you, Roslyn," he told her softly, then turned to exit the room.

Roslyn didn't want to hear words of love, she wanted finality. She wanted to send him packing back to London so she would never have to submit to him, neither did she want to admit to him what she had done. It would be better that way. Wouldn't it?

After a prolonged moment spent in silence, she began to wrestle with her conscience, to wrestle with the need to rush into his arms begging forgiveness for her hurtful words. She turned toward him with words of apology resting on her tongue only to be left gasping at the empty space where he had stood. He was gone. What have I done?

Chapter Fifteen

"It was settled before yer father died. Did ye not read the contract?" Fergus asked before stuffing a piece of ham into his mouth. "The contract states that upon marrying Roslyn ye would become my heir as I have no sons. Tis why we made the agreement to begin with." He continued chewing heartily.

"Only your eldest child can inherit your title," Luther argued.

"Ye are not heir to my title. She is the heir to my title. Ye are my chosen heir to become laird of the Clan McClarent. Tis a different issue. I may name whomever I choose to become laird upon my passing. I never intended for Roslyn to be burdened with such a position. It requires great strength to join two clans; the strength of a man such as yerself," he told him.

Luther was stunned to hear this. He had not read the contract in full and, apparently, Roslyn hadn't either.

"This is not fair to Roslyn. She has believed all these years that she would one day become laird of her people. She has worked hard to prove she is worthy, she has earned it and now you just simply rip it away from her. It is cruel beyond measure. Can you not change your mind?" Luther asked him.

"Life isnae fair and no, I cannae change my mind. The course was set ten years ago, and it was sealed with a blood promise on yer father's death bed. Roslyn will just have to understand that she was never meant to be laird of the Clan McClarent," Fergus railed at Luther.

"You have doomed our marriage to fail with such nonsense. I don't know if she will ever speak to me again as she believes that I have had a hand in this," Luther complained.

"Are ye a wee mouse or man? It doesnae matter what she thinks. Ye must make her submit to yer will as a husband. She cannae deny ye yer due," Fergus counseled.

"You clearly have no idea who your daughter is or you could never say such things. She is a strong woman that could never allow herself to be subjugated in such a way. Do you not know her at all?" Luther asked rhetorically.

"Och man, ye think I dinnae know the lass is hurtin'. I know it, but what is done is done and cannae be undone. Now, I have said all I'm goin' to say on the matter."

Luther turned to leave Fergus in his study where he had been taking his midday meal, but before exiting the room, he turned to ask one last thing.

"Would you have made her marry Magnus had I not consented?"

"No force on this earth could have compelled me to give her to that no good black heart of a devil. No, had ye not married her, I would have given her to yer brother," Fergus told him.

Luther let out a harsh shaking breath at Fergus's latest revelation. He felt as though he had been punched in the gut by Poseidon himself. The words nearly sent him to his knees, now he wanted nothing more than to wrap his hands around old Fergus's throat to choke the life right out of him. The man was unscrupulous, how could he be so heartless where his daughter was concerned?

After he had composed himself from the desire to harm the old man, he turned on his heel, exiting the study. He was sickened, disgusted on so many levels that he couldn't even organize his thoughts. One word seemed to loom large in his mind above all others, however; interloper. He felt like an interloper, he didn't belong here. Roslyn would never love him now, how could she?

Two days had passed since he had left Roslyn in her room after their quarrel. She had not ventured out, nor had she allowed him audience. He had tried numerous times to speak to Fergus but found the simple concept of conversation nearly impossible with the old man as he seemed to drift in and out of the present quite frequently. Today he had been rather lucid, so Luther had thought to seize the opportunity for answers. Well, he certainly had answers, but now there was a new question. Why am I here? Clearly, Roslyn didn't want him; she had said as much.

Then there was Trapper. Poor Trapper loved Roslyn, he could even now, this very minute, be her husband instead of himself had he simply refused to cooperate. This last idea sank in Luther's heart heavily as he envisioned a happy union between Roslyn and Trapper, the image causing a painful stab to his already aching heart. Perhaps there had been more to the story of their relationship than he had concluded. He didn't want to believe it, he couldn't.

Driven by the sudden need to escape, he made the quick decision to leave Duneath. He would go to Huntley to take refuge from this awful debacle. Perhaps there, he could have time to think about how he should go forward. With that decided, he made his way down the hall to his quarters. Once there, he quickly gathered his meager belongings. He stopped outside of Roslyn's room, trying one more time to speak with her. He lightly tapped on the door, speaking her name as he did but was answered only with silence. So be it!

As he made his way down the stairs, he heard the clanging of a bell coming from the bailey. He picked up his pace, quickly finding himself outside confronted by a horrific sight. There, amidst a gathering crowd was an old cart, covered within with dried blood; barely recognizable was a young man with long blond matted hair that could only be his brother.

"My lord, we found him in a boat, floating down the river," said a solemn young man.

Luther swallowed hard as he took in the horrible scene. What could have happened to Trapper?

"Is he … is he dead?" he asked.

"I dinnae think he is dead. I thought I heard him moan when I moved him into the cart," the man told him.

"Has anyone called the surgeon?" Luther asked.

Everyone looked about confused as though they had never heard the word before, so Luther clarified. "Doctor? Has anyone called the doctor?"

"There be no doctor here at Dunheath; only the healer, and she's helpin' with a birth in the village. There's only our lady Roslyn to help him now," the young man told him.

Just then, Roslyn came bursting through the crowd, shoving everyone aside. Once at the center of the disturbance, it took her only a moment to see what was there before issuing a sound so woeful that it rocked Luther's soul, undoubtedly it would stay with him for the rest of his days.

A sound so sorrowful that it had to have been heard to the heavens above as she drew Trapper up in her arms, cradling him lovingly while rocking from side to side as she would a child.

There was absolutely no response from Trapper as he hung limp in her arms. One thing was certain; if Trapper weren't dead, without immediate aid from a doctor, he would be soon.   Luther moved nearer to Roslyn to get a closer look. From his vantage point, he could see his brother's back had been torn to shreds. The sight could only mean one thing. Someone had flayed him.

"Allow me to carry him inside," he instructed softly.

She looked at him with tears pouring forth then back at Trapper before nodding her head in consent. As gently as he could, he lifted his brother from the cart, placing him over his shoulder to avoid injuring him further. Roslyn realized then, the nature of the injuries, then fell to her knees retching to release the contents of her stomach.

Luther was torn between carrying Trapper or helping his wife, but knowing that she was a strong woman, he knew she would quickly compose herself to follow, so he soldiered on with his burden. The crowd parted allowing him a clear path to the keep. Once inside, he labored up the stairs with his brother then took him to his own quarters. There, he pulled the covers back on his bed then gently lay Trapper on his stomach, careful to make sure he would be comfortable. He then went in search of a maid to help him with hot water and supplies to allow Roslyn to administer aid to him.

On his way down the stairs he passed his wife, they briefly paused to contemplate one another. Whatever issues that lay between them would have to wait. What was most important now was saving Trapper then finding out who had done such a thing and why?

****

Roslyn could hardly summon the courage to look at Trapper's wounds, but she knew she must if she were to try and save him. From the look of him, she wasn't sure there was much hope as he seemed to have lost so much blood, his wounds so brutal, the likes of which she had never seen, and she was sure there was a fever.

"Who did this to ye, Trapper?" she whispered as she began removing his boots.

Of course, there was no answer. He was lost in a deep sleep, barely breathing. Who could have done this to him? One name sprang to mind, but she couldn't imagine a reason for it. Magnus would have had no cause to do such a thing to Trapper unless he were sending her some kind of message, but that made no sense. Perhaps he had run afoul of some woman's husband, perhaps some girl's father.

She shook off the thought as she continued to undress him, careful not to move him too much. Removing his breeches was a difficult task in his current position, but she didn't dare roll him onto his back for fear that she could cause more harm to his injuries. Roslyn tried to relax, to allow her mind to think of other things as she went about her task so as not to become overwhelmed by the true horror of the sight before her. It wouldn't do for her to lose her composure as she had in the bailey if she were to be of any real use to the situation.

It no longer mattered that she demonstrate strength as a leader in front of her clan, but she still had her pride. Her father might not have any confidence in her as his heir, but she didn't want to allow that to govern her behavior. She had never been weak in the stomach before, but seeing her best friend in such a state had been more than she could endure and she had succumbed, losing the contents of her stomach as though she were some kind of delicate flower.

She had seen the look in Luther's eyes when he was trying to decide who to lend his strength to; she or Trapper. In the end, he had decided to leave her to her own devices, choosing to carry Trapper instead, and rightly so. Perhaps he was still angry with her from their fight the other night, or perhaps he was angry because she had chosen to refuse him audience since.

She had been so ashamed of her behavior that night hoping that she could be spared further humiliation from having to see him again, or that he would just leave, but he had stayed as he promised he would. But why? She had treated him deplorably from the very beginning, yet he continued to exhibit a rare strength in character, one that she found most humbling.

Could this be the same Luther Rollins who had shown so little concern for her or her people for all these years? Perhaps losing his memory had been a good thing for him. It allowed him to become an outsider to his own life, helping him see his folly with a whole new perspective. One thing she was starting to wonder with more apprehension was whether or not she was deserving of him.

"I have brought warm water and bandages, and the cook provided me with some ointment for his wounds. I trust you have the necessary implements to stitch him up?" Luther said bringing her out of her musings.

Roslyn turned to the sound of her husband's voice as he was putting the items on the nightstand. She had been startled to see him there as she had been so deep in thought that she wasn't even sure how much time had passed since she let her mind begin to wander.

Rising from the bed, she stood in front of him for a brief moment; she thought to say something, anything to mend the rift between them, but now didn't seem like an appropriate time, so rather than speak she quickly fled the room in search of the supplies he had requested.

Truth, she needed to compose herself because she didn't feel at all strong right now. She felt like the slightest touch or the softest breeze could shatter her into a million pieces as if she were indeed a delicate flower, nothing more than a dandelion.

Chapter Sixteen

The long day turned into night as they kept their vigil at Trapper's bedside with no encouraging signs that he would survive, causing a deep anxiety to permeate throughout the keep. Early in the evening the healer had arrived to assess Trapper's condition, stating that it was in the Lord's hands now; though she had remained to oversee his care just the same.

Roslyn was grateful that she had been relieved of such a heavy responsibility being not at all equipped with the knowledge it would take to nurse him back to health. She had cleaned and stitched him up as best she could, embarrassed when Elsbeth had examined her work, though quite relieved by the praise, which had put her concerns for her incompetence to rest.

Roslyn had taken great care to make sure that she made her stitches as fine as possible, drawing from her memory of the time she and Trapper had made hats out of a pig's hide, noting with a shivering revulsion at the similarity in texture. It was horrible to consider that such a wonderful day had actually trained her for such an endeavor, but she would have been at a complete loss had it not been for that experience.

Now as she sat in the semi-darkness at Trapper's bedside, her eyes began to grow heavy with fatigue. She wasn't certain of the time, but she surmised that it had to be well past midnight. Luther had been ever present alongside her with barely a few words, but she could feel his strength, taking comfort in its warmth.

"Ye should get some sleep," she found herself saying.

"Aye and you as well," he returned softly.

Roslyn hadn't planned on leaving Trapper's side, but she knew Luther must be getting tired so she thought to offer, "Ye can sleep in my room. I'll just make a pallet on the floor here in case Elsbeth has need of assistance in the night," she told him.

Her spine tingled as Luther's silence spoke volumes to her suggestion that she would not be leaving Trapper's side.

"Ye just go on with yer husband, my lady. If there be any change in his condition, I'll alert ye," Elsbeth said breaking the silence.

Roslyn had thought the old woman to be sleeping, silently cursing her interference in the matter.

"Thank you, Elsbeth. We will be just down the hall if you should have need of anything; don't hesitate to call us," Luther told her as he stood offering his arm to Roslyn.

Roslyn thought to refuse but really didn't want to cause a scene as she had in front of the seamstress, so reluctantly she rose, allowing herself to be escorted from the sick room. Once they were out of Elsbeth's range of hearing, she would make certain Luther understood that she would make her own decision in this and return to Trapper's side.

Luther led the way to her room, never uttering a word along the way. Once they were at the threshold, he opened the door then gently shoved her inside, quickly closing the door behind him where he placed his body to block her escape.

"Now then, get undressed and get in the bed. I'll not have my wife driven to exhaustion when there are servants to care for my brother," he commanded.

Roslyn gasped at his audacity before attempting to refuse.

"Now!" he ordered.

"I told ye before Luther Rollins, that ye'll not be tellin' me what to do," she protested.

"Woman, I am your husband, and it is my wish that you get into that bed and get a good night's rest. If Trapper makes it through the night, you can see to him in the morning. Until then, do as I bid and get some sleep," he told her, his tone growing more severe.

Roslyn could see that he was hell-bent on having his way in this, so perhaps now was not the best time to force an issue such as this, but she wanted nothing more than to tell him that Trapper was not his brother; that she had every right to keep vigil at his bedside. Instead, she took a deep calming breath. Damn the man!

"I guess ye think to be beddin' down with me?" she asked more defensively than she meant to.

"Where else would I sleep but with my wife?" he asked with a raised eyebrow.

Roslyn knew there were other rooms available to sleep, but most of them had been closed up for years, requiring much in the way of preparations for which they simply had no time. Would it be so awful to allow him to sleep in her room? They were husband and wife; who would gainsay them for sharing a bed? Roslyn sighed in defeat.

Yes, he would have to bed down with her, so without further argument she began to disrobe. She had all but forgotten that she was wearing one of the skirts and blouses that the seamstress had sent over just this morning. She had been so impressed with the practicality of it that she had donned it right away never thinking about it again after the bell had rung to alert them of Trapper's arrival.

She looked up to see that she had Luther's complete attention as she began unbuttoning her blouse. Pausing briefly to revel in her apparent ability to distract her husband, she boldly continued to undress until she was wearing only her shift.

Luther wanted her; she could see it in his eyes as they wandered over her nearly naked body, causing her own body to thrill in response. Hoping that he wouldn't notice his effect on her, she quickly turned away from him to crawl into her bed where she quickly pulled the covers up to shield herself from his view.

Perturbed by her own desire, she tried to settle her accelerated heartbeat but found it an impossible thing to do, knowing that he was about to lie down with her. Straining to hear the soft sounds that he made over the sound of her own blood as it pulsed through her ears, she realized that he must be disrobing; again her body thrilled with anticipation. Her breath caught and held when Luther pulled the covers back before sitting down on the edge of the bed.

Would he have expectations? Did she? Choosing to appear unaffected by his presence, she rolled on her side, presenting him with her back, but it did little to quiet the thundering of her pulse. She felt his weight beside her as he lay down, but when his arm draped over her as he pulled his body against hers, she nearly died from the pleasure of his nearness. Though it was a wonderful feeling being wrapped in such warm strength as her husband exuded, her body soon stiffened when she felt the proof of his desire against her backside.

The devil taunted her with an easy grind as he settled closer against her. As if her rear-end had a mind of its own, she arched her back to press into him as well, causing him to issue a soft chuckle.

"Just what do ye find so humorous, husband?" she asked.

"Oh, tis not humor but delight," he told her with a smile apparent in his voice.

"Delight ye say?" she wondered?

"Indeed, I thought I would never know what it was like to snuggle against my wife in such a way. Tis truly delightful," he told her, then bumped her from behind for effect.

"Och, ye are the Devil," she bantered but said nothing further to admonish him.

Just then, he drew her closer still until she could feel his breath upon her shoulder, engulfing her in his essence. He smelled of masculine comfort that made her feel safe and secure. It was a pleasure to her senses that sent a warm sensation along the length of her body that settled into her nether regions where it began to simmer. The heat in her loins began to make her feel restless with wanting as though she hungered with an appetite that only he could satisfy.

As if he understood her need, he began a slow sensual massage of her breast, first with slow strokes of his thumbs along the underside until boldly as though sure of himself, he began to squeeze and knead with the skill of a master sculptor with his clays, softening her to his will. Arching her back with her pleasure, she moaned softly as he taunted her senses further by dragging his hand down the length of her belly until it rested between her thighs where he cupped her heat with his large, capable hand. Her body responded with a hot tightening of her flesh where she needed him most.

"Luther," she cried out as she reached for his hand to press it firmly to her need.

"Shh, let me give you pleasure," he advised softly.

Like a kitten, she seemed to purr as he began to massage her woman's mound, the sound sending Luther into a euphoric state as he sought to give her release, grinding his erect shaft between the globes of her shapely derriere while rubbing her fleshy nub with his fingers. He wasn't sure if he could hold his own release back, but at this point he couldn't care as he finally had her right where he wanted her; in his arms writhing with pleasure.

As though she were aware of his discomfort, she lifted her leg, entwining it with his, allowing him access to her sheath where in one swift move he soon found himself home in the center of her heat. Together they cried out in pleasure at the joining, then he began slow, swift strokes, never taking his hand away from her sensitive flesh as he did. He could feel her tightening around him, he knew that it wouldn't be long before she crested, taking him with her on the crashing wave of her orgasm.

Lost in the blissful moment, he began to suckle at the base of her neck as he deepened his thrusts; her body's reaction was instantaneous. Immediately, she crashed into him hard, pulsing, pulling him in deep where he soon surrendered to his own release.

Luther held tight to her for several moments, allowing his seed to flow into her where he hoped that it would soon take root, making her fat with his babe. He hadn't planned on this, but seeing her nearly nude had been his undoing. Gone were his noble plans to allow her to get the rest she needed, replaced by his need to possess her.

All afternoon, he had wrestled with jealousy of his brother who lay dying as his wife lovingly tended to his wounds. He knew that it must be done if Trapper were to survive but found that he could hardly bear witness as her hands touched another man.

It had been an ordeal, one he was ashamed of, but now after such a passionate joining with his wife, his jealousy had been subdued. Trapper was just a boy, he could never give her the kind of loving that he had just given her. It took a man to command a woman's body to respond as she just had.

Still, he wanted Trapper well so he could go on to live his own life as he should. He knew that his brother was in love with Roslyn, but he hoped in time he could find happiness elsewhere. He didn't want him under the same roof pining away for his wife, or she feeling conflicted by his presence.

The wounds of separation were too fresh for the lifelong friends; Luther wasn't sure Trapper would allow them to be happy. No, it was best to keep Roslyn fixed by his side while his brother was in residence to avoid future complications. Seduction was the answer. He would romance her, lavish her with his attentions, show her how wonderful life with him could be. Soon, with any luck a child would come then any fears he had of losing her would virtually disappear. He wanted her to thrive as a woman of leisure, never again having to worry for the welfare of her people. He knew that she was still hurt by her father's decision, but in time he felt sure that she could accept it, even be pleased by it.

Gone too, was the need to flee Dunheath, he no

longer felt like an intruder. After giving careful consideration to all that had occurred, he knew that he was where he belonged. Their fathers had planned their future, but he and Roslyn controlled it. They could work out their differences, they could even find love between them despite their recent quarreling. He already loved her madly, he just needed to be patient, give her time to accept him as her husband and protector, then in time, she would grow to love him too.

He was brought out of his reverie by the soft sounds of his wife snoring. The sound made him smile. The poor lass was exhausted.

"Rest well, my love," he told her, then gently kissed her upon her neck.

She whimpered slightly when he eased himself out of her sheath but snuggled back into him when he drew her into his arms, holding her securely while she slept.

"I will love you forever," he told her before closing his own eyes, allowing sleep to overtake him.

Chapter Seventeen

The following day turned into night as the newlyweds continued to cement their bond as a couple through passionate lovemaking. Roslyn would never have imagined that she could find the kind of peace as she had with Luther since last night, but she had done so. Just lying nestled against him filled her with a sense of rightness as all her cares began to melt away.

When they weren't lost in the throes of their passion, they were speaking of the future. Luther told her of his plans to improve conditions for their clans with such conviction that despite her earlier reservations, she found that her faith in him to achieve the seemingly impossible was increasingly absolute. Too, she began to suspect that he had recovered his memory in full but confirming it with her confession was still something she couldn't bring herself to do as the possibility of losing him now would be utterly devastating if he had no knowledge of her misdeeds against him.

However, her concern over his memory or lack, thereof, was becoming more confusion than one of fear the way he talked as if he remembered Trapper as a child. He even spoke of the anger he had felt toward his father for abandoning him with such passion as if it were true so that she really began to wonder.

When he first began to speak of it, she thought that perhaps he had created the memories somehow. Then as she listened, she began to question what she knew or had always known to be fact. Was it possible that Trapper really was his brother? If so, why had no one ever told her of it? Why had Trapper never told her of it? Why did everyone go about pretending that he was merely the stable master's son?

Truth, if Trapper really was his brother, then her crimes against Luther were not so bad. All she did was ... kidnap him and give him amnesia. She inwardly shook the thought aside; that was bad enough, but was it bad enough to prompt him to leave her? He had told her many times how much he loved her, that he would never leave her again. He even told her that there was nothing she could ever do or say that would make him leave her. Was he trying to let her know that he knew? She wasn't sure anymore.

She didn't want to continue to harbor secrets when they had so many other issues to overcome. Presently, there was the pressing matter of finding out who had done this thing to Trapper. Luther had selected a group of men to go about with an ear to the ground in hopes of learning something to aid them in the discovery. It was possible that they may have to wait until Trapper had recovered enough to name the villain himself; if so, they could be in for a long wait.

Another issue they would have to overcome, sooner rather than later, was how to go about joining the two clans as her father had said they were to do. Most of Luther's clan had been dispersed, many absorbed by her clan and others by Magnus. How would they ever bring them back to unite them under one banner? Then there was the matter of Luther's estate falling to ruin. He hadn't even had a chance to go see about it with all that had transpired since their return to Dunheath.

She had reconciled her heart and mind to her new situation as the wife of the future laird, as there was nothing she could do about it anyway. In her heart, she knew that she would be inadequate for such a responsibility but had been willing to take it head on just the same. If the clans were to be united, it could only happen under the leadership of a strong man such as Luther. He, of course, would have his work cut out for him in trying to garner respect from a people that he had forsaken for the last decade. She would have to give him her full support if the people were to ever give him a chance.

It was unlikely that the members of Luther's clan that had gone with Magnus would ever return, but Luther didn't seem at all worried about it. When she had pointed this out to him, he had merely told her not to worry as it would work out the way it was supposed to. If she were to give him her full support, shouldn't she give him her full honesty too? This was the thought that brought her concerns full circle. She had to say something; she couldn't let it linger between them to fester like a splinter under one's fingernail.

"Luther?" she ventured as she lay snuggled close to him.

"Hmm," he responded lazily.

"There's something I need to say to ye," she told him.

Luther turned toward her so that they were nearly nose to nose, then with a gentle hand, he began to rub her back soothingly. She briefly wavered in her confidence as the risk of losing moments so precious as this would be too costly. Just as she opened her mouth to make her confession, Luther silenced her with a kiss, then placing his forehead against hers, he took her fears away.

"I know what you and my brother did Roslyn, and I know why you did it. I love you anyway, so rest your mind and think no more about it," he told her with his eyes closed.

Roslyn gasped at his declaration. So it had been true, he had known it all along, but he had stayed beside her to prove his devotion. Her heart soared with relief, but she wanted clarification so she continued.

"But we gave ye amnesia," she protested.

"Aye, and I'm a better man for it, now go to sleep," he told her.

Roslyn couldn't sleep, she couldn't leave it there. Was Trapper really his brother? She had to know, she couldn't allow him to continue on believing it if it weren't so.

"I need to know something," she told him.

"Yes, my love, what do you need to know?" he asked turning to her with one eye open.

Roslyn sat up. She wasn't sure how to pose this question without shedding a bad light on the extent of her duplicity if it weren't true.

"If ye know what we did, then ye know everything?" she asked, caution present in her tone.

"Everything?" he questioned?

Luther was alert now. What was his wife about to confess? He had told her that he knew what she and Trapper had done, yet she seemed adamant that there was more to be told. His stomach clenched at the possibility that she was about to admit to a relationship with Trapper beyond what had been apparent.   He wasn't at all sure that he wanted to hear her confession, but he braced himself for it with his breath held.

"Aye, are ye sure that ... well, are ye sure that Trapper is yer brother?"

Luther sat up now as he found her question unusual, not at all what he had prepared himself for. Of course, Trapper was his brother. What was she talking about?

"I'm not sure I understand the question," he told her.

"I don't know if he really is yer brother. I think he was just tellin' ye that to make ye cooperate with us," she admitted.

Luther nearly broke apart with relief as the indication of her question lent proof to his belief that there had been never been a romantic entanglement between them. Lovers spoke of such things, did they not? Aye, if they had ever been involved at such a level, she would have known such things but she had not. She had merely believed the story that their fathers had conjured to cover the shame so Trapper could lead as normal a life as possible.

"Roslyn, I guess you didn't know this, but your father helped my father hide his dirty little secret by giving Trapper to his stable master. I remember it distinctly as it shamed me deeply to know what he had done. I couldn't understand how he could simply throw the boy away, and I simply found it impossible to forgive him. It was one of the reasons that I was so angry with him and why I had left after he died. I was disgusted by him and felt that he had no right to try to map my future out by forcing a marriage contract upon me when he had been so unscrupulous with his own life."

Roslyn hadn't known this, frankly she was stunned to hear it now. She had thought that Trapper had been a fine actor when he had told Luther he was his brother that day in the old abandoned shack, when in reality, he had been acting his entire life by hiding it from everyone, even her. Poor Trapper. Her heart suddenly ached for him.

All these years, he had known that he had been an unwanted bastard, never telling anyone about it. He had been her best friend all this time, had always taken care of her as though she were his sister, never once complaining about the injustice of his birth. Her heart ached at how hard it must have been for him to go along watching his father show favor to Luther while ignoring him so completely. She felt hot tears roll down her face followed by Luther's thumb as he traced them down her cheek.

"You love him, don't you?" he asked her.

"Aye," she said on a sob.

Luther was at a loss for words. He closed his eyes against the hurt of her admission before turning away from her. They may never have been lovers, but there had been an abiding love just the same. Perhaps someday they may have overcome the obstacles set between them to marry, but now he stood in their way. Just as he was about to remove himself from the bed, he felt her hand on his.

"Luther?" she said.

He stiffened his back but said nothing.

"Luther, I love ye as a husband, but I love Trapper as a brother," she told him.

His shoulders sagged with relief, she said she loved him, she had never come close to saying those words before. He turned to her to see tears spilling from her eyes; he couldn't help himself, he was overcome with need. She had said she loved him, but the words had been lacking passion. Without thought, he pulled her into his arms, kissing her with all the heartfelt love he could put behind a kiss. Pushing her back onto the bed, he took her by her wrists, securing them above her head then commenced to ravish her body with unfettered heat. He wanted her to feel his passion, his love for her so she would no longer think of his brother.

He needed to dominate her, mark her as his own in such a way that she would never forget that she belonged to him. He didn't want her to love him as a husband, he wanted her to love him as a soul mate, as lovers that were created for one another, solely for one another and no other. He wanted to pour himself into her so deeply that they became one body, one soul united together forever.

 Forcing her legs apart with his own, he paused before going further as it occurred to him that his young wife might not understand the meaning of love or maybe she was just telling him what he wanted to hear. Either way, he had a desperate need to know.

"How do you love me?" he asked.

Roslyn's breasts were heaving with desire, "like a husband," she panted.

Luther rammed himself home with swift brutality before stilling himself, "How do you love me?" he asked again.

"Like a husband," she responded with her eyes closed to the pleasure.

He removed himself from her, "Woman, how do you love me?" he demanded as he sat suspended just outside her entrance.

Roslyn's eyes flew open to see his eyes penetrating hers with a deep intensity that she didn't understand, but she could see that he fully expected a different answer. The one she had given seemed to have angered him, now she had no idea what she was supposed to tell him. He was her husband, her lover; what else was there to say? What did she need to say so he would finish what he started? She needed him to finish what he started, she had a hot ache to be assuaged.

"Please Luther, I dinnae know what ye want me to say," she pleaded.

Luther rammed himself home then removed himself again leaving her bereft.

"I love ye, Luther. Och! I need ye Luther, please give me what I need," she begged.

Luther slammed home again, this time he stayed seated, but he didn't move. He could feel her sheath tightening around him, but he willed himself to ignore the pleasure.

"You love me like a husband?" he taunted.

"Aye! Ye are my husband," she told him as she tried to encourage him to move by bucking her hips toward him.

Luther removed himself from her yet again, only this time he rolled off of her, his member raging at him for doing so.

"I'll not finish until you figure out just how I want you to love me. When you figure it out, let me know," he told her before removing himself from the bed.

Luther had no explanation for his behavior. He knew that he was being irrational to leave her in such a state, when he too was suffering from the same affliction. But damn the woman! Why could she not see what he needed? He needed to know that she loved him as much as he loved her. He felt as though his very life depended on it.

Seeing her cry for his brother had been more than he could endure. The jealousy that he had been wrestling with reared its ugly head again, he couldn't go on unless he wiped her love for Trapper out of her head. He knew that Trapper was in love with her, and now part of him suspected that she had been in love with him too. Before he could have believed that she had been oblivious to his brother's affection for her but now ...

They had grown up together, had spent years together doing who knows what, in the way of experimentation with one another. Trapper had probably given her her first kiss. He had probably even seen her naked. The thought was maddening. He had to get away from her if he were to retain his sanity.

He reached for his breeches and began putting them on with his back to her. He couldn't bear to look at her at this point. He grabbed his shirt and put it on, tearing it as he did, he didn't care, he just wanted to get away from her. Just as he was about to put his boots on, he felt a solid object hit him in the back before it fell to the floor with a thud. He looked down to see that she had thrown a candlestick at him.

"Coward!" his wife shouted at him.

"Madam, I'll thank you not to throw anything else at me. I wouldn't want to lose my memory again if you should accidentally hit me in the head too hard," he told her before picking up his boots then storming out of the bedroom, slamming the door behind him.

His escape made, he stood outside the door trying to collect his wits. What have I just done? Was he a fool? His wife had confessed to him as he had wanted her to. She had told him that she loved him but what did he do in response? He turned into a lunatic, created a quarrel then left her loving arms. For what?

Chapter Eighteen

'Bidh gaol agam ort fad mo bheatha, thusa 's gun duine eile' she remembered telling him in her tongue that day at the loch. 'I will love you my whole life, you and no other.'

Roslyn woke with a start, sitting up straight in her bed with the memory of that beautiful day at the loch. This was the answer she had been searching her mind for the last three days since her quarrel with Luther. Finally, she understood what it was that he had wanted her to say. Didn't the insufferable man know that she had already said those words?

Growling with determination to set him straight, she threw her legs over the edge of the bed with the intention of going to his room to do just that. Set him straight! The man was a blind fool if he couldn't see how much she loved him. She loved him, God how she loved him, had always loved him. She had to let him know before any more time could pass. The last three nights without him beside her had been miserable, and it had all been for naught.

She had been confused with passion when he began to try to pull her confession of love from her and hadn't been aware of how serious the moment had been to him. He wanted validation, but she had failed to realize it. Were all men so insecure where matters of the heart were concerned? She didn't know, but her husband was insecure about her feelings for him, of that she was sure.

Of course, if she really stopped to consider the way she had treated him so far, she could see how he might feel that way, but it had only been to protect herself from his rejection when he learned of her part in his amnesia which it turned out, she never needed to be afraid at all because he loved her just as much as she loved him.

From the moment she had reunited with him, she had done nothing but snip and snipe at him at every possible opportunity to the point that she was surprised every moment that he remained by her side. Her husband was a wonderful man with strength of character like no other, but in this he was as weak as a new born pup. She smiled as she remembered the way he had sought to mark her with his passion so all would know that she was his woman.

Yes, he needed to be validated, he needed to hear her say how much she loved him and she would; never again would he need to feel unsure of her feelings for him because she would make sure he understood those words through her actions. She would strive to be a proper wife for him too, one that he could be proud of.

She would do whatever it took to learn the ways of the nobility so that she could accompany him anywhere, even London if the occasion ever arose. Giddy now with excitement, she vowed that she would hire a tutor to instruct her in the arts of decorum, dancing and proper speaking. She would even allow the seamstress to have her way so she could dress as a woman of her station should.

From this day forward, Luther would always know that she was happy to be his wife, his lover, and one day, God willing, she would be the mother of his children too. The thought caused a flutter in her belly; could she be with child now? She giggled at the notion as she continued to dress herself. Oh, how she would love to give him a son, daughters too but first a son.

Her dressing finished, she quickly ran a brush through her tangled locks then stood in the mirror to make sure she was presentable. It would have to do, she was in a hurry. She had to go to him right away to tell him just how foolish she had been. Flinging her bedroom door open, she nearly ran into Elsbeth as the woman had been poised to knock upon her door.

"Come my lady, he be awake and he's askin' for ye," she urged.

Roslyn stood blinking at the woman as if she had no idea whom she was referring to.

"Young Trapper, my lady. He is awake and he's askin' for ye. Ye had best hurry because he may not have long before he goes back under," she explained.

In her excitement to reach her husband, she hadn't given a thought to Trapper or his condition. Of course, she would go to him right away. What else could she do? Luther was probably still asleep at any rate so a few more moments couldn't hurt one way or another.

"Of course, we must go to him," she agreed.

The two women quickly scurried down the hall to the room Trapper lay in, but before reaching it, Roslyn stopped just outside the door next to it, which was Luther's room, to touch the door briefly with the palm of her hand. After a silent promise to return as soon as she could, she took a deep breath before entering Trapper's room.

The breath she had been holding escaped her lips in a harsh sound as she took in the sight before her. The fool was on the edge of the bed trying to stand up. She quickly ran to him, extending her arms out to lend him her strength.

"Och ye fool! Are ye tryin' to kill yerself?" she asked as she stood before him.

Trapper pulled her into an embrace, burying his face in her shoulder then began sobbing as though he were in awful pain. She was at a loss as to where she could touch him, so she stood with her arms low near his buttocks so as not to cause further injury to his back.

"There, there now. Just ye sit down here, Trapper. Ye shouldnae be tryin' to get up," she told him.

Trapper didn't let go of her but continued to hold on to her with all of his strength as he continued to cry into her shoulder.

"I thought I had lost ye forever my bonny Roz," he cried.

"What's this now? Of course ye havenae lost me. Go on, sit down now before ye fall to the floor," she told him as she gently guided him to sit down on the edge of the bed.

Trapper was overcome to see that Roslyn was safe. In his sleep, he had been plagued with all manner of nightmarish dreams where Magnus had managed to bring harm upon her and Luther.

"Roslyn, I have to tell ye something. Where's Luther?" he asked as he took his seat on the bed.

"Ye need to get yer rest is what ye need to do. Now hush, lie down," she admonished.

Trapper knew he had to warn her while he had strength enough to speak. He knew that once he explained the situation she would be angry, but he couldn't allow himself to worry about that now, Luther and Roslyn's life were in danger.

"I have to tell ye now, it cannae wait. Where's Luther?" he asked again.

"I'm sure whatever it is, can wait until later. Just ye rest now, darlin," she pressed.

"Roslyn, ye dinnae understand, I thought I lost ye forever. I failed ye before, but I willnae fail ye again. I cannae go on like this, where's Luther?" he tried again.

"Ye could never fail me Trapper. Hush now, get some rest, my love," she told him.

Trapper could feel his strength waning. He knew that he didn't have long for his confession as he could feel the pull of unconsciousness threatening to overtake him. Desperate to voice his concerns, he plowed forward in a rush.

"Listen to me, my bonny Roz, I love ye, ye know I love ye. I wouldnae ever do anything to hurt ye. Everything I did, I did because I love ye. I wanted to be yer husband. It was the only way, but I failed ye. Luther has to know so we can make it right. I cannae go on like this, he must know," he told her with slurred, barely coherent speech.

Roslyn had no idea how to respond to his fevered ramblings. Clearly, he had suffered from some terrible nightmare and was under the impression that the whole thing had been real.

Poor Trapper; he was a mere shadow of the man he had been before this had happened to him. Gone were his youthful muscles, replaced by a frailty that frightened her as his ribs were visible under his skin. He had felt so weak as he had held onto her as though he could be crushed to a fine powder with the slightest of effort had she returned the embrace.

He had lost so much weight that his eyes had sunk into their sockets, aging him horribly so that she hardly recognized him.   How would he ever be nursed back to his former state of health? Could he ever be what he was before?

****

Luther stood in the opened door that adjoined his room to his brother's with an aching heart as he listened to Trapper confess his love for Roslyn, she had called him her love. He could listen no more, he had to get away.

Feeling as though he had been a fool, he turned away from the scene and quietly closed the door. A tear escaped his eye as he put on his jacket. He wasn't sure where he was going, but he had to get away from here. He had to think! He needed time to think! He left the room stopping briefly at the closed door where his wife was now offering comfort to his brother. He closed his eyes as he touched the door with the palm of his hand, making a silent promise to himself. Never again will I be such a fool.

Taking a deep fortifying breath of resolve, he set out for the stables to retrieve his horse. Perhaps, he would go to Huntley to see just how bad things really were there before heading back to London. He would spend a week, maybe two, to get things in order, then send word to Roslyn that he would not contest an annulment if that were her wish. He could seek out a man of business, hire a new steward too, to look after his interests here so there would be no need for him to remain.

Why would he want to remain? Roslyn didn't love him, she never had. She had only used him to avoid marrying another. Clearly, she hadn't planned on him falling in love with her as it had been her hopes all along that he would go back to London once she had accomplished her objective.

He really had to hand it to her though, she had given the impression that she was trying to make it work after her father had informed her that she wouldn't be his heir. She had even begun to soften up a little, or maybe she was just biding her time until she could figure out how to be rid of him once her lover recovered. Now that he thought upon it, she had really given up quite easily; she must have had some kind of plan in mind though the mechanics of it eluded him.

Stopping to leave a note for Fergus, telling him of his plans to leave, he went down the stairs with a heavy heart. Roslyn didn't love him, she never would, how could she? He had failed. Ten years was a long time to cultivate failure. He should never have run from his responsibilities so long ago, then perhaps they could have been happy together now.

Now, all was lost to him. Later, perhaps, he could sift through the ashes of his desolate life to see if anything could be salvaged, but he couldn't do it here. He couldn't bear to look upon Roslyn knowing what a fool he had been. He needed to escape.

Once in the stables, he readied his horse himself, mounted it then set off in the direction of Huntley. The hour was early, the sun lazily rising in the east; if he were lucky, he could make Huntley within a few hours, putting him there well before noon.

He had been delaying this trip, preferring to stay at Dunheath to prove his loyalty to his wife. He had wanted to make her life easier by making improvements there first, knowing full well that his own home was in near ruin. He hadn't regretted it at the time, but now he felt all the more foolish for believing that she had actually wanted him there.

For days, he had waited for her to come to him

to tell him what he had hoped to hear. He had wanted her to recognize what he had become to believe was a very special bond between them. To him, it had felt like the other half of his soul had been found within her; two halves of the same whole.

To him, it felt as though he could be with no other ... he still could be with no other. His love for Roslyn was the most profound experience of his entire life. He wasn't at all sure he could go on without her now that he had found her. How will I go on without her?

Chapter Nineteen

Roslyn sat in complete disbelief as Trapper laid out for her all that he had done against his own brother in an attempt to secure her hand in marriage. He had schemed with the Devil to kill the man she loved! The fool! So her first instinct had been correct! It had been Magnus who had committed this horrible deed as he had repaid Trapper's treachery by trying to kill him in return. If he were not already in such a state, she would thrash him within an inch of his life herself. How could he have done such a thing?

Her blood ran cold as she listened to Trapper's warning that Magnus would finish what he himself hadn't been able to accomplish.

"I willnae ever forgive ye for this, Trapper," she told him with tears pouring from her eyes.

"Aye, I deserve yer loathin' but ye are in danger, so is my brother. We are all in danger now. Where's Luther? We must warn him too," he told her, trying to stand again.

Roslyn shoved him back on the bed, taking no care that she could cause pain to his injuries with her rough handling. Roslyn never would have believed her lifelong friend capable of such perfidy; she was disgusted.

"It's no yer business now, ye've done enough. As soon as ye are able, I want ye out of my house and out of my life for good. Do ye hear me?" she shouted.

Just then, Fergus came bursting through the door with fire blazing in his eyes as he waved a paper at his daughter.

"Just what do ye know of this Missy?" he demanded.

Roslyn took the paper from his hand to see what had her father in such a lather. After reading the words her husband had written, she gasped in despair. Luther is gone? He believed that she was in love with another, now he is gone? Suddenly she was reminded of Trapper's confession; he is on his way to Huntley with no idea that Magnus wanted to kill him.

"It says that he can no longer compete for the love of a woman in love with another. What nonsense is this?" her father demanded.

"I've no time for this now, I need to go after him," she told him, shoving her way past him.

"Stop her Fergus! For God's sake stop her, she's in danger," Trapper wailed as he tried to get up from the bed.

She heard Trapper's warning but didn't let it

stop her as she went to her room to change her clothes. Yanking off her skirt, she quickly donned her leather breeches then strapped her knife to her leg. Donning her jacket, she then tucked her pistol inside her pants. She had to go after him, she had to warn him, she had to bring him back! Roslyn would do or say whatever she must to get him back.

As she turned to exit her room, Roslyn staggered, knees nearly buckling beneath her when the true magnitude of her crimes against her husband struck her. Bracing herself on the sideboard near her bedroom door, she steadied herself while her mind grappled with these developments. How could she have treated him so poorly when all he had shown her was love in return? What if she could never convince him to come back? Or worse, what if Magnus got to him before she could warn him?

Swallowing back the sob that threatened to overtake her, she straightened herself, resolve stiff in her spine. She would get him back, she must because she simply couldn't face a life without him in it.

"Pardon my intrusion my lady, I know it's no my business, but I thought ye might like to know that yer husband left only a half hour past," Tess, her lady's maid told her from her opened doorway.

Roslyn spun around at the sound of her voice.

"What do ye know of it?" she demanded.

"I know we shouldn't gossip, but Elsbeth told me that yer husband had been standing in the doorway when the young man was tellin' ye, or rather ... confessin' his love for ye, my lady," the young woman told her, nervously looking down as though she found something of great interest near her shoe.

"Where is Elsbeth now?" she demanded.

"In the kitchen, my lady," the girl told her.

Wasting no time, Roslyn rushed past the young woman, nearly knocking her over in the process as she went in search of Elsbeth. She needed to know just what Luther had heard so she could get a better idea of what had happened. She hardly remembered her conversation with Trapper or that he had confessed a love for her. She had become so enraged by his revelations of treachery that she had forgotten everything that had been said before.

Storming into the kitchen, she grabbed the old woman by the arm then pulled her out of the kitchen.

"Tell me what ye saw. Tell me everything!" she demanded.

The old woman quickly rattled off what she knew, causing Roslyn's heart to sink like a stone. It couldn't be any worse. It must have appeared to him that she and Trapper had been love's from the way the old woman told the story. His note to her father made perfect sense now, but how could he have believed such a thing after the passionate loving they had shared?

Memories flooded Roslyn's mind as she began to answer her own question. Hadn't she told him that he was not her first lover that night on the bank of the loch? Luther had seen her run after Trapper moments after they had married; he had seen them locked in an embrace right there in the street just outside the smithy's and now this.

It must have appeared to all who had witnessed it that they had been lovers. For the love of all the saints, how many times had she had told Luther that she loved Trapper? All these memories slammed into her head, causing her stomach to pitch and roll. How could she ever convince him of her love for him when everything she had said and done had painted a different picture? Was it any wonder that he had left her?

"Ye look sick my lady," Elsbeth told her.

Just then, Roslyn's stomach began to heave as though she were about to lose the contents of her stomach. She pushed the old woman aside as she desperately made her way back to the kitchen where she found an empty bowl on the work table. She grabbed it and began heaving into it, but as her stomach was empty, all she managed to do was gag as her stomach warred at her.

"Perhaps ye should eat something," the old woman suggested, holding out a piece of bread. "Have ye had yer courses?" she shrewdly inquired.

Roslyn looked at the old woman with confusion before taking the bread she offered. Taking a small bite, she chewed slowly before swallowing. It landed in her stomach seeming to calm the rolling, so she took a bigger bite realizing that she had best eat something if she were going to go after Luther. She might not be able to catch him before he reached Huntley. It could shape up to be a very long day with an empty stomach threatening her all along the way.

"Here, wash it down with some milk, then ye will feel better," the woman told her as she handed her a cup of cool milk.

"What shall I do," she voiced her thought before taking the cup.

"Ye eat yer breakfast, then ye go and fetch yer husband and tell him there be a bairn on the way. He'll come home with ye," she advised.

"A bairn?" she asked with eyes wide.

"Ye've no had yer courses?" the woman inquired.

Roslyn thought about it then realized that she should have had her courses a few days ago but had not. Was it possible? It seemed too soon to know such things, but if it were true, then she had conceived that day at the loch. Her stomach fluttered as if in response to her question. Could it be true? Was she carrying Luther's child? She threw her hand to her mouth, closing her eyes to the wonder of it.

"Och, just tell the man to put such foolish notions that ye could love another aside. It's plain as the nose on yer face that ye are in love with yer husband," she said patting Roslyn on the back to comfort her.

"Is it? Oh Elsbeth, I've been a fool! A terrible, terrible fool! I have treated him so badly, he willnae ever come back," she cried.

"Hush now, lassie. The man is in love with ye too. He'll come back. Now eat yer breakfast then ye can go and fetch him home. Tis very romantic, if ye don't mind me sayin' so," she told her.

Roslyn didn't know about romance, but she did know that she wanted her husband back. Whatever it took, she wanted him back.   All her life, she had dreamed that they would one day be together; she would be damned if she let him slip away now.

With that thought, she began to shove the bread

into her mouth with gusto until she had all but finished it. She quickly swallowed down the milk then stood, surprised at how much better she felt. Fortified with determination and a good meal, she knew what she had to do.

"Ye're right, Elsbeth. He's comin' back, even if I have to bash him upon his skull and kidnap him again, he's comin' home!" she declared before leaving the kitchen.

Chapter Twenty

Luther knew as soon as he left that he wouldn't be able to stay away from Roslyn for very long. He felt like the coward she had called him that night when he had tried to get her to confess her love for him. Why had he done it? He went over what he had seen and heard in his mind several times, searching desperately for something that would change the obvious into something innocently misunderstood.

In his heart, he didn't, couldn't believe that she was guilty of any deceit. He knew in his very soul that she loved him. Try as he might, he couldn't allow his mind to conjure any images of she and Trapper engaged in carnal relations. He knew she had been a virgin that first time at the loch, so why had he been so quick to jump to conclusions? Hadn't he promised her that there was nothing she could say or do to make him leave her again?

The further he traveled from Dunheath, the more his heart ached for her. Many times, he had thought to turn back, but he was afraid. He was afraid that his suspicions would continue to grow, causing no end to the problems that might result as long as his brother was in residence at Dunheath. Since Trapper was so severely injured, he didn't have the heart to banish him just yet.

Perhaps a week, maybe two at Huntley would

serve to allow Trapper's recuperation, then he could go back to his own home. It was an idea that lifted his spirits somewhat as he reached the outer perimeter of his ancestral home. He could send a note to Roslyn, even invite her to come here where they could spend time alone. He hoped that he could explain his jealous impulse away enough to smooth things over with her. She might not want him back now that he had broken his promise of loyalty so soon after he had made it. A man was only as good as his word; his word wasn't worth shite now. Could he blame her if she wanted nothing to do with him ever again? No.

If he had to explain his reasons for being jealous of his brother, he would have to admit that he was resentful for all the time he had spent with Roslyn over the years. He had been there for her during her youth, watching her grow into the beautiful woman she was today while he himself had forgotten that she even existed. Rather than being grateful for the gift he had been given by both their fathers, he had viewed it as an imposition. He had refused to see the beautiful potential in the little girl that so obviously adored him.

Trapper had remained by her side when everyone else had left her life in one form or another. He had been her ever-present companion, guiding her along as best he knew how. All things considered, she had turned out to be a woman of great character and strength. He could only surmise that it had to have been Trapper's influence.

Therein lay his greatest shame; he had no right to be angry at his brother for harboring a deep abiding love for Roslyn, but he was. Perhaps he was only angry with himself.

Trapper had taught her so many things that it was natural for Luther to think that perhaps he had taught her about love too. It was madness to believe that he could have spent so much time with her yet not be in love with her. Of course, he had to love her, how could he not? If he were in Trapper's position, he would have done whatever he could to secure a future with her too, so how could he be angry with him for doing just that?

Understanding didn't make it easier to witness as his brother had confessed his love for her. It had made him feel as though he were an intruder, that he should leave so they could be alone together; thus he had fled like the coward she had named him. For that brief moment, he hadn't felt that he deserved Roslyn, that she was far too good for him. He felt as though he had done them both a great injustice by coming back. Her father's words hadn't helped on that score by saying, had he not returned, he would have given her to his brother.

Trapper had done a thing Luther wasn't sure he himself could have done if their roles had been reversed. He could never have assisted her with finding then capturing another man so that she could marry him. Nay, he could never have stood by as she married the other man while his heart must have been breaking apart, but he had loved her enough to step aside so she could.

How could he blame Trapper for trying one last time to sway Roslyn to his side by confessing his love for her? He couldn't. Still, in the face of understanding his brother's feelings and motivations, it would be best if he went on to live his own life somewhere else. If he were Trapper, he wouldn't want to hang about as the woman he loved, lived her life with another; he would want to get as far away as he could. He was still young, surely he could find another woman to love. Of course, she wouldn't be Roslyn, but there was bound to be a woman perfectly suited for him out there somewhere.

Luther was pulled from his brooding when Huntley Manor came into view. Nestled in a lush valley, the stately old manor sat at the center of the village that supported it, boldly proclaiming its former wealth and significance. Though it had long since crumbled to ruin, Luther's original ancestral home had been an old castle at the top of the highest peak above the valley, long since given to the ghosts of his ancestry.

Roughly a hundred years ago, it had been replaced with a more modern estate house, though it was still enclosed by an outer wall with a grand gate entrance that included a watchtower on either side. However, they appeared to be little more than useless fixtures of ornament now as they were vacant with the gates flung wide open. During his father's lifetime, the place had been a well-secured fortress, but now as he entered the gates, his heart skipped a beat when he realized that it appeared to be totally abandoned.

From his vantage point, he could see that moss and weeds had begun to overtake the place. It appeared too that many of the windows had been broken, accompanied by what seemed to be a gaping hole in the roof. Roslyn and Trapper had been telling the truth about the place falling to ruin.

Where was Mr. Hook, the steward that he had been paying all these years or the groundskeeper or even the other servants that he knew to be employed til this very day? Had they all vacated, leaving the place to the elements? Aggravated by the sight of his home, Luther spurred his horse to a gallop with blazing determination to get his hands on Mr. Hook. The bastard had been fleecing him, just as Trapper had told him. When he got his hands on him, he would thrash him within an inch of his life before severing their business arrangement.

Upon reaching the portico leading to the front door, he jumped from his horse, not caring to secure the animal before trying to enter the home. Surprised to find the door locked, he set about pounding on it to see if he could gain a response from within. Just as he was about to give up in favor of finding another entrance, he heard what sounded like the voice of an old woman from inside. He stilled himself as he waited nearly an insufferable moment before the lock turned and the door began to slowly creak open revealing the suspicious eye of an old woman. Maude or Mildred, he thought her name was though he couldn't quite remember, looked him over from head to toe before the dawning light of recognition showed in her eyes.

"Is it ye my lord? Have ye come home then?" she asked with sarcasm dripping as she opened the door to allow him entrance.

"Aye, I have returned Mrs ... forgive me, I cannot remember your name," he told her as he entered.

The woman who had been the cook when he was a lad looked somewhat offended that he could forget her but aided his memory by providing him with her name.

"Ah yes, now I remember, Mable. Mable, where are the other servants? Why is the Manor in such a state as I have found it?" he inquired without further ado.

The woman shuffled a few feet backward as though suddenly stricken with fear, but squared her shoulders before answering his question with an authority that quite surprised him.

"When ye abandoned us to our own devices,

that no good Mr. Hook decided that he were lord of the manor and went about terrorizing all of the servants until only a few remained. Ye still have Mrs Dunhagen, the housekeeper, though lately she's been down with the ague. Yer, groundskeeper died two years past, God rest his worthless soul. Yer butler's a filthy drunkard, layin' about, day in and day out, finishin' off yer wine stocks and the scullery maid? Well, she be a hoor that ran off with the last of yer footmen to God knows where. All told, ye have six servants left to manage the place," she explained.

Luther looked around, noting that the place was in a surprising state of cleanliness considering the exterior state, still there would be much work needed to restore it back to its former glory.

"Where is Mr. Hook?" he asked rather sharply.

"Och, he ran away when he got word of yer return to Dunheath. So ye come back and married the girl, did ye? We heard tell that she dragged ye back in chains," she said with a chuckle.

So the villain had fled! Good riddance! He would catch up with him later and call him to account for his dastardly deeds, but there were far more pressing matters at hand, but make him pay, he would. Luther was somewhat embarrassed by her last comment considering how much truth there actually was in the malicious gossip that seemed to be circling about, but he suspected much worse had been said; all richly deserved.

"Aye, Lady Roslyn and I have wed so you had best accustom yourself to having your lord in residence again. On that note, round the staff up and tell them to meet with me in an hour in the kitchen ... and Mable, if you have anything cooked, I would appreciate a quick repast," he told her.

"There be some smoked trout, cabbage, potatoes and some blackberry tarts with a bit of cream if ye like," she told him, pleased with herself for her preparedness.

At least his servants had been eating well, that was something to be thankful for. With great shame in his heart, he silently vowed that he would put matters back to right. He wanted Huntley to be restored right away as it was a much grander home to raise a family in than Dunheath though he suspected Roslyn would have to be pried away with a team of horses. All things in due course, but first he had a mess on his hands.

"I will be there in a few moments. I want to take a tour about the place to assess our needs," he told her.

Mable did her best to curtsey but only managed to accomplish a wobbly bobble before quickly shuffling away to perform the mission she had been tasked with. It had been ten years since she had been required to make such a gesture, so he tried not to laugh at her efforts though it had been quite comical; he wouldn't want the old girl to come after him with a cleaver for the insult.

****

Later that evening, he was confident that he had made a good start to set the estate back to order. All the servants had been counted and assessed as well as plans to bring up many more from the local village tomorrow. After touring the manor, Luther determined it wouldn't be as costly an undertaking as he had originally thought. All the place really needed was full staff and a good cleaning.

The hole he had thought he saw was only a darkened patch of straw that must have blown in from a storm some time past. With no one about to clear it away, it had rested there undisturbed for many weeks potentially causing rot to the shingles.

He would have to replace the windows though bringing panes in would be no quick, easy thing as he would have to send off for them from Inverness. He had learned that there had been a terrible display of temper by Mr. Hook when he learned of his return, resulting in the damage; all the more reason to seek him out for restitution. Thankfully, the weather had not grown too cold just yet, but it probably wouldn't be long now so it would have to be put at the top of list.

He was surprised that so many of the tenants had remained behind to work the land and could only speculate what their needs might be. Later in the day, he had spoken with one of the farmers, who on first meeting him had regarded him with suspicious hostility but calmed somewhat after the promise to hold a meeting in the morning here at the manor to hear the plights of the other farmers. The man obliged Luther's request to spread the word and left with a much more pleasant attitude. Perhaps, it wouldn't be as difficult to gain their respect as he had begun to fear.

He was further pleased that he had managed to find a local lad to deliver a message to Roslyn apologizing for leaving so suddenly as well as to invite her to come here to spend some time with him. He wasn't sure if she would come, but one could only hope. If she didn't want to come, he would go there, but the need was so great here at Huntley that their reunion would have to be postponed for at least two weeks.

Two weeks without her would be a small eternity of torture, but if she would only respond to his missive accepting his apology, the separation could be endurable. He realized that she may not want to abandon Trapper to his injuries when they were so great but vowed to accept her will in any case. What else could he do? He loved his wife and would do whatever it took to make her happy.

During his tour of the manor, he had found his way to the master's chambers, surprised to find that much was as his father had left it. While sifting through one of his old trunks, he found his father's tartan and kilt. When he donned the items, he was reminded of a conversation he had with Roslyn while on the road to Dunheath. She had told him that he had been loathe to wear the colors of his clan when he had been a young man.

With his memory recovered, he remembered now that he had been embarrassed by the garb of his people as a child because he had been conditioned by his mother to believe that the Scots were an inferior people to her own. He had loved his mother dearly but in this she had wronged him by tarnishing his view of his heritage, thus preventing him ever growing an attachment to his homeland.

Perhaps she had been more embittered to have been married to his father than he had realized. She had been considered a diamond of the first water in her season. She could have had her pick of any titled gentlemen of her class, but his father had been a wily old Scotsman nearly twice her age, snatching her up before she'd even had a chance to be noticed by anyone else; how it must have rankled in the mind.

In hindsight, she must have tried to turn her son from his people as some kind of punishment to his father. Perhaps his father had not forsaken her but she him, thus bringing about the birth of Trapper. He knew that his father had loved his mother with great passion, yet he had left her bed and sought out the comforts of another woman.

Speculation about the dynamics of his parents' marriage would serve him nothing now except he could use the insight to go forward. He was a Scotsman now, had always been. Despite his mother's best efforts to the contrary, he would embrace it with pride, happily wearing the colors of his people for all to see. He was the Chieftain of the Clan McRoolins for better or worse.

Luther was so absorbed in these revelations as to be startled when the sound of horses outside drew his attention. The hour was late so he couldn't imagine who it could be, but clearly riders had arrived. Jumping up from behind his desk, he hurried downstairs to see what the commotion was about.

Whoever was there began beating furiously upon the door, giving him pause to answer, and that's when he heard him. Hawk! Luther threw open the door and was quickly rushed by his friends as they carried on in greeting. He should have known that his brothers would come for him.

Chapter Twenty-One

"You left her? Why did you leave her? Have you gone mad?" Dylan asked his lifelong friend.

Dylan himself had done much the same, worse even, to his wife Claire just before they were married, all due to jealous insecurity. Now that Luther thought on it, he truly had been a fool to just walk away from her without giving her benefit of explanation. It served no purpose other than to keep them apart unnecessarily, which resulted in unbearable suffering by them both.

"You are one to talk," Gabriel reminded his friend.

Dylan shot a dagger-laced glare at his friend, "tis, precisely why I know that he must have gone mad," he retorted.

Luther had spent the last two hours regaling his friends along with their traveling companion, Harold Jackson of Bow Street, of his adventures since he had been kidnapped by his wife and his brother, much to their great amusement. It lightened his heart to have his friends here.

"Dylan is correct. I must have been mad, which is why I have sent word to her, inviting her to come here," he told them once again brightened by the prospect of having her here.

"Why wait? Why not go to her instead? Right now?" Gabriel asked.

The impulse to run to her as fast he could was suddenly strong within him yet so was the concern that she would reject him after he had acted so rashly. It would be best to await her response from his missive before he rushed to any decisions.

"Perhaps she will reply to my invitation and come here, instead. There is much work to be done here, and I have set up a meeting with the tenants in the morning. I had best be here for that if I am to secure their trust," he told them.

He knew that he was groping for reasons to avoid a painful encounter with his wife, and he knew his friends could see through his response. They had always been a close-knit group, knowing one another better than they knew their own families.

"Perhaps we could go and fetch her for you," Dylan suggested with an arched brow.

Truly Dylan subscribed to the theory that a couple in love should be together rather than suffer apart. He had to commend him for his wisdom but still, he would wait until tomorrow before he made any plans.

"That won't be necessary," he told him.

"Fool! I happen to know that it is very necessary and need I remind you that while you sit here nursing your jealous pride, there is another man vying for your woman's affections this very moment," Dylan told him.

"Unlike you were able to do, I have quickly concluded that my wife is innocent; therefore, I trust that our reunion can wait a day or two to allow the meeting that I have arranged to take place in the morning," Luther told him with more bravado than he felt.

Luther didn't want his friends to see his insecurity, but he knew it was painfully obvious. In truth, he wanted to go rushing back to her this very instant, the meeting be damned, but he would compose himself to wait.

"I'm sure his brother is even now sleeping soundly with the injuries that Luther has described. I'm sure that he can wait until morning to return to Dunheath," Gabriel said as though he were trying to spare Luther further humiliation; for which he was grateful to his friend.

"Indeed, the hour grows late. I think we should retire for the night," his friend went on.

Luther sighed as the weight lifted from his shoulders. He would go to her after the meeting if he did not receive a response from her by luncheon. With that decided, he rang for a servant to ready rooms for his guests. Tomorrow, he would reunite with his wife.

****

Trapper was awakened by the ringing of the bell from the bailey as it sounded the alarm. Something was wrong! Lifting himself to a sitting position, he strained to listen to the commotion outside; perhaps Roslyn had returned from Huntley. Maybe Luther was with her; however, he had a deep foreboding in his gut as he continued to listen.

Chaos! There was chaos in the bailey as shouts rang out. Trapper positioned himself on the edge of the bed, then lifted himself to stand on his weakened legs. He stood for a moment allowing a rush of dizziness to pass, then went over to the window to see what was afoot.

Below, he could see that the guards had gathered around a horse; Roslyn's horse, but where was she? Fergus entered the bailey, flailing his arms about while shouting hysterically, clearly he was disturbed by something. Trapper could stand it no more, he had to know what was happening.

He searched around until he found his breeches and boots, then with much agony he began to put them on. Once he had slipped his feet into his boots, he was surprised to find that the pain he had felt when he first rose to his feet was somewhat endurable now. Perhaps it was fear driving him forward, he didn't know. He only knew he had to get out there and fast, his injuries be damned.

As quick as he could manage, he made it to Fergus's room to rummage through his clothes, finding a shirt to slip into then turned to make his way down the stairs. Feeling stronger with every step he took, it wasn't long before he made it outside to the bailey.

"What's happening?" he asked one of the guards as he grabbed him by the arm to stop him as he was passing by.

"Our lady's horse has returned without her," he responded frantically.

Cold dread passed through Trapper's soul as he realized the implications, Magnus must have gotten his hands on her. Searching about for Fergus, he located him in the stables sitting on an overturned crate in one of his stupors, he would be no use to anyone now. Trapper knew that he would have to take command if they were to find Roslyn.

Turning from Fergus, he located one of the guards looking on in confusion at the chaos as the untrained men went about blaming one another for various issues. This one was blaming that one for allowing her to go alone while others were trying to decide if they should wait until daylight to look for her.

"Ye there! Take old Fergus into the keep and see him to his room," he told the man.

The young guard looked grateful to be given an order as he quickly set about his task, lifting the old man to his feet. Trapper then instructed another to ready a horse. He wasn't sure what he was going to do, but he did know that he would need a weapon, so with that thought in mind he turned back to the keep to find whatever he could for his mission.

God willing, his strength would hold, but he knew that he was no match for Magnus in his current state of injury. He had to get to Luther with all possible haste to let him know what had happened. He silently cursed Fergus for a fool for allowing her to go alone, and himself for passing out from exhaustion after she had left before he had been able to warn him of the danger.

He had failed her again, but he refused to believe that it was too late. In order for Magnus to achieve his goals, he would need Roslyn alive at least until he could marry her so he would most likely use her as bait to bring harm to Luther. He had to get to Luther first, before Magnus could lure him into a trap. He only hoped that it hadn't already happened. He wasn't sure how long Roslyn had been gone, but he was surmising that it had been nearly a full day as the hour seemed to be approaching early morning. The sun would be rising soon, so he had best hurry.

****

Roslyn regained consciousness to the harsh reality of her predicament. Though she couldn't see anything, she knew she was in some sort of dungeon. It was cold and dark as she lay trussed up on a stone floor waiting for the return of her captors with only her fears to warm her.

She had been in hot pursuit as she sought to catch up with Luther on his way to Huntley when she had been thrown from her horse when he stumbled over something in the road then tumbled, sending her flying to the ground. The horse had been spooked after he regained his footing, and she had been unable to convince the beast to return to her; thus, she had found herself alone.

As she began what she believed would be a long walk to Huntley, she had encountered two riders, men with which she'd had a recent encounter. Magnus's men had found her and were all too pleased to wrestle her weapons away from her when she had drawn one of her pistols to warn them away.

After a brief struggle, she had been rendered unconscious until now, thus she began to weep silently at the futility of her situation. All the years that she had thought herself as good as any man seemed to mock her now when she realized how truly weak she had been against her abductors.

They had easily brought her low in spite of the fact that she had been well armed with protection. Who knew how long it would be before help came? Her father would assume she was at Huntley, Luther would believe she was still at Dunheath for days, possibly weeks even.

She let out a woeful sound beneath the gag that had been tied around her face, then began to struggle against her bindings in frustration. If only she could free her hands, she could possibly escape. She still had her boots on, so with any luck she still had the small dagger that she had tucked within. She rarely went anywhere without her dagger.

Trapper had always told her to keep a small weapon tucked away where no one would see it, so she had always heeded his advice. Trapper! He had wrought this on her by scheming with Magnus though she suspected he would have found other ways to make mischief with or without Trapper's assistance.

She wasn't worried about herself so much as she worried about Luther being caught unawares. He had no idea that Magnus was a madman seeking to destroy him so he could get to her ... her land. She had no idea what Magnus had planned, but she knew that he would most certainly use her as bait to ensnare her husband.

She had to escape somehow. Again, she struggled with her bindings but try as she might, it was no use. They were tightly wound around her wrists with absolutely no slack. With that realization, she began to see if she could free her ankles from their bindings, but again, there was absolutely no slack there either.

"Rest yerself lass. Ye need to keep yer strength up," a deep voice spoke from the darkness.

Roslyn cried out as the voice had startled her. She had thought she was alone. Was it Magnus?

"Shh! Ye don't want to bring him down here, do ye?" the voice asked.

Roslyn quieted. She had no idea who this person was, but she knew one thing, he was right; she didn't want Magnus to come.

Chapter Twenty-Two

Luther had been impressed with the number of tenants who had turned out for the meeting after such short notice. All had been eager to air their grievances, so he had nearly been overwhelmed by the commotion created when he had told them of his marriage to Roslyn, along with the subsequent plan to merge the two clans under one banner.

Initially, most had been adverse to the concept until he explained that he was a very wealthy man; therefore, he would be able to meet the demands of all those who would be in need of certain provisions to ensure a profitable harvest. Many had complained that their houses were in dire need of repairs; those that had, calmed quickly when he assured them that their needs would be met without delay.

A scant few had left, refusing to give allegiance to a derelict lord, citing that he could hardly be trusted after he had abandoned them for the last ten years. Luther couldn't blame them for their lack of confidence, surprised too, that many more hadn't followed after they had made their damning statements.

Just as the meeting was concluding, the doors to the great hall burst open, shocking all those within to silence at the sight of his brother as he stumbled forward before collapsing at Luther's feet.

The sight of his brother could only mean one thing. Something awful had happened!

Luther bent to help Trapper to his feet, noting that the poor lad was near death from exhaustion, but with chest heaving, he began to pant out his warning.

"He has her ... Mag ... her horse ... we must save her," he tried just before swooning.

Gabriel rushed forward with a flask of whiskey, then began feeding it to Trapper as he lay unconscious. The fiery liquid soon roused the young man from his stupor as he began to cough and sputter as he came round.

"Tell us what happened," Gabriel urged.

"Quickly man," Luther put in with a shake of Trapper's shoulder to keep him alert.

One could have heard a pin drop as Trapper with labored breath began to explain what he knew.

"Roslyn went after ye when she learned that ye had taken it into yer head to leave her. Then early this morn, just before daylight, her horse returned without her. I tried to get old Fergus to stop her by tellin' him of the danger, but he wouldnae listen. He was so angry that ye had left that he dinnae stand in her way to try to bring ye back. Now Magnus has her, and we must do what we can to save her," he told them.

Everyone stood speechless as they considered what Trapper had told them. Luther couldn't fathom a reason for Magnus to abduct Roslyn. It was more likely that she could have had some kind of riding accident.

"Perhaps she was merely in an accident and was unable to remount her horse to return home. What reason would this Magnus fellow have to abduct her?" Dylan reasoned as though he had heard Luther's own thoughts.

"No, ye don't understand," Trapper tried to tell him before being cut off by Luther.

"There is no time to waste, we must go search for her. She could be wounded or worse," he declared.

The thought of Roslyn lying wounded somewhere in harm's way made more sense than what Trapper had suggested. There was no reason for Magnus to go after Roslyn. What could be gained from it? She was of no use to him now that she was married, so the idea didn't take root in his mind as a real concern.

No, it was far more likely that she had been thrown from her horse or something similar, he reasoned. Time could be critical if she had been stricken with a head injury or broken bone; he had best go and search for her now. With that singular purpose, he began to give instructions for all those willing to help.

Trapper tried again to make Luther listen, but the excitement to find Roslyn had taken center stage, causing Luther to ignore him completely. The clamor of the crowd drowned out Trapper's attempts to explain his reason for believing that Magnus was the culprit in this. He felt helpless to be heard as Luther and his friends were forming their plans to go search for her with the apparent help of the clan.

"Ye must listen to me," he tried again, but to no avail.

His voice was too weak to be heard over the din of voices in their excitement to start their search. Trapper struggled to his feet with determination to stop Luther before he could go but was greatly relieved when the man who had asked the question earlier was beside him to aid him to his feet.

"Please Luther, ye have to listen to me," he called out, but it was no use. Luther couldn't hear him as he was now on his way out the door followed by a group of farmers.

"Tell me what you know," he heard the man say.

Trapper looked to heaven with relief that someone would listen to him, so he began to unload his conscience to the only person that had taken an interest.

Dylan had noticed that the young man was overwrought with worry. The lad had been brutally wounded, nearly causing his death just days ago, yet he had made the journey here to tell Luther of Roslyn's disappearance.   Something very serious was afoot.

It took a few minutes for Trapper to tell Dylan of his treachery against his brother and the consequential beating he had suffered for betraying Magnus by aiding Roslyn to marry Luther.

He had gone on to inform him that Magnus had taken great pleasure in relaying his plans to kill Luther and Roslyn so he could take their lands. First, he would kill Luther then Roslyn after he forced her to marry him. Trapper assumed that Magnus must have thought him dead when he had disposed of his body, but somehow by the grace of God, he had survived.

Too, he told Dylan of his confession to Roslyn and how she had told him that she wanted him out of her life. But when he had learned of her disappearance, he knew that Magnus must be behind it, which was why he had come here to warn Luther.

Dylan listened with a heavy heart to the tale that Trapper had unfolded. Brief though it had been, it spoke volumes about his character. He didn't believe the lad was bad but had been horribly misled by a silver-tongued devil because of a genuine love for Roslyn. Still, when Luther learned of it, there were sure to be serious consequences for the lad. Dylan wasn't sure how to handle it, but he knew he had to stop Luther then guide him on the correct course to find his wife. Time was of the essence.

"Thank you for telling me this, and when the times comes, I will do what I can to influence Luther in coming to the correct course of action where you are concerned," Dylan told him as he left him standing there to go in search of Luther.

Dylan located Luther, mounted on his horse, looking for all the world as the clan leader he had become as he gave them instructions to form a grid to include any shortcuts between Dunheath and Huntley, leaving no stone unturned to find his bride. The men were about to depart when Dylan stopped them.

"Hold!" he shouted as he made his approach.

"Luther, you need to hear what your brother has to say before you start your search. He has critical information that you must have if you are to bring her back alive," he told him.

The last word of his friend's statement struck Luther like a stone to his head. Alive?

"What do you mean, alive?" Luther asked, confused by the usage of the word.

Dylan was well versed in the history of the Scots culture with their tradition of stealing brides of rival clansmen. He had thought the practice had mostly died out under English rule, but apparently there were still pockets of rebellious behavior where such practice still prevailed.

"After listening to the boy, I am quite convinced that this Magnus has taken her," he told him as calmly as he could.

The crowd began to grumble after hearing the words that Dylan spoke. It was clear that everyone present believed that Magnus could be behind it even without knowing the details of it. It was also clear that all knew of Lady Roslyn and would do anything to rescue her as the word 'battle' began to be whispered with enthusiasm.

Gabriel moved to Dylan's side then leaned in to whisper, "Looks like we have arrived just in time. Our Luther is about to become engaged in clan warfare," he told him.

****

The hall was filled with vibration as Luther raged at

his brother when he learned of the danger that Roslyn was really in. The fact that he had colluded with Magnus and attempted to kill him had angered him. When he learned that Magnus had beaten him within an inch of his life while telling him of his plans to harm Roslyn, he had been moved to near insanity with the need to plunge his fist through his brother's heart. Had his friends not been there to hold him back, he surely would have killed him.

"We must form a battle plan," Gabriel suggested when Luther calmed enough to be reasoned with.

"I will go there and take the bastard's head right off his shoulders with my bare hands," Luther growled.

"That's all well and good, but first we have to find out what his demands are," Mr. Jackson put in.

"We know what he wants," Dylan offered with a meaningful glare at Luther.

They all knew what Magnus wanted. He wanted Luther's death, there would be no need for negotiations.

"We need to do some reconnaissance. We need to find out how many men he has as well as where they are posted around his keep. I would imagine that he has already enhanced his security since Roslyn's abduction," Gabriel advised.

Luther knew they were right. He had to keep a cool head; he needed a clear plan of action.

Trapper spoke up then. "He keeps a personal guard of ten men at the ready. He has another fifteen that can be called upon whenever he has need within a moment's notice as they reside within the walls of his keep. If he had time to properly ready his clan, he could have no less than one hundred men ready for battle within a couple of days," he told them.

Luther glared at him. Clearly his brother had spent enough time with his nemesis to know him well.

"Are they battle hardened?" Dylan asked.

"The twenty-five are paid for their loyal service," Trapper said with disgust apparent.

Luther thought about the odds. He and his friends along with their companion were no match for twenty-five men. He didn't want anything to happen to them that would prevent them going home to their wives and children. This was his fight, he would have to meet it head on alone.

"Perhaps I should go alone," Luther said, putting voice to his thoughts.

"Have you seen the gathering of men outside?"

Dylan asked. "I don't think you going alone will be an option for these Scots," he continued with a raised brow.

Chapter Twenty-Three

Roslyn didn't know how much time had passed since she had been abducted, but she suspected it had been many hours, so she was beginning to despair that she would ever escape. Though she had been kept in darkness, she realized that the man who had warned her to be quiet before was not a prisoner like herself as she had thought but rather, one of Magnus's men. But why had he showed her kindness?

Since she had awakened, he had been ever present as though he had been appointed her personal guard, disappearing momentarily to bring back food or water every few hours. After he had convinced her to remain quiet, he had removed her bindings then handed her a pot to relieve herself in for which she had been thankful for both, it and the darkness when nature dictated that she relieve her bladder.

She had thought to make conversation with him to try to extract information, but apparently, his kindness toward her ended where his loyalty to Magnus merged. She had been able to gain absolutely nothing from him. Perplexing though it was, thus far she had not been plagued by Magnus's presence; therefore, she could only speculate with dread what he might want from her. Considering the condition he had left Trapper in, she was truly grateful for his continued absence.

As soon as she had been able, she checked to see if her small dagger was still in her boot, taking comfort when she discovered it undisturbed. Her abductors had not thought to search there so with any luck she could possibly find a use for it. Her guard would be leaving again soon to bring food, so perhaps she could have a go at the lock to her cell in his absence.

She had never picked a lock before, but she knew that it was possible if you had time and patience. She wasn't sure how much of either she had, but she knew she must do something. She couldn't just wait like a timid lamb to be slaughtered, she had to act; her husband needed her.

****

Luther was touched to see the growing support of the Clan McRoolins within the great hall of his ancestral home. Men were showing up from the village in fairly impressive numbers, all wearing their tartans, well armed for battle. Many were sporting axes, or scythes as they were first and foremost farmers, but when the call to arms could be heard, those tools became fairly effective weapons. Many more had bows with their quivers bursting with arrows while others had various types of swords most likely handed down from days long past when battles with the English had been a daily threat.

Luther rolled the sound of his ancestral

surname around his tongue. McRoolins. Why had his grandfather changed it? Why had he not taken pride in it? It was a good, solid Scottish name. Perhaps that had been it. His grandfather had been married to an English woman with connections to the house of George ll. His grandfather had been chieftain during the time of one of the Jacobite wars known as the forty-five though he had not thrown his support behind Charles. No doubt his grandfather feared reprisals from the English king had he not given the appearance of fealty after the embarrassing loss of the Jacobites who had sought to overthrow him. He would petition the crown to have it reversed as soon as possible.

He would think on that later, but now nightfall had come as Luther, with the help of his friends along with a few of the local elders who knew the layout of the land, were formulating their plan. They would leave within the hour so as to be in position just outside the perimeters of Magnus's estate well before dawn.

The idea was to catch his security unaware, allowing them to storm the keep to rescue Roslyn before they could send out the call to arms to the villagers. He didn't know how long it would take for Magnus to rally his villagers to his cause, but he knew that he had at least twenty-five well-trained fighting men within the walls of his keep. Twenty-five well-seasoned men could easily fend off four times that amount if they were properly outfitted for battle, which they almost certainly were.

Luther knew that the men who had come to his aid were not battle hardened, which caused him a serious amount of apprehension. Too, he didn't like the idea that his friends would be joining in the fray. He didn't want to have to carry them home to their wives, explaining how they had lost their husbands so he could save his wife.

The idea settled in his stomach like a jagged stone, causing him great discomfort, and after much arguing they had vowed that Luther would have to kill them to stop them from this mission. Both Gabriel and Dylan were well skilled in all manner of the arts of combat, but they had never engaged in such a mission as this could prove to be. Mr Jackson, the Bow Street man, however, seemed to be relishing the prospect. Perhaps he had a little Scotsman in him somewhere.

Luther would rather try to sneak in alone to secretly extricate his wife from danger while they were all sleeping, but according to his brother and the elders, entrance into the keep would surely be detected, thus he had relented. He would need all the help he could get.

"You had best give your speech to rally your troops," Dylan whispered in his ear.

Luther knew that he would have to express his gratitude to these men who had taken the time to put their lives in harm's way. He had already surmised that it was their love for Roslyn that drove them further, proving that his wife was a wonderful woman whom the locals viewed as a living saint. The way they referred to her as 'Our Lady Roslyn' put a lump in his throat when he choked back the tears that threatened every time it was said.

It seemed that Roslyn had adopted his clan as her own a long time ago by making monthly rounds to hand out food or medicine to those in need. Remarkable! They loved her, and it was that love that would help save her now, God willing. Luther looked over his farmer-warrior troops with reverence before clearing his throat to speak.

"My good men, may I have your attention?" he proceeded.

Luther had never been a great speaker, but he sensed that he would need to articulate very carefully to impress upon these men his gratitude. He had been a derelict lord for the last decade, leaving them to their own devices; therefore, he had no right to ask anything of them, but here they were ready to put their lives on the line.

"Truly, I am touched by the show of force I see here tonight. It must be a true testament to Lady Roslyn's character that she could have touched your lives so completely that you would put aside my sins against you these long ten years past to assist me in her rescue," he humbly spoke.

"I do not deserve such loyalty and do not speculate for even a moment that you are here for me. Nevertheless, I am deeply humbled and swear to you all that from this day forward, I will be your loyal servant. Never again, will I forsake my people for a life of debauchery, as my beautiful wife likes to term it, while your families suffer as your needs go on unmet," he said allowing a pause as the din of the crowd grew animated by his comments.

"When Roslyn and my brother found me in London, I had no thought for you all or this place ... nor to my great shame, even her. I was quite content in my dereliction, but she was a determined woman who refused to be ignored a moment longer. Determined as she was, she traveled a great distance with my brother in a conspiracy to kidnap me then force me to marry her over the anvil, if need be," he informed them and was rewarded with a din of laughter laced with crude comments.

"Well here I am, a married man because they had to bash me upon the head so hard, causing me to forget who I was so I could finally discover who I am, so that I might become the man I should have always been. My wife, being the loyal woman that she is, has given me the chance that I did not deserve. She saw in me something worth salvaging and brought me round to my true reason for being. Now, I stand before you a man in love with her so completely with all my heart; this woman, Roslyn, who forced me to marry her over the anvil that I cannot imagine my life without her," he told them as he again choked back tears.

Finding his calm, he continued. "You know, Lady Roslyn and I have discussed the future, and we believe that our clans, when brought together will prosper greatly for many generations to come. It was the will of our fathers to join us in marriage, thereby uniting our people to usher in a new era of prosperity. It is now my will to see their dreams come to fruition, but I cannot do this alone. I need Roslyn by my side to guide me with her loving conscience to better serve you, to be a better man," Luther told them, unable to continue as the crowd rallied with chants of 'Our Lady Roslyn' vibrating the hall.

Luther held his hands up to quiet them before continuing.

"And so it is in the spirit of my wife and Our Lady Roslyn that I will take great pride in having all of you at my side when we go take care of the black-heart, nay, this devil who would seek to harm her. We will show him the error of his ways with our passionate might. We will lay him low for daring to take her away from us; she is OUR LADY," he vowed with his fist held high in the air over the roar of excited battle cries.

****

Trapper listened to his brother with wondrous pride. After hearing his brother's words of love for her, he knew in his heart that Luther and his bonny Roslyn belonged together. He was proud, that in the end the right man would be by her side. His brother.

As the crowd dispersed to reconvene outside for their journey, he went to his brother. He knew that he had much to account for and in time he would. But now, right now, he wanted to be with his brother. He wanted to be by his side when they stormed the doors, doing whatever he could, weak though he was, to bring Roslyn home safe.

"Luther?" he spoke.

"Brother?" he returned with something that sounded like ... respect?

"I know that I dinnae deserve yer forgiveness, but I would ask fer it. Maybe not now but some day, ye could find it in yer heart to give it," Trapper told him with his shoulders squared in earnest as he looked his brother in the eye.

"Today is a great day for forgiveness. I have learned through all of this that I am really no better than you. During the course of our lives, we do things we are not proud of. What matters is how we continue on once we have learned the error of our ways. I know how much you cared for her, and I know that she is the woman she is today, mostly because of you. You are forgiven, my brother. Think no more on the matter," Luther said with a hand firm on his brother's shoulder.

"May the saints preserve ye, brother and our bonny Roz. Do ye think she can forgive me too?" he asked with hope in his voice.

"We are talking about Roslyn! She is a great lady; of course, she will forgive you," Luther returned with a chuckle, "though you might want to prepare yourself for another thrashing when she gets her hands on you," he said with a broad smile.

Trapper smiled too so that both men stood smiling at one another, with the dimples that their father gave them both caved deeply in upon their similar faces.

"Let's go get my sister," Trapper told him.

Chapter Twenty-Four

"Listen! He comes! Have no fear, Lady Roslyn fo he willnae hurt ye. Just say nothin' to provoke him," her guard warned her.

How could she not be afraid? The devil was coming to do what, only God knew. Other than her small dagger, she was helpless in the face of these men. She had removed it from her boot the last time her guard had gone to bring food for her, but after several attempts to trip the lock, she realized that she could not escape.

Suspecting that her guard was more than what he appeared, she clung to his wise counsel, meeting Magnus as meekly as possible, when within moments of the warning of his arrival, the outer door opened and a shaft of lantern light directed him on his way to her cell.

When he reached her, he stood looking her over with something like disgust apparent on his face before saying, "I thought I told you to keep the bait fresh."

Roslyn understood his meaning. Her cell stank and because she had been forced to endure it for nearly three days she must surely stink too. She didn't let the sleight offend her as he had hoped it would, rather she lowered her head in mock shame, biting her lip as she did.

It wasn't so long ago that she had demonstrated great bravado in his presence when she had been flanked by her husband, but now she was alone and presumably by him, unarmed. How she would love to plunge her dagger into his throat, but now was probably not the time. She would have to be patient with the hope that an opportunity could present itself neatly.

Magnus took the keys from her guard to open her cell. Her heart skipped a beat as he entered, bringing him within inches of her person.

"Could it be true that you have been reduced to a lowly female, after all? Where is all that raging bluster now, hmm?" he taunted.

She wanted to spit in his face, but she knew that would only bring his wrath down upon so again, she bit her lip while keeping her head tucked. Clearly, Magnus was not one to be ignored as he reached out to place a finger below her chin to lift her face.

"I wanted you to know that we will have a special guest later today. I sent word round to Dunheath, informing your husband of your terrible spill and the resulting injuries that necessitated my offering you hospitality until he could come and fetch you. As I told him in my missive, I can't imagine why you would have been riding at such a dangerous pace onto my estate as you were, but that you had suffered a sprained ankle and a nasty bump to your head, so you simply couldn't travel. Naturally, I had to take you in," he told her with a sniff through his beak-like nose.

Roslyn's eyes twitched in anger to his dastardly scheme. He had laid a trap for Luther to fall in, but the jest was on him. Luther wasn't at Dunheath. She started to tell him so but remembered the wise words of her guard. Say nothing. Her ire was not lost on him, however, he smiled, pleased with himself.

"After he arrives, I will offer him a drink from my aging stocks, and as he is a gentleman and a known drunkard, he won't refuse. Of course, it will be poisoned, and he will die soon after partaking, but that is not for you to worry. We will marry soon after it is concluded that he suffered an apoplexy after rushing to his bride. He is a rather big man you see, big men often die suddenly from apoplexies. Tis a shame really," he told her.

Dread began to bubble in the pit of her stomach. What if Luther had returned to Dunheath? What if he had received the missive to come and retrieve her?

"You needn't worry that we will remain wed for long. I will keep you tightly secured until I get an heir off you then I will set you free," he informed her.

Roslyn felt as though bile were threatening to rise to her mouth. She swallowed hard in an attempt to keep it at bay. She would not allow him to see her fear, so she continued to say nothing. She didn't dare give him reason to believe that Luther might not be coming.

"I never really wanted a wife. It's a ghastly business; keeping a wife, that is. They ceaselessly whine and complain about this or that while spending all your money on ridiculous balls and house parties to the point that you can barely stand to look upon them let alone bed them down long enough to sire an heir. Tis why my first wife had to die. It became apparent that she was barren, but the lack of pregnancy didn't stop her from blazing a trail through my wealth while trying to gain the upper hand within the household. She suffered an apoplexy too; she was rather large like yourself. Perhaps you too might suffer such a fate. One can never really know such things," he laid out his confession with ease as if the murder of his former wife had been a trivial thing.

Roslyn was mad now. She put her hand behind her back to reach for her dagger. She would make a quick lunge for his throat so fast that he would never see it coming. She felt the cold steel of her blade to rally her confidence. She had to save her husband! She had to save herself!

"My lord, would you like for me to arrange a bath for the wench?" her guard suggested quickly as though he knew what she was about to do. How could he?

"That is a wonderful idea. Please see to it, but when she is cleaned up, I want her back in her restraints. We have been far too hospitable, but it was necessary, I suppose. We wouldn't want it said that we didn't take care of the poor dear," he said before quickly spinning on his heels to leave her cell.

Roslyn's body shook as he walked away whistling a happy tune. She had been mere seconds away from ending his murderous life.

"Put yer dagger away, my lady," the guard told her.

Roslyn snapped her head in his direction. He knew she had the dagger! But why had he allowed her to keep it if he knew she had it?

"How do ye know about my dagger?" she asked.

"My lady, I am very good at what I do. I searched ye from head to toe before I set yer bindings," he told her.

"Who are ye?" she demanded.

"Let's just say that I willnae allow anything to happen to ye," he told her.

****

Luther and his band of warriors had been traveling for several hours when he noticed a rider approaching as he crashed out of a trail cut out of the forest that connected his land to Magnus's.

"Hold," he heard himself say.

The troops stopped immediately to allow the rider to come closer. The rider had been coming in fast, so they didn't have long to wait before he met with them.

Panting and bleeding from scratches he had suffered from limbs beating at his flesh as he raced through the forest, it took him a moment to compose himself, but it was obvious from his colors that he was from the clan MacClarent.

"Praise be the saints that I have found ye so soon. Magnus has Roslyn and has sent a message to ye to come and fetch her because she is injured from a fall, but it be a trap. Fergus sent me to warn ye that he has men waiting to charge the keep to bring her home ... but I see ye too have men," he said before scratching his head in confusion.

"Aye, we are aware that he has her, thanks to Trapper's efforts," Luther said indicating his brother to his left.

"Och, we didn't think Trapper would live long enough to warn ye, so old Fergus sent me to tell ye," the man told him.

"As you can see, he is well, and we too are on our way to rescue my wife. So make haste man and lead me to old Fergus ... time is of the essence if we are to take Magnus unaware," he told him.

Luther's confidence was bolstered by the fact that Fergus had men waiting as well, as Magnus would surely be quite confident that he would come alone and probably wouldn't have increased his security detail by much, if any.

The men too were bolstered with confidence as they began to run the last leg of the journey. There weren't enough horses for the majority of the men, but that didn't stop these hardy Scots. He suspected that each man had the endurance of a stallion, easily able to run for hours at such a pace. Fortunately, they were within a few miles of the outer perimeter of their target so at this pace they would make it there rather quickly. Soon, he would have his beloved back in his arms. Magnus had better pray that not a single hair upon her beautiful head had been harmed or his death would be no easy thing.

Within less than an hour, the two clans convened in the forest near their destination. Old Fergus sat tall in his saddle as he awaited his son-in-law's approach. The rider had ridden up ahead to inform Fergus of the developments and as promised his men were ready and waiting.

"Thanks be to the saints, I thought we would have to go on without ye. That bastard has my girl!" Fergus roared with fire from his belly.

"He had best have a friend in hell because that is where I plan to send him," Luther told him with fire from his own belly.

"Have ye a plan?" Fergus asked.

"We plan to fell a tree for a battering ram and a few smaller trees for ladders to climb over the walls. Kill as many as we can until we find Roslyn," he told him.

"Och, it's as good a plan as any though I hadnae thought of the ladders. We already felled the tree, but how long do ye suppose it will take to make ladders?" Fergus asked.

"Perhaps an hour, but first my men need to rest. They have been running hard for near an hour after we met with your rider. I want them primed and ready for action when the time comes. Have you any carpenters?" Luther asked.

"We're all carpenters, there isnae a thing in this world we Scots cannae build," Fergus declared.

Luther and the other men who had benefit of horses along with Fergus's men quickly set about their task, and as promised it wasn't long before they had constructed several lightweight though very sturdy ladders. Their construction was a crude, simple fashion composed of young trees still dressed in their bark, but as they were meant to be temporary solutions, they would serve. They still had an hour of darkness for cover, so after rallying the men, they began their stealthy march to Magnus's sanctuary.

Luther thought about his wife and the fear that she must be in, using it as fuel for what lay ahead. Throwing silent prayers heavenward that she had remained unharmed, he sent a message of love ahead of him. He knew she wouldn't know that he was coming, but he felt the need to do it anyway. She was his soul mate, perhaps she could feel him near.

Chapter Twenty-Five

"Ye had best wake and ready yerself, my lady. The time grows near," her guard told her.

Roslyn had no idea how long she had been sleeping, but the fog of sleep was rather stubborn as she responded to his command.

"What's afoot?" she asked groggily.

"Listen! Yer husband comes," he told her.

Just then, Roslyn heard a thunderous boom from above mixed with the shouts of men, many men. Her heart skipped a beat as she tried to reason it all out. It sounded as though the keep were under siege.

"Yer husband is a resourceful man, it seems. He has assembled a band of men to assist him in yer rescue," he told her with something that sounded like pride.

"But how?" she asked.

"He must have been informed of your capture long before Magnus sent word. Ye had best listen to me if ye are to survive. When the time comes, dinnae worry, no matter what you see or hear, just stay close to me, and I'll be sure ye are safely returned to yer husband," he advised.

"But who are you?" she asked him.

"I am Amos Dunbar of the Clan McRoolins at yer service, my lady," he said with a bow.

"Och, ye are from the clan McRoolins?" she asked surprised.

"Aye, yer husband is my cousin and now he is my chieftain," he told her.

"I see, but how do I know I can trust ye?" she asked.

Just then, there was another thunderous boom from above, this one shaking the keep furiously. Roslyn quickly gathered herself, taking her dagger into her hands in preparedness.

"Ye have no choice, the keep has been penetrated. We must go now," he said taking her by the hand.

He was right! She had no choice, she had to trust him. Then a thought occurred to her.

"Ye're in danger," she told him.

"Dinnae worry about me, I'm quite skilled," he told her.

Roslyn was worried about her would-be savior.

If Luther didn't know that he was helping, then he could be killed, or if Magnus figured out that he was a traitor, then he could be killed. Either way, things didn't look good for Amos.

"But ye are no match fer bullets," she insisted as they reached the end of the corridor leading to the steps.

Just then, he took her through a passageway hidden in the darkness just before reaching the steps, tugging her behind him as he went. Down a long hall, they traversed until they reached a set of stairs as he dragged her along taking the steps two at a time. Roslyn managed to keep up with him though her knees felt like jelly as fear spiked its way down the length of her body.

"We must hurry," he warned her.

Roslyn could hear the battle above as the men fought one another, causing her heart to race as she thought about the danger her husband must be in. She had no idea how many men Luther had managed to pull together or how many men Magnus had, but she could tell the battle was being fiercely fought.

"Hold!" came a loud command from the top of the stairs.

Magnus! He was there, flanked by two guards, awaiting them. Was this some sort of trick? Had

Amos set the whole thing up to gain her cooperation? Roslyn didn't know, but once again she drew on his wise counsel from before. Say nothing.

"Master, what has happened?" Amos asked.

"Someone must have tipped Luther off because he's arrived with a number of men crashing his way into my keep. Where are you going with the girl?" Magnus asked with hostility barely contained.

Roslyn's blood ran cold as she palmed her dagger to keep it hidden from his view.

"I was bringing her to safety," Amos calmly told him.

"Safety?" Magnus repeated with suspicion.

Roslynn knew that Magnus was no fool. If her would-be protector weren't careful, Magnus would see through his ruse.

"When I heard the commotion, I realized that I had better hide her," he explained.

Magnus seemed to consider his words as he continued to look upon them with suspicion while assessing them for some sign of deceit. It was as though the sudden siege upon his keep had rattled him, causing him to trust no one.

"Aye that was wise, now hand her over to me. She's just the weapon I need to neutralize Luther and his men. Seeing a knife pressed to her throat will put things back into proper perspective for my cousin," he said taking her roughly by the forearm.

Roslyn briefly considered putting up resistance but thought better of it, for now at least. She wanted desperately to see her husband by any means necessary, and it sounded as though Magnus planned to take her to him. Patience! She cautioned herself silently, clutching her blade as she was led to where, she knew not.

The further along the route of the corridor they traversed, the louder the sounds of battle became. Men shouting, pistol shots ringing out, swords clashing all made for a horrible cacophony. Fear struck deep in her soul at the realization that somewhere amidst all of it was her husband fighting to save her.

Roslyn sent a silent prayer to the heavens asking God to protect her husband along with all his men during this perilous endeavor. Surely, God would not be so cruel as to take him away from her now that they had found each other. Now that they had experienced a love so profound as to surely have been written in the stars as their true destiny.

Roslyn soon found herself led onto a balcony above a great hall that allowed her a view of the battle being fought below. Frantically, she searched for Luther until her eyes settled upon him. There he was, a giant of a man, swinging his sword to and fro as he fought his way through the fray.

Just as she was about to shout out his name, Magnus, drew her in front of himself then quickly made good on his threat to put a blade to her throat.

"Now, you can scream," he told her.

Roslyn didn't want to be his pawn. She knew if she did scream, Luther could become distracted, possibly allowing someone to run him through with their sword. Too, she knew that Magnus wanted to stop the fight because he feared defeat. He was seriously outnumbered, it seemed, and many of his men were falling to Luther's men.

"Perhaps, I didn't make myself clear. Scream now!" he ordered her as he applied pressure to her throat with his blade.

"I will not aid ye in yer attempt to murder my husband!" Roslyn ground out through clenched teeth.

She felt the sting of the blade as it cut into her skin followed by the wet trickle of her blood as it made a snaking path downward. She knew the cut was small but served to illicit her cooperation. She would rather die than submit.

Palming her blade, she thought that this would

be the time if ever there was one to try to make her escape, but how far would she get before they recaptured her? Would Amos help her? She wasn't sure, but she had to do something. Now!

"Shoot the bastard," Magnus told one of his men.

Several things happened at once, so fast that Roslyn wasn't sure of the sequence of events. She twisted out of Magnus's hold, lunging at him with her blade, but his man was fast as he slapped it out of her hand before slamming her body to the ground.

Too, there was a scuffle behind Magnus as Amos made some sort of attempt to save her but was brought low when the other of Magnus's men plunged his dagger into his belly for his effort. She feared he might be dead but could do nothing to help him. Then the shot rang out, and she did scream when Luther went down on one knee in response. He had been shot!

Just then, there was an eerie hush in the hall as all the fighting came to a halt. Two men she had never seen before rushed to Luther's side, the one with dark hair putting himself in front of Luther, effectively shielding him with his own body as he trained his pistol toward the balcony with a look of deadly determination. She had no idea who he was, but clearly he valued Luther's life above his own with such a loyal demonstration.

She didn't have time to ponder the identity of the two men further as she had been roughly drawn to her feet once again with a blade to her throat.

"Gentlemen, welcome to my home," Magnus declared with mock hospitality.

That's when Roslyn heard it; a gut-wrenching howl that sounded more animal than man as it was issued by her husband when he saw her trapped by Magnus. Their eyes locked with one another in desperate dread for the other's safety, both knowing that the situation could turn deadly at any moment.

With a promise in his eyes that was meant to calm her, Luther rose to his feet with the aid of his friend with the light colored hair and there, just behind him was Trapper, standing tall and fierce with fire blazing in his eyes as he glared at Magnus.

Roslyn took comfort in seeing the two brothers together, clearly united, even though she knew much of this could be laid at Trapper's door. But there he was, as close to death as she had ever seen any man just days ago, armed with a sword, standing behind his brother, bloody from battle. Overcome with a mixed rush of emotions, joy, sadness, anger, hope even; she wept.

Chapter Twenty-Six

Luther's heart was gripped with cold icy tendrils of fear at the sight of the blade at his wife's throat. Seeing her trapped in Magnus's clutches with tears spilling from her eyes was more than he could endure. His hands clutched tightly into fists with the intense need to rip her away from him, to bring her back into the safety of his embrace.

How he wished that he could grow wings to take flight so he could pull her away from the villain then slay him for daring to harm her. Alas, he was only human with his feet planted firmly on the ground with her just out of his reach, several feet above him.

"I see that I have your attention now, cousin," Magnus taunted.

"Release her!" Luther quickly demanded.

Luther knew that it wouldn't be as easy as that. Magnus was a crafty devil with an agenda to be fulfilled, clearly Roslyn would be his vessel for bargain to have it realized. What Luther needed was a way to turn the tables to ensure that his own plan would rule the day. He had to get Roslyn away from him by any means.

"Really cousin, do you take me for a fool? Ah ... Trapper, I see you have been resurrected from the dead. How truly miraculous," Magnus said with genuine astonishment apparent in his tone.

"It would take more than the likes of ye to kill me," Trapper boasted before spitting on the floor.

Magnus twisted his face to indicate that he smelled something foul, then rolled his eyes for bored effect.

"Tell me cousin, did your bastard brother tell you of his plans to kill you so he could steal your bride?" Magnus asked Luther.

Luther seethed with every evil word that Magnus spoke. As soon as he could manage to get his hands on him, the villain would pay.

"A plan laid out by a black heart of a devil to encourage a young man to stray from the path of righteousness," Luther countered with vehemence.

Magnus roared with laughter, "Is that what he told you? But then how would you know for sure, you lost your memory, did you not? You have no idea who is telling you the truth," he told him.

Luther could feel the sting of his injury to his right thigh as the blood left a trail down his leg. He was sure that it was only a flesh wound, but the blood loss seemed significant. If he were going to save his wife, he had better find a way to act soon as he would no doubt weaken from his wound before too long.

"I can assure you, cousin, that my memory is quite intact. I am well aware who the real villain is. You have always been a rotten scoundrel, no doubt, worsening with age. Let my wife go now, and I may spare you yet," Luther told him as he continued to search his mind for a solution to this stand-off.

"Tell your men to drop their weapons, or I will toss her over the balcony. You won't mind having a crippled wife, eh, cousin?" Magnus countered as he bent Roslyn forward, demonstrating his intentions.

Luther's heart skipped a beat at the sight of his wife bent over the rail. Their eyes connected with silent messages exchanged. His eyes told her to have faith that he would see her safely returned though hers were telling him not to give in to Magnus's demands, but damn the woman's bravado; how could he allow her to remain another minute in that evil bastard's clutches? An idea occurred to him then.

"Perhaps this could be settled between us," he told Magnus as he waved his sword tauntingly at his cousin.

Luther remembered that Magnus was reputed to be quite the swordsman. With his injuries, Luther suspected that Magnus might consider him an easy match. However, Luther himself was considered a force to be reckoned with, sword or no. It was unlikely that Magnus would have knowledge of this, which would give Luther a possible advantage.

Magnus twisted his face into a sinister grin as he considered Luther's offer. He could see the wheels turning in his twisted mind and hoped that he had gauged him correctly. The last thing Luther wanted was for anyone else to be killed or injured. It would best if it were settled between the two of them.

Anticipation was thick in the hall as everyone waited, breath held for the words Magnus would say next. Luther himself felt a clenching around his guts as he too waited. Time seemed suspended briefly before his decision was made.

"Up for a little fencing are you cousin?" he taunted.

Luther tried hard not to smile; he had him. He knew it would be difficult for Magnus to pass up an opportunity for an easy kill on a weakened opponent.

"I'll grant your request upon a few conditions," Magnus suggested.

"Conditions?"

"First, you will have your forces leave my hall.

Second, this will be a fight to the finish. Third, are you listening?" Magnus asked.

"Out with it!" Luther demanded.

Magnus pulled Roslyn close to him then holding her firmly in place with his blade once again at her throat, he ran his tongue along the length of her face from her chin to her brow.

"Third dear cousin, winner takes our fair Roslyn here," he said, clearly relishing the outcome.

Roslyn bucked and squirmed at his comment causing quite a commotion by Luther's men. Feeling the same way, he knew that they wanted to storm the stairs to slaughter Magnus then feed his entrails to the dogs, but he couldn't take that risk. He had to get Roslyn out of his reach. He had no choice but to accept these conditions.

"Allow me a moment," he requested, turning to his men he said simply, "trust me."

"I'm staying," Dylan told him.

"Me as well," Gabriel insisted.

Luther knew his friends would not leave him in such a situation. He surveyed the room, taking in the number of wounded and was astounded to see that nearly all of Magnus's men were down with the exception of a few who seemed keen to have an end to the massacre, but nearly all of his own men were still fit for battle. It didn't appear that he had lost anyone.

Fergus stood still in the center of the hall with his eyes locked on his daughter. Luther knew that a team of wild stallions wouldn't be able to budge him away. Then there was Trapper, wounded and pale, but standing bravely, ready to rip Magnus to pieces with his bare hands.

A thought occurred to Luther then, what if I fail?

Luther looked to Dylan, "If I should fall, shoot him between the eyes," he told him quietly.

Dylan nodded in affirmation.

"You will not fall," Gabriel told him.

Luther felt he would be able to handle himself against his cousin. He was much taller as well as younger after all, but there was always the possibility of failure. He knew he had best plan for it.

Turning back to Magnus, "We need witnesses. I have selected four men to stay; you can do the same."

Magnus didn't appear to like this proposal as he stood considering it.

"As you will cousin," he consented before turning to his two men standing at his side, "If I should lose, slit her throat," he advised one.

He shoved Roslyn into the man's arms, then looked to the other, "You will accompany me below."

Roslyn made an attempt to wiggle out of her captor's arms, but it was no use; he was even bigger than Magnus and his hold was much tighter. She sagged in defeat and watched as Magnus and his man descended the stairs to meet with her husband below. All but his two friends, her father and Trapper had exited the hall to serve witness to what she prayed would be a victorious outcome for her husband.

Chapter Twenty-Seven

Armed with their Claymore swords, neither man wasted any time engaging the other. With quick, precise movements meant to gauge the level of skill their opponent had, each man advanced, deflected and faded the other with equal dexterity.

Gone from Magnus's mind was the belief that Luther would be an easy kill, marked by the sweat quickly beading on his furrowed brow. Determination set firmly in his jaw, Magnus made multiple attempts, lunging toward the wound in Luther's right leg, but Luther, despite his large stature, proved to be quite agile on his feet, easily avoiding the strikes.

Pride began to swell in Roslyn's heart as she watched with fascination. She couldn't help but admire her husband's calm, collected demeanor as he demonstrated his prowess, reminding her of some Viking warrior from legends of old. Confidence showed bright in his eyes as he jousted with his opponent, no sign of distress visible on his brow.

Hope reigned supreme when a moment later, Luther landed his blade upon Magnus's upper arm, the wound immediately issuing a stream of crimson fluid that began to drip in copious amounts onto the stone floor. That's when she heard it; the sound of her captor's grunt of agony followed by the loosening of his hold as he fell to the ground behind her.

"Go to yer father, my lady," Amos told her.

"Amos!" she gasped.

"At your service," he told her with a slight bow.

"But ye … I thought ye ... that is to say ... lord, ye are ... oh, tis a miracle!" she blathered.

"Was nothing more than me padded vest," he told her with a grin as he lifted his shirt. "See, tis only a flesh wound," he demonstrated.

In this light, she could see a family resemblance to her husband, with the same tall, brawny stature, light colored curls upon his head and, of course, dimples. Giddy with relief, a silly thought occurred to her then; perhaps my sons will have dimples too. Compelled by an urge of gratitude, she threw her arms around him then kissed him on the cheek, she would be sure her husband knew of his kindness toward her as soon as she was able.

"Och, ye are a sly one," she told him grinning widely at her newly acquired family member.

"Let us go below," he told her taking her by the

crook of her arm.

As she was being led below, the battle continued, but clearly her father and Trapper had seen what occurred above as they rushed to meet her at the bottom of the stairs. Her father hugged her tightly before shaking hands with Amos, bestowing him with words of undying thanks for the safety of his daughter.

Once delivered into the safe arms of her father, she was quickly ushered to a position in the hall where she was quickly met by the two men that had protected her husband from before. Now, instead of protecting him, they had positioned themselves around her, nearly blocking her view of her husband as he fought valiantly on.

Surrounded by these five men, Roslyn was no doubt the safest woman in the world as must have been noticed by the few remaining men that Magnus had standing. One by one, they began to slip away to escape what they must surely fear would be their fate in moments yet to come.

Luther too had observed her rescue, "Your prize has slipped away," he taunted.

Magnus growled as he swung his sword wildly, trying to find a fleshy mark, but again her husband's swift feet allowed him to evade the desperate maneuver. Again, Magnus roared as he lunged at her husband, again he avoided injury with ease. It almost seemed as though he were beginning to enjoy himself as he toyed with the villain.

****

Luther was enjoying himself. Knowing that his wife had been delivered safely away from harm, he was allowed to focus solely on the man who had dared to harm her. So far, he had managed to land several nicks at various places on Magnus's body but none was bleeding quite as badly as the one on his arm. Magnus was weakening fast with the knowledge that he would soon be utterly defeated apparent on his face.

Luther lunged forward again, this time making significant contact with Magnus's thigh, again producing a rich stream of blood. He grunted in response, staggering slightly, but quickly returned an ineffective thrust back toward Luther. Luther merely side-stepped the attempt before landing yet another blow, this one to Magnus's left shoulder. Pain etched across his face, but he stubbornly continued to go at Luther with no ill effect.

"Had you survived, my wife would never have submitted to you. No doubt, she would have cut your bollocks off while you slept," Luther boasted.

Magnus grunted as he tried to lunge forward, but Luther lunged forward too, driving his sword through his gut. Magnus stood there as if refusing to believe that he had been impaled while Luther slowly withdrew his sword.

"You really thought you would win?" Luther asked him before rearing back with his meaty fist wrapped around the hilt of his sword to deliver a savage blow to his cousin's nose. Magnus went down, but Luther wasn't done, he followed, straddling him.

Grabbing him by the collar, he lifted Magnus's head, "You dared to harm my wife; for that you will die," he told him before delivering another savage blow.

Blow after vicious blow, he issued before his hand was finally caught in mid-strike. "He is finished," Gabriel's voice assured him.

Luther let go of Magnus's collar and allowed his head to fall back unconscious upon the stone floor. It was done. Magnus was dead. Never again could he harm his precious Roslyn. Remembering the blood trickling from her throat at the madman's hands, Luther wished he could kill him again as he sat astride him a moment, gathering his breath and his wits.

The hall around him was quiet, but sounds of his victory could be heard outside as the men began to chant his name. Taking a deep breath, he lifted himself to his feet, turning with eyes seeking his wife. He had to go to her, he had to wrap his arms around her so he could smell her sweetness to assure himself that all was truly well.

He found her safe amidst the circle of her protectors. Their eyes met, freezing him in place at the sight of her beauty. Love sparked from her hazel eyes as they blazed at him with promise of a life filled with passion. She was so beautiful, he could hardly imagine she was meant for him.

Slowly but surely, with the aid of his friend beside him, his feet, heavy with fatigue, he moved toward her. Time seemed to slow down, stretching out the length between them. Eyes forward, he tried to close the gap between them until he became aware that the love he had seen in her eyes seconds before had changed to that of absolute horror.

As if in a nightmare where everything moved in slow motion, he watched as his wife did the most amazing thing. Grabbing the pistol that Dylan had tucked in his holster while simultaneously shoving him to the side, she then charged forward. For one absurd moment, he thought she had gone mad, having finally decided to kill him.

"Get down," she shouted as she pressed toward him with her arm outstretched, pistol tightly clutched in hand.

Luther hadn't time to react before Gabriel grabbed him around the shoulders, pulling him to the ground just as she fired the pistol. They rolled out of harm's way in time for him to see what had driven his wife to her actions. Magnus had risen it seemed, with his sword held high about to deliver a death blow to his back. After a brief moment, with a small hole between his eyes, Magnus swayed then finally fell to the ground when his knees buckled under his dead weight.

Dropping the pistol to the ground, Roslyn ran to her husband, throwing herself upon him, kissing him furiously about the face and lips.

"My husband," she breathed into his mouth.

"My wife, my own," he returned before kissing her passionately in return.

Coming up for air, Roslyn hurried out the words, "Bidh gaol agam ort fad mo bheatha, thusa 's gun duine eile," she told him.

Luther remembered those words. She had said them that night at the loch when they made love for the first time though then as well as now, he had no idea what they meant.

"What does this mean?" he asked her, cupping her face in his hands.

"It means that I will love ye my whole life, you and no other. This is how I love ye. Forgive me, but I was a stupid, stupid woman, never letting ye know just how much I loved ye, but I was scared ye would reject me. Ever since I was a wee lass, I loved ye, Luther Rollins, ye and no other. I waited for ye to come back, and when ye dinnae, I came for ye because ye belong to me and I belong to ye. I need ye as I need the air that I breath. The blood in my veins warms my body as it flows for ye. Ye are the moon and the stars in my sky. Ye are my everything. This is how I love ye. Can ye ever love me as I love ye?" she asked with tears flowing.

Luther's heart soared with her words. He drew her tightly into his embrace, nearly swooning from his joy.

"Yes, I love you just as much, but it was I that was stupid for I tried to forget you all those years. Can you ever forgive me?" he asked.

"Tis already done, my love," she told him with a passionate kiss upon his lips.

In that instant, his wife had banished all of his suspicions. She loved him, had always loved him, just as Trapper had told him. He truly had been a fool not to see it sooner. Never again would he entertain doubts or jealousy where his brother was concerned, for though Trapper loved her, she had loved only him. From this day forward, he would wrap her in his loving devotion to prove to her that he was worthy of that love.

Luther became aware of their surroundings, then silently cursing that he could not take her here and now to cement their bond, he pulled away from her sweet lips.

"Let us leave this place. We have much need of our bed," he hotly whispered in her ear.

Roslyn turned the most beautiful shade of red, when she too made the realization that they were not alone.

"Let us hurry, dear husband, for I find that I cannae wait to have my way with ye," she whispered.

Together, they rose followed by a procession of their friends cheering as they made their way out of the place that had been her prison. Home, they were going home.

Chapter Twenty-Eight

"Congratulations," Dylan said to Luther at the celebration being held to commemorate the marriage between him and Roslyn. "You are a living legend it seems, my friend," he went on to tell him with a clap on his back.

Luther didn't know about legends, but he did know that the two clans seemed to have embraced him as their leader after he had defeated Magnus so soundly two days before, evidenced by the massive turnout here tonight. The festivities had to be moved to the grand courtyards outside of Huntley Manor to accommodate the swelling of guests that continued to arrive from points all over the region.

Word had spread quickly that Luther was Magnus's heir; thus, his clan too would come under his protection, allowing many members who had defected to come back where they belonged. Luther recognized so many faces among the crowd that his heart swelled with pride to have their support, so he welcomed them with open arms. He didn't know what tomorrow would bring, but if tonight was any indication, the future seemed bright, indeed.

It turned out to be rather fortuitous to have had a Bow Street man along with two dukes of the realm to witness the events that led to Magnus's death, thus it would be unlikely that Luther would suffer legal repercussions in the matter. Indeed, after the inquest was complete, the crown would officially award his cousin's title and property to him. He really didn't want it as he had told the magistrate, insisting that they search Magnus's family tree to find a more suitable candidate. He knew they would find none, but one could only hope. He would have his hands full enough bringing two clans together as it was, adding a third clan to the mix could be too much of a burden.

The local magistrate had seemed all too pleased to thank Luther for ridding them all of such a pestilence whom through his many deeds of villainy had wrought harm on so many. It seemed that everyone regarded Luther with a particular reverence for lifting them out of the bonds of terror that had been inflicted upon them by his cousin in his long absence, as words of cautious praise could be heard filtering through the din.

"I have much work to do before I gain their respect, I fear," he said more to himself as he watched his wife dancing with Gabriel.

"She is a beauty," Dylan observed.

"Aye, but she doesn't know it," Luther responded with a smile.

Roslyn was dressed in a beautiful pale green gown that drew the eye to the well-rounded figure beneath, prompting a memory of their lovemaking the night of her rescue. They had come together so explosively that he had been reduced to shuddering tears, as a result.

The idea that he could have lost her had lent a volatile element to their loving that had left his soul raw and exposed. His wife had understood his needs with great intuition as she held him tenderly, softly cooing words of comfort while he had sobbed like a small child afraid of monsters hiding under his bed. He had been embarrassed by his emotional display but found that he could do nothing to stop the flood once it had started, but she would have none of it. As soon as he recomposed himself to a more manly demeanor, she had ravished him until he had become a mindless servant to her needs.

It should have been the other way around, he should have been comforting her, but his wife was a strong, valiant woman who had saved him from so many things, chief among them, himself. The experience had been humbling, but one he would cherish for the remainder of his days. He had been wholly restored by this woman he hadn't wanted. He would live the rest of his life with absolute faith that she had been a gift, a wonderful gift from God.

Feeling like the luckiest man alive, he smiled at his wife. Though she was dancing with his friend, her eyes remained firmly fixed on his with promises of carnal delights to be shared between them when they once again came together later this eve.

"Who would have dreamed that there would be

a woman so perfectly suited for you?" Dylan responded.

"Perfect," he murmured as though he hadn't really heard his friend's words.

Dylan watched his friend as he gazed upon his bride, like a lovesick fool. Though he was happy for him, he would miss having him close by when he and Gabriel returned home in the morning. It had not gone unnoticed by him or Gabriel that Luther had become a man of great significance in these last few weeks. He had transformed from the happy, carefree member of their group, one that they had often teased for his dim wit, to the leader of a very large people, which would no doubt come with great responsibilities.

It was obvious to him now that Luther had never been a dimwit, rather he had been set adrift from his true purpose as though he had amnesia for the last decade, only now being reawakened. The thought gave Dylan pause as he considered that he nor any of the others had ever recognized Luther's potential for greatness. Neither had they seen that he was lost, had not helped him back on course. As his closest friends, they should have seen it, but they had been blind. When Jasper heard of it, he would no doubt find it hard to believe. Why hadn't Jasper seen it?

Since the men had been young lads, Luther had always sought Jasper out as his closest companion.

It was an odd duo to be sure as the two were exactly opposite in every way imaginable, but they had always been inseparable. Surely Luther had shared things with Jasper that he had not revealed to anyone else? Though if he had, Jasper had never betrayed his confidence.

Dylan had always thought that Jasper enjoyed keeping Luther around to exaggerate his own intelligence, but perhaps Jasper had seen what the others had missed and had been nurturing a future leader all along. These were thoughts to ponder on his way home on the long ride back to England, but now he needed to make his move if he were ever to have his dance with fair Roslyn.

"I believe I see an opportunity to pry our good friend away from your wife so that I may secure the next set," he told Luther with an elbow to his ribs.

"Just mind yourself," Luther warned him with a smile as he watched him go.

Moments later, Gabriel returned to Luther's side. "Fascinating creature," he remarked.

"She saved me," Luther commented as he watched her dance with Dylan.

Luther knew that his wife had no idea how to dance, but with the aid of his friends, she seemed to be gliding effortlessly through the movements. He himself had not been able to secure a dance with her yet but had instructed her to save a waltz for him.

"I believe you are correct sir," Gabriel said with a nod of agreement. "Have you given any thought to our discussion earlier?" he asked after a few minutes of companionable silence.

"Indeed. I believe it is a fine idea to petition the king to knight my brother for his heroic efforts in the rescue of my wife. In fact, I have already drawn up a document that I would have you take to my man of business in London when you return. I am of the mind that a young knight will need a place to call his own; therefore, I am going to gift him with one of my estates," he told him.

"Which estate would that be?" Gabriel asked, surprised by this revelation.

"The Belmont estate," he told him.

Gabriel issued a low whistle at this information, "But that is the source of most of your wealth," he proclaimed.

True, Willowbrook is a very wealthy estate, which is precisely why he would give it to his brother. Never again would he be looked down upon by others as a lowly bastard; instead, he would be a man of great wealth and consequence. With a knighthood bestowed upon him, he would be able to enter society, mix with the ton, he could even attract a bride of nobility at some point if he wished.

"Will you take him under your wing?" he asked his friend.

"You needn't ask it of me, you know I will look after the lad," he told him.

"Good," Luther said simply.

"Are you doing this to keep him away from Roslyn? She will be hurt by it, you know," Gabriel warned.

Yes, he still wanted Trapper away from Dunheath, away from Roslyn. He didn't want to banish him from their lives, only give him a new direction that would allow him a chance to find happiness elsewhere. If Trapper remained here, Luther would always be suspicious of his brother's motives with regard to Roslyn. He didn't want to live that way, it wouldn't be fair to any of them. In time, his brother's broken heart would mend, but the mending would be much more swift if he were given a distraction, such as Willowbrook would surely prove to be.

"It is for the best," was his reply.

"When will you tell him?" Gabriel asked.

"I told him this morning. I think he was pleased though somewhat suspicious. When I informed him that he would be considered for a knighthood, he looked at me as though I had gone daft. When I asked him how the title Sir Calum Rollins of Willowbrook sounded to him, he smiled then burst into a fit of laughter, then told me to quit jesting. I assured the lad that I was most serious, but he doesn't believe me. That's why you will be taking him to England with you. Seeing is believing as it were," Luther told him with a raised eyebrow.

"How do you propose to make a grown man go to England if he doesn't wish to go?" Gabriel asked.

"Why, kidnap him, of course," Luther told him as though it should be obvious.

The two men laughed at the prospect before Gabriel said, "You're serious aren't you?"

"But, of course, he did the same for me, only let's spare him the head injury, shall we?" Luther told him.

Luther turned his attention back to his bride. He could stand the separation no longer, then without realizing he had moved toward her, he found himself tapping Dylan on the shoulder, "I would like to dance with my wife," he stated.

Dylan bowed after handing Roslyn over to her husband then excused himself.

"Finally," he breathed in her ear.

"Och Luther, I'm havin' a most wonderful time," she told him.

"Dancing with all these men?" he asked her with mock concern.

"Aye, tis true. I never imagined I would be dancin' at our weddin' celebration, tis truly marvelous. Then I've been watchin' ye watch me all night while bein' tossed about by one man or another with anticipation growin' in my belly until ... well ... can we sneak away now? I have a most desperate need of ye," she told him conspiratorially.

She need say no more. Luther quickly sprang into action, whisking his wife away so he could satisfy both their desperate needs.

****

"Shh, we don't want to wake him," Dylan advised Gabriel as the two men stood outside Trapper's bedroom door.

"I can't believe we are about to do this," Gabriel grumbled.

"Shh, just stick to the plan," Dylan cautioned.

Carefully, Gabriel turned the knob to allow them entrance into the bedchamber, relaxing when he heard deep rhythmic snoring from within. The men split up to position themselves on either side of the bed so they could quickly subdue their prey.

"It's time to go home, Calum Rollins," Dylan told him as he cocked his pistol near Trapper's ear.

The End.

ABOUT THE AUTHOR

My father was a great story teller and always said that one day, he would like to write a novel. My sister is a writer as well, so naturally I'm a dabbler. I thought I'd try my hand at writing romance novels because I love to read them. Romance novels have everything you want, mysteries, villains, wonderful character's and I easily find myself living in the moment with the story. I hope that readers will find my stories as entertaining as I have found so many. I like to mix tragedy and comedy together with a cast of colorful characters that I create from people that I have met in my life. I will visualize a person that I know as this or that character and the rest is history.

I hope you enjoy my warped sense of humor and the stories that I tell. If you happened upon this book first, please go back and read My Sweet Alyssa, the first of the Brother's In All series and Resurrecting Dylan, the second book of the series.

Gina Rose is the pseudonym for a very prolific author who spins tales in the Regency Romance genre.

Look for many more or her books to be available soon on Amazon and most other online bookstores.

Check her website, ginarose-author.com, often for more information and reviews.